In the Flesh

In the Flesh

SYLVIA DAY

writing as Livia Dare

KENSINGTON PUBLISHING CORP.
www.kensingtonbooks.com

KENSINGTON BOOKS are published by

Kensington Publishing Corp.
119 West 40th Street
New York, NY 10018

ISBN-13: 978-1-61773-056-6
ISBN-10: 1-61773-056-4

First Kensington Trade Paperback Printing: October 2013

10 9 8 7 6 5 4 3 2 1

Printed in the United States of America

First Electronic Edition: October 2013

ISBN-13: 978-1-61773-057-3
ISBN-10: 1-61773-057-2

This is for all the readers
who've been waiting for Sapphire's story
for five long years.

I hope you love it!

Acknowledgments

My gratitude goes out to Sasha White, Annette McCleave, and Jordan Summers. Thank you all for your input. And thank you for the support and encouragement over the last few years while you waited impatiently for this book to release. What great friends you are! I'm blessed.

Prologue

"**I**s he dead, Your Highness?"Closing the bio-scanner, Wulfric, Crown Prince of D'Ashier, rose from his low crouch and stared down at the corpse at his feet. Desert sand swirled around the body, eager to bury it. "Unfortunately, yes."

He lifted his gaze and scanned the berms around them. "At the next check-in, make the report. No need to call this in early and risk the signal being detected."

They were too close to Sari to chance discovery. The Sarian king was always on the lookout for any provocation to go to war, hence the border patrols that never ceased.

Once every two months Wulf accompanied a platoon of D'Ashier soldiers on their rounds. His presence wasn't required, but for him it was a necessary task. A good ruler lived the trials experienced by his people. He saw the world through their eyes, from their level, not from so high above that he lost touch with their needs.

"Was he coming or going, Your Highness?"

He glanced at the young lieutenant next to him. "I can't determine. It's so hot today I can't even tell how long he's been dead."The bio-suit Wulf wore protected him from both dehydration and the scorching sun, but he could see the heat waves shimmering above the sand.

After the recent Confrontations, the border had been closed abruptly, which left many families divided. The unfortunate result of this was the death of many citizens who tried to cross to their loved ones. Wulf attempted to reopen treaty negotiations with Sari on a regular basis, but the Sarian king always refused. Despite all the years that had passed, Sari still held a grudge.

Two centuries ago, D'Ashier had been a large, prosperous mining colony of Sari. After years of disagreements and injustices claimed on both sides, a bloody revolution had freed the small territory from its homeland, creating a permanent animosity between the two countries. The people of D'Ashier had crowned the popular and well-loved governor as monarch. Over the years, Wulf's ancestors had expanded and strengthened the fledgling nation until it rivaled all others.

But the royal family of Sari still looked disdainfully upon D'Ashier such as a frustrated parent would look on an upstart child. Sari remained steadfast in its decision to ignore D'Ashier's power and sovereignty. The talgorite mines of D'Ashier were the largest producer of the coveted power source in the known universe, well worth every battle and war waged in an effort to reclaim them.

"Something is off." Wulf lifted his field-sight lenses to scan the sky.

He and the lieutenant stood on a mound several kilometers away from the border. His *skipsbåt* hovered nearby, waiting. D'Ashier guardsmen kept watch all around them. There were a dozen of them altogether, the requisite number of every patrol. From this vantage, he could see a good distance and should feel relatively secure, yet the hair at his nape stood on end. He'd learned long ago to trust his instincts.

Surveying the situation anew, he said, "There's something posed and artificial about this, and there are too many unanswered questions. This man couldn't have traveled so far without transportation. Where is his skip? Where are his provisions? Why hasn't the sand buried him?"

As his headset crackled to life, he lowered the lenses.

"There is no sign of anything of note, Your Highness. We've searched the surrounding two kilometers."

"Any more unusual readings, Captain?"

"Nothing."

He shot a glance at the young lieutenant who stood expectantly beside him. Wulf's patrols were always officer heavy, usually with many newly commissioned. The general had made that request years ago in an effort to demonstrate to his subordinates how the weight of command should be carried. It was a mantle Wulf had worn without strain since birth. "Let's go."

They moved swiftly to their abandoned skips, using the economical movements that were innate to inhabitants of a desert planet. Just as they prepared to mount the slender bikes, the ground rumbled ominously. The source was easily recognized, and Wulf cursed his failure to foresee the trap. Loosening the restraint of the glaive-hilt holster attached to his thigh, he yelled out a warning. Leaping onto his skip, he engaged the power and tugged hard on the controls, flying away just before the small enemy borer emerged from the sand.

"I can't get a distress call out!" cried the panicked lieutenant. The rest of the patrol assembled into the V-shaped group formation, and sped farther into D'Ashier territory.

"They're blocking it." Wulf's tone was grim. "Damn it, they must have been boring their way through the sand for days."

"Why didn't they show up on the scanners? We were directly over them."

"The power was off. Without that signature, they were effectively invisible."

Wulf was highly conscious of the powerful hum of the borer behind them. The warning blip that had sparked their investigation must have been made as the transport entered D'Ashier from Sari, before the engines had been turned off.

The corpse was merely the lure that ensured the anomaly wasn't dismissed as a malfunction.

"How the hell could they stay under without environmental controls?"

"With desperation," the captain muttered, flying upward as a warning shot from the borer spewed sand into a cloud before him. *"That's not a Sarian borer. They're mercenaries."*

Studying the upcoming landscape through his navigational scanner, Wulf said, "We can't outrun them. Break up over the rise. Circle the rock outcropping."

Clearing the embankment, the patrol separated into two lines. Another shot from the borer hit its mark, sending a skip spinning briefly before it exploded and killed the soldier who rode it. The rest of the men bent lower as they sped toward the multi-towered rock formation that rose as monoliths from the desert floor.

Wulf cursed when a well-aimed shot from the borer crumbled a tower of red rock. Blood-colored dust billowed as a horrifying cracking sound rent the air. Glancing down at his console, he saw transport-sized debris break loose, crashing down upon the other half of his patrol. From the loss of readout, he knew only a few survived.

Rounding the corner, he saw an opening that could give them a fighting chance.

"Dismount," he ordered, weaving his skip between the monoliths. "Draw them out in the open."

In the center of the rock outcropping was a circular patch of sand. They set down, alighted, and fanned out, forming an outward-facing circle. Drawing their glaives, they engaged the powerful blades and waited, the tension palpable.

Phaser fire shook the ground beneath them, but they were safe inside. The gaps and crevices between the various obtrusions were large enough for a skip to enter, but not the borer, which was much bigger. If the attackers wanted to kill them, they'd have to come in on foot and fight hand to hand.

The waiting was endless. Sweat coursed down Wulf's temple. The rest of his skin stayed dry only by benefit of the *dammr*-suit, which regulated his body temperature.

"We just want the prince." The words echoed around them. "Give him to us, and the rest of you can live."

Wulf felt the anger that spread through his ranks.

"You'll have to kill us first!" the captain challenged.

"I was hoping you would say that," came the laughing reply, then blaster fire lit the air and was deflected by the quick movement of a glaive, the powerful laser blade more than a match for the inelegant handgun.

Almost before he could blink, Wulf found his men surrounded. As he thrust and parried with almost innate reflex, he knew there had to have been more than one borer. All these men could not have fit inside one of the small transports. He also knew there was no chance for victory, not when they were outnumbered four to one.

The urge to surrender for the lives of his men was strong. Despite the risk his ransom would present to D'Ashier, Wulf was about to yield when his headset crackled.

"No, Your Highness." The captain shot him a sidelong glance. *"They will kill us regardless. Let us at least die with honor."*

And so he fought on, his chest tight with regret and frustrated anger. Every one of his soldiers gave their all, despite knowing the inevitability of the outcome. They kicked at those who got close enough, cut down those who stumbled in their path, and kept as near as possible to Wulf in a vain effort to spare him.

One by one they fell, the air thick with the smell of burnt flesh. Bodies, both soldiers and mercs, littered the sandy floor. But all too soon, he stood alone against the many.

In the end, Crown Prince Wulfric of D'Ashier went down

with the knowledge that he could not have done any more than he had.

For him, that was enough.

Sari, the Royal Palace

Sapphire lounged in the small private atrium that was attached to her quarters and absently studied the design of the Sarian palace on her compu-pad. Birds called out from their hanging cages, singing in chorus with the splashing water in the fountain. Sunlight poured onto the large plant fronds that lined the walls and shielded her in shade, the scorching rays diffused by the low emissive skylights above.

The other *mätresses*, royal concubines like her, were gossiping in the *seraglio*, but she didn't want to socialize today. In fact, over the last few years she'd found herself growing more dissatisfied with her life in the palace. She was an active woman with a variety of interests. The indolent life of a concubine, while highly respected and esteemed, was not suited to her temperament.

Despite this, Sapphire remained grateful that the King of Sari had chosen her from among the many women graduating from the Sensual Arts School in the capital city of Sari. Her graduation had come soon after the end of the D'Ashier Confrontations, a drawn-out war with a neighboring nation that had drained Sari's resources. For a time, concubines became an unaffordable luxury, and many graduates had been forced to auction their contracts to the highest bidder. The king's interest saved her from a similar fate, and created her high social status. All she'd had to relinquish was her name. She was now known as Sapphire, the royal stone of Sari. The appellation was an undeniable declaration of the king's possession, and the driving force of her fame.

But she possessed her king more surely than he would

ever possess her. His love for her was obsessive, his desire insatiable. He demanded her presence at all public events. Since their first night together, he had never taken another woman to his bed. Not even the queen.

This last result pained Sapphire greatly. It was obvious the Queen of Sari loved her husband. Sapphire had no personal experience with that powerful emotion, but she imagined the pain would be devastating—loving a man who in turn loved another. She hated to be the cause of such misery.

Over the last few years she had taken every opportunity to speak highly of her queen. She pointed out Her Majesty's beauty, poise, and ease with command, but her praise fell on deaf ears. Her best efforts to help the other woman all met with failure.

Setting aside the compu-pad with a sigh, Sapphire rose to her feet and began to stroll along the tiled path.

"I hate to see you so bored," came a lilting voice from the doorway.

Sapphire turned her head and her gaze met eyes of soft, pale green. Dressed in flowing pink robes, the blonde woman who'd spoken was a welcome sight. "Mom!"

"Hi, sweetheart." Sasha Erikson opened her arms and Sapphire rushed into them, curling with pleasure into the maternal embrace. "I've missed you. Tell me what you've been up to."

"A great deal of nothing, sad to say."

"Oh, sweetheart." Her mother kissed her forehead. "More and more, I think I did you a disservice by not seeing where your true calling lay."

Sasha had loved the life of a concubine and urged Sapphire into pursuing the career. Retired now and a tenured professor at the Sensual Arts School, Sasha was widely appreciated for her beauty and the adoration of her idolized husband. Sapphire's success was largely attributed to the tutelage of her mother and she was grateful for that advantage. However, she'd realized too late that she was far more suited to her father's military occupation than her mother's sensual one.

"You know better than that." Sapphire's tone was softly chastising. Linking arms, she pulled her mother into the atrium. "I wouldn't have pursued this career if I hadn't wanted it. My expectations were off. That is no one's fault but my own."

"What did you expect?"

"Too much, apparently. I can tell you what I *didn't* expect. I never expected the Confrontations or the sale of my contract to the king. I didn't expect that the political marriage between our monarchs was in fact a love match for only one of them. I never would have accepted His Majesty's offer if I'd known." She wrinkled her nose. "I was naïve."

"You? Naïve?" Sasha squeezed her hand. "Sweetheart, you are one of the most pragmatic women I know."

"You wouldn't say that if you knew what I'd hoped for then. I wanted to find what you and father have. You have a great love story—the handsome, heroic general who falls in love with and marries his beautiful concubine. You said when you first saw him it was as if your blood caught fire. That's so romantic, Mom." She sighed dramatically and her mother laughed. "See? You think I'm silly. Girlish fantasies and day-dreams."

Her mother shook her head. "The majority of people don't find love in the course of their employment. But I don't think you're silly."

Sapphire arched a dubious brow.

"Oh, okay," Sasha conceded. "Maybe a little silly."

Grinning, Sapphire rang for a *mästare* to bring wine. Then she sat on the tiled lip of the fountain and settled in to experience much-needed excitement through the words of her mother.

★ ★ ★

In just a few moments, her husband would leave the exotic haven of their private rooms for the bed of his concubine.

Desperate to reach him before he left, Brenna, Queen of Sari, spoke bluntly. "You have to make love to me, Gunther, if you want me to conceive. I cannot do it alone."

As the king began to pace in front of her, his frustration was clear. He was such a handsome man, tall with golden hair and skin. In all of her life, she had never met a man who could equal him. With every breath she took, she loved him more than the last.

"The precedence is clear and unbreakable. I cannot be artificially inseminated," she reminded him ruthlessly. "All royal heirs must be conceived naturally."

Running a hand through his hair, Gunther shot her a scathing glance. He strode past where she sat on the velvet-draped divan. "I know the rules!"

His reluctance to bed her cut deep. As she thought of his concubine, her nails dug into her palms. Sapphire was the *karimai*—most prized of all the *mätresses*.

The concubine's quarters remained full with women of every description, but for five years now the other *mätresses* had exclusively been sexually pleasured by the *mästares* who protected and served them. Only Sapphire shared the bed of the king—a place that should be Brenna's, and would be again. Soon.

"Send her away," Brenna suggested, as she had a hundred times. It always sparked an argument, but she refused to stop trying. She would get rid of her rival. Somehow. "Sari must have an heir."

He growled and paced faster. "I weary of your harping."

"We have been married for years! The people grow restless. They begin to doubt our fertility."

"You lie. No one would dare speak of such things."

She leaped to her feet. "They think it. They whisper it."

Coming to a halt, Gunther's gaze darted around as if he was trapped. No doubt he felt as if he was.

"Gunther?"

"Do it, then."

Her breath caught.

"Tomorrow, Brenna. Before I change my mind."

"Yes, of course."

Gunther stared at her for a long moment. Then he shook his head and made his egress.

To go to her. *To Sapphire.*

Brenna fought back the bile that rose in her throat. She had only hours left to wait until the *mätress* would be gone.

Then the king would be hers again.

As Sapphire made love to the King of Sari, her mind was firmly on her job. She barely registered the opulence of her surroundings, heeding them only in passing recognition of their enhancement of her duties. Simulated candlelight and smoky incense drifted lazily through the room. White stone arches draped in blue velvet circled the divan where she pleasured the king. Beyond was a shallow bathing pool; the tinkling melody of water pouring from the fountains was masked by the rhythmic sounds of sex.

She concentrated instead on the king's body signals—the rapidness of his breathing, the impatient upward drives of his hips, and the glazed look in his blue eyes. Using the powerful muscles of her thighs, Sapphire raised and lowered herself with practiced grace above him, conscious of her appearance because she knew the king liked to watch her. She was rewarded by the masculine satisfaction that curved his lips.

Soon he was gripping the pillows around him, hoarse cries torn from his throat as she serviced him. The all-powerful King of Sari groaned, sweat breaking out over his handsome features.

Sapphire arched her back as the king's orgasm pulsed

within her. Her job done to his satisfaction, she closed her eyes and reached her own climax. Her moan of release echoed through her bedchamber along with the king's.

Replete, she sank into the king's embrace with a sigh. He was a tall man with a sinewy strength she admired. The monarch was golden from the top of his blond head down to his manicured toes, and he was kind to her.

Once she'd dreamed of falling in love with her king, but in the end it was impossible. The King of Sari placed his pleasure paramount to hers. He knew nothing about her and made no effort to learn. After five years, she was still served food she didn't enjoy. They listened to music he liked and the clothes provided for her were made in colors and materials he chose with no care for her preferences.

Once a concubine accepted a labor contract, she was bound to her chosen protector until he decided to release her. Sapphire wondered if the king would ever allow her to go. How long would she be asked to remain his concubine? His interest showed no signs of waning.

Sapphire wanted to find someone who cared for her as she truly was—inside and out. She wanted to make love to a man because she was giving herself to him with her heart, a gift of herself for the man she loved.

That would never happen if the king never released her.

Nuzzling against his neck, Sapphire gave a throaty laugh as the evidence of his renewing desire swelled inside her. Her eyes met his.

"Give me a moment, my king." Her voice dropped to a throaty purr. "And I will pleasure you again."

He gripped her face between his hands, his gaze fierce. "No matter what happens in the future, you must promise me that you'll always remember you are my *karisette*. You have been from the moment I first saw you."

The intensity of his tone startled her, as did his words. *Karisette*—"true love."

"My king—"

"Promise me!"

She caressed his chest soothingly, turning her voice into a gentle croon. "Of course. I promise."

He rolled her beneath him and took her again.

Restless and edgy, Brenna paced the length of the throne room. Whenever she felt powerless, she found this location—the seat of her power—to be soothing. It had been dark when she first came here. Now the massive chamber brightened as the sun rose, spilling light through the domed skylights above.

"Your Majesty."

She turned her head and saw the prostrated messenger by the door. "Rise."

He stood swiftly, straightening the blue and gold vest that proclaimed his position as a member of the royal staff. "I have a message for the king."

"You may tell me," she said, needing the distraction. "His Majesty is occupied."

"A family near the border reported a disturbance they likened to blaster fire. A unit was dispatched to investigate and in the ensuing fight a mercenary was captured." He paused. "It is Tarin Gordmere."

Brenna's brows rose. Gordmere was a well-known irritant to Gunther. He had no qualms about raiding certain sectors, often costing the royal coffers a great deal of income. If she were to present the mercenary to the king, it would put him in a good mood, which could only be conducive to softening his feelings toward her, if only a little. "Where is he now?"

"At the southern detention facility."

"Excellent." She gifted the messenger with a bright smile. "I will see that the king hears of this. You are dismissed."

"There is more, Your Majesty."

"What is it?" Her tone was curt, an audible sign of her thinning patience.

"Gordmere's lieutenant approached the jail soon after the incarceration and offered an exchange."

"He has nothing we want," she scoffed.

"He claims he has Crown Prince Wulfric of D'Ashier."

She stopped midstep. "Impossible."

"The captain assures you that he would not bring this information to the palace without proof. The mercenary carried a signet ring bearing the royal shield of D'Ashier."

Stunned, Brenna attempted to reason out the implications of this new development.

Gordmere. Prince Wulfric.

How delicious, if the tale was true. Certainly if she presented Gunther with the prince, he would admire her daring. She would prove to him that she was fit to be his queen and worthy of Sari. He would see what he'd been blind to all these years—that she was perfect for him.

"Guardian," she called out.

"Yes, Your Majesty?" responded the masculine voice of the palace computer.

"Inform my guards to prepare for my departure." She strode past the servant, needing to change and depart before her husband was made aware of the day's events. "I leave within the half hour."

Sari, the Borderlands

Adjusting the train of her velvet robes, Brenna disembarked from the antigrav-craft. As she took in her surroundings, her nose wrinkled. The vast cave they'd been directed to made her skin crawl, and the smell of uncleansed air was offensive.

"Where is he?" She was eager to finish the distasteful business ahead.

The large sandy-haired man who waited at the end of the ramp bowed at the waist, a grave insult since he should have dropped to his knees and prostrated himself. "This way, Your Majesty."

Brenna could order her guards to force Tor Smithson down and would have if the mercenary didn't have something she wanted. But he did, so she followed, surrounded by her guardsmen. They traversed a long hallway, then turned a corner.

The sight that met her made her gag.

Covering her mouth, it took a few moments to find breath enough to speak. "If he's dead," she choked out, "you get nothing!"

"He's not dead." Smithson shrugged. "I just had a little fun with him."

A little fun.

Her stomach roiled violently. The man was mad. What she saw before her was near carnage. The stone walls around them were spattered with so much blood she couldn't believe it belonged to one person.

Hiding her nausea beneath chilly hauteur, Brenna moved forward. The man they said was the Crown Prince of D'Ashier hung unconscious before her, his wrists shackled and chained to opposite walls. The entire weight of his body was supported by those metal bonds. His powerful arms and broad shoulders were stretched to the tearing point, his hands a dark purple from supporting his large frame.

Reaching him, she used both hands to lift his slumped head and gasped. Aside from her husband, she had never seen features so finely crafted. Each line and plane had been etched by a master hand to create perfection.

Sadly, his face was the only part of him not covered in blood, or cut or burned or whipped. The rest of him—a warrior's well-honed body—was gravely, perhaps mortally injured.

She listened closely for sounds of life, and caught his breathing—shallow and erratic. The sounds of a man dying. "Take him down." She stepped out of the way.

Smithson growled. "Give me Gordmere first."

"No." Brenna raked his massive frame with a look of pure disgust. She'd never in her life met so vile a creature. "Once the prince is safely in my transport, I will release Gordmere."

The exchange was completed within moments, a perfectly healthy Gordmere exchanged for a man who had only hours left to live. The antigrav-craft lifted off and navigated carefully out of the cavern.

"Send out a call for troops," she ordered. "I want that place destroyed."

The distance to the palace was quickly traversed, but the prince's condition seemed to worsen considerably over the journey. Afraid to move him further, Brenna left him in the craft when they landed She wanted to present a live captive, regardless of whether he died shortly after or not. Running against the clock, Brenna hurried from the transport bay in search of her husband. The fastest route was through the *seraglio*, so that was the path she chose.

Rounding a corner, she skidded to a halt at the sight of the king. She was about to speak when she realized he wasn't alone. He was with *her*. Sapphire.

As Brenna registered the intimacy of his pose, her eyes widened. Gunther stood in the doorway of the concubine's room with her cheek cupped in his hand. Bent over her possessively, his lips clung to the *mätress's* with obvious affection. When he lifted his head, the torment on his handsome features was clearly visible.

He loved her.

Brenna collapsed against the cool plaster wall, shocked by comprehension. She could not win his heart, because it was no longer his to give. He was taken.

Something inside her cracked, then broke completely.

Sending the concubine away would not be enough. As long as Sapphire drew breath, she would be a threat.

Straightening and moving away before she was seen, Brenna reminded herself that she was queen and had unlimited resources. She could, and would, deal with this threat once and for all.

Everything she needed was right at her fingertips.

Sapphire entered the queen's receiving chamber, admiring as always the beauty of natural light flooding the room from the domed skylights above. As the palace computer slid the door closed behind her, she prostrated herself just inside the threshold, her forehead touching the cool tile floor. "Your Majesty, I am here as you ordered."

The queen's regal voice echoed across the vaulted ceiling and down the long, narrow chamber. "You may rise, king's *mätress*. Come and sit at my feet."

Moving as she was bade, Sapphire walked the massive length of the throne room toward the beautiful Queen Brenna. Golden, like her husband, the queen was the day to Sapphire's night. Tall and blessed with a willowy gracefulness, the queen stood a head higher than Sapphire and possessed none of her generous voluptuousness. However, it was not the blonde's figure that had discouraged the king's passion but her frigidity. As Sapphire approached the monarch, she swore she felt a radiating chill even through the queen's warm velvet robes.

Once she reached the end of the room, Sapphire took a seat on the bottom step of the royal dais and waited.

"We both understand our respective positions well, *mätress*, so I will be brief. Sari needs an heir. I have discussed this with the king and he agrees."

Sapphire took the news without a blink.

The queen watched her closely. "The thought of the king in my bed does not affect you adversely."

It was a statement, not a question.

Inclining her head in acknowledgment, Sapphire said, "Of course not, my queen. The king is yours. I have never thought otherwise."

Brenna leaned back in her throne with a grim smile. "I see you are not as taken with the king as he is with you."

Sapphire said nothing, which in turn said everything. She had never professed to love the king. He was a good man, a handsome and kind man, but he was not her *karisem*. She could never love a man who saw her only as a possession and not as an individual with thoughts and feelings of her own.

"That is fortunate for you, *mätress*, considering what I have to say. The king does not feel he can share my bed if you remain in the palace." Bitterness was evident in the regal voice.

Sapphire lowered her eyes to hide her pity, her heart going out to her queen.

"You are to be retired with the honor due you as the king's *karimai*," Her Majesty said. "As his most favored, you will be moved immediately to a home on the outskirts of the capital. You will be provided with fourteen *mästares* who will serve you until you die. Your every wish will be granted, *mätress*, for your exemplary service to the king."

Sapphire sat for a moment in shock. *Retired*. More than freedom, more than she had ever allowed herself to hope for. She was being pensioned off, after only one contract.

Usually when a *mätress* was released, she was free to find another protector, her value now greatly enhanced for having shared the bed of the king. Her wages became ever more exorbitant, her worth increasing with every protector until she acquired the funds to support her indolent lifestyle. But such was not to be Sapphire's fate. The king valued her and loved her so much he was willing to retire her.

Retirement. The word swirled in Sapphire's brain with a heady delight. It was what she had worked for, the reason her parents had encouraged her to become a concubine. Not only was the position well respected, it was also one of the few careers where hard work guaranteed a luxurious existence for life. In addition to her pension, she was also being gifted with fourteen *mästares*—handsome, virile men who would dedicate their lives to serving her.

"I'm grateful, my queen." Her words were heartfelt.

Brenna waved her hand in dismissal. "Go. Your belongings are being packed as we speak. The king has left the palace and will not be saying farewell. I'm certain you are clever enough to discern why."

"Yes, Your Majesty." Now she understood the king's driving urgency of the night before and his passionate declaration. He'd known it would be their last time together.

Sapphire backed out of the room in a bow. The doors slid open with a hiss as she approached, then closed again when she departed.

Unbelievably, freedom was hers.

Brenna waited until the doors sealed shut behind the retreating *mätress*. The fact that the concubine could so easily disregard the king's love solidified the queen's already firm resolve.

"Guardian," she called out to the empty chamber.

"Yes, Your Majesty?"

"Has my gift been delivered to the new home of the *mätress* Sapphire?"

"Of course, my queen. With the utmost discretion."

Her mouth curved in a feral smile. "Excellent."

Chapter I

Sapphire alighted from the royal antigrav-craft, her palms damp with anticipation. The home given to her by the King of Sari was, in fact, a small palace. Bright white with multicolored windows, it was set in the golden hills of sand like a sparkling jewel.

As five of her new *mästares* unloaded her belongings, she approached her front door. The hot breeze that coursed over her skin was a welcome and pleasant sensation. She'd spent the last five years inside the palace, her skin tanned by artificial means, her lungs filled with purified air. On excursions with the king, she had always entered the cooled antigrav-craft through equally cooled landing bays.

Taking her first deep breath of natural air in years, Sapphire smiled at the slightly gritty sensation left in her mouth. She enjoyed the heat of Sari and relished the fine sheen of sweat on her skin that evaporated instantly in the dry desert environment.

Placing her palm on the recognition pad, she waited a split-second as the system acknowledged her prints. The door slid open and *"Welcome, Mistress"* rang out in the melodious feminine voice of the house computer.

Sapphire entered her new home and was immediately assaulted with chilled, cleansed air.

"Guardian."

"Yes, Mistress?"

"Purify the air, but cool it only in the bedchambers."

"As you wish."

Absorbing her new surroundings with wide eyes, she found the balance of her *mästares* lining either side of her long entrance hallway. The resemblance the men bore to the king was noted with a smile. Tall, blond, and possessing sinewy lines of muscle, they were all remarkably handsome.

Sapphire walked through the gauntlet, then paused at the end with a frown. "There are only thirteen of you."

The *mästare* nearest to her dropped to his knees. "Mistress, my name is Dalen."

Resting her hand on his head, she slipped her fingers through his silky hair. "I'm pleased to meet you, Dalen."

He stood, and smiled with boyish charm. "The other *mästare* is still in the healing chamber, Mistress."

Her frown deepened. The healing chamber took only moments to heal slight injuries. *"Still?"*

"He was gravely injured when he arrived. He's been in the chamber for half an hour now. While he should be healed shortly, he'll need some rest before he can assume his duties. But the rest of us stand ready. We'll more than make up for his absence."

"I've no doubt you will all please me. But I'm concerned about the injured one. How was he so badly hurt? And why was he sent to me in such a state?"

"I'll take you to him, Mistress. I have no answers to your questions. You'll have to ask him when he emerges."

Offering his arm, Dalen escorted her through her palace. Sapphire took in the size and beauty of her surroundings with astonished pleasure. There could be no greater testament of her worth to the king than this show of largesse.

They crossed the large receiving room with its massive divan and traveled down an arched hallway to the center atrium. The sight of a large bubbling bath surrounded by lush greenery filled her with joy. The rest of her life would begin in this home, and her blood quickened at the thought of the freedom she would enjoy here.

Dalen stopped before a door nestled along the rear wing of the courtyard and waved his hand over the lock pad. The door slid open, and she stepped inside. In the center of the small room stood the cylindrical glass healing chamber. She took one look at the unconscious man inside and her instinctive response to him was so powerful, she ordered Dalen to leave her. When the door slid shut behind the retreating *mästare*, Sapphire walked closer to the chamber.

The injured man took her breath away. Tall, dark, and devastated with whip marks that were slowly healing before her eyes, he still boasted raw potent masculinity. He was nothing like the king or her *mästares*. He was nothing like any man she'd ever seen.

Rich, gleaming black hair blew gently around his nape as the swirling air pressure inside kept him upright. His skin was deeply tanned and stretched over powerfully defined muscles. She'd never seen a man with so many ripples of power beneath his skin; not even her warrior father displayed such strength.

His facial features were strong and bold, like the rest of his body. High cheekbones and an aquiline nose gave him an aristocratic cast; the powerful jaw and sensual lips made him dangerous. He was simply magnificent. She wondered what color his eyes were. Brown maybe, like her own? Or perhaps blue, like the king's?

Sapphire circled the chamber slowly, wincing at the myriad wounds that striped and gouged his flesh. The man had been tortured most grievously. The length of time he'd already spent in the chamber told her he must have been near death when they brought him to her. Who would have selected such a man for her? He was as different from the other *mästares* as she was from the queen. Even unconscious, this man radiated mastery. He was no *mästare*.

Returning to the front of the chamber, she continued her heated perusal, her nipples puckering as desire quickened her blood. His broad and powerful chest was almost healed now. A thin strip of hair led her eyes down the ripples of his abdomen to his cock and testicles below. Her mouth went dry as she noted the carefully trimmed curls at the base of his shaft and his heavy sac that was completely denuded of hair. She stepped closer to the chamber until her hands and breasts were pressed against the warm glass, her eyes riveted to his groin. Even flaccid, his penis was impressive. She wondered how it would look when aroused.

As if it could read her mind, his cock suddenly twitched and began to swell. Rising slowly, it took on commendable size. Becoming aroused by the sight, Sapphire rubbed her breasts against the glass, then stilled as the stunning phallus grew in response to her wantonness. Startled, her gaze flew upward and was arrested by dazzling green eyes. Emerald bright, they raked her body hungrily, able to see her completely through the sheerness of her gown. Her skin tingled and grew warm as the man studied her with breathtaking boldness.

Nakedness imparted no vulnerability to the man's undeniably arrogant bearing. She was so hot for him she was on fire, this stranger with the battered body and handsome face. For the first time in her life, Sapphire felt the pull of true desire, heady and overwhelming.

"Who are you?" she whispered, even though she knew he couldn't hear her through the glass. He reached out a hand, pressing opposite hers against the barrier that separated them. Sweat misted her skin at the thought of touching him. She wanted to curl her fingers and lace his long digits with hers. She longed to caress his bronzed skin and see if it was as smooth as it looked.

He was almost healed. Soon, he would exit the chamber. Prolonged, intense healing was exhausting. He would most likely collapse at her feet. With a sigh of regret, Sapphire stepped back and was startled when he lunged toward the glass as if to catch her. *Don't go,* he mouthed. The stark plea in his eyes made her chest tight.

"Guardian." Her voice was a hoarse whisper. "Who is this man in the healing chamber?"

"He is Crown Prince Wulfric of D'Ashier."

Chapter 2

Taken aback by the introduction, Sapphire recoiled from the glass. Wulfric remained against it, watching her with a narrowed, alert gaze.

The D'Ashier crown prince.

Sari's refusal to acknowledge the full power of D'Ashier often led to war. The General of the Sarian Army had become a national hero with his victory in the D'Ashier Confrontations only a few years past.

The stunning man before her was the legendary warrior son of the present king of D'Ashier. Wulfric was the eldest, the heir to the throne. He was re-nowned for his ruthlessness and his military genius. It was rumored that it was he who truly ran D'Ashier, while his father acted mostly as a figurehead.

Her voice shook with confusion. "Why is he here?"

"He is one of your mästares."

She shook her head. "That's impossible. This man rules a country. He cannot remain here. His presence in Sari could restart the war."

"His countrymen believe him to be dead."

The fiercely intelligent green eyes studying her knew the exact moment she realized who he was. His lips thinned and his gaze hardened.

Sapphire's hand went to her throat. "I cannot keep him."

But she wanted to. With a primitive hunger she'd never experienced before. There was fire in her blood, such as her mother had told her about. And the way he looked at her . . .

Sweat broke out on her skin.

She knew that look. He wanted her, too. Yet Prince Wulfric was dangerous in every way imaginable. He was a master to her slave, a prince to her concubine. She'd just been released from that life and she would never go back to it.

"How am I expected to keep him here, and why? Who chose him for me?"

"He is a gift from the queen, Mistress. She bids you to tame him as you did the king."

A dry laugh rasped from her throat. This man was no gift. He was a spiteful punishment for stealing the affections of the king. The queen probably hoped the prince would kill her. Or that she would kill him first.

"The queen has provided seven of her personal guardsmen to assist you."

"I see." Sapphire licked dry lips and watched as an answering smolder lit Wulfric's eyes.

Looking at him, she felt a strangely profound regret. She would never be allowed to enjoy him the way he should be enjoyed. They were at odds without saying a word. He was a prisoner and she was his keeper, but given the slightest chance, he would easily reverse their roles. He was hot. Her resistance would melt. And while she would most likely glory in every minute of it, Sapphire couldn't allow it to happen.

She offered a mournful smile. Wulfric's mouth curved up on one side, his gaze still burning with desire but sharp with challenge. She could read his response to her withdrawal in his eyes. Relentless, ruthless—that's what the media said about him. He got what he wanted, and he wanted her.

"Guardian, what if I wish to release him?" she asked.

"But you do not. Your vital signs tell me—"

"I know what my vitals are telling you. That's precisely the reason he has to go."

"Yes, Mistress. No order was given forcing you to keep him. I conclude that leaves the choice to you."

Sapphire held the prince's gaze. Something passed between them, an awareness that intensified with each passing second. How could she feel this way about a man she'd never touched or spoken to? For all she knew, he could be a cruel and selfish man.

Yet she sensed he wasn't. His gaze was too direct. He allowed her to see everything he was feeling—attraction, desire, defiance, determination.

She sighed. "The queen knows I will do nothing to bring attention to this. We could both be executed for treason. Brenna's bitterness must truly run deep for her to resort to this reckless and ill-conceived plan of revenge."

"As you say, Mistress."

"How could she predict my reaction to this man?" she wondered out loud. *She* was startled by this depth of feeling. How could a stranger know?

"My conclusion is that she expected hatred, due to your father's position."

Sapphire stiffened. Her father. If he were to discover Wulfric . . .

She had to hide him.

The moment the thought was conceived, she rejected it. What was she thinking, wanting to protect the prince? Only two men had ever held important places in her life—her father and her king. The prince was their enemy. Why was she considering his welfare first?

"Guardian." Squaring her shoulders, Sapphire turned toward the door. "Send for three guardsmen. His Highness is almost healed and will be released from the chamber soon." The portal slid open as she neared it. The heat of Wulfric's gaze burned her back until the door closed behind her. She refused to return his look.

"What are your orders in regard to Prince Wulfric?"

"Have him dressed, fed, then locked in his room to sleep. You will advise me when he awakens. In the meantime, gather all the information you can about him and give me a report. I want to know what I'm dealing with."

"Of course, Mistress."

"Pull up the architectural plans for this palace. I'll need to study them, and set in place the means to confine him."

"You could ring him."

A mental picture of a confinement ring came to mind. The innocuous-looking but deadly band of metal was placed around a prisoner's ankle. As long as a ringed individual remained in the designated areas, there wasn't a problem. But should they venture too far, the ring would burst in an explosion that annihilated the wearer.

With the virile beauty of Wulfric still fresh in her mind, Sapphire shuddered at the thought of killing him. "No. I won't go that far. If he escapes, I'll hunt him down myself."

"As you wish. Do you require anything else?"

"Yes. Send a thank-you to the queen for her thoughtfulness."

Wulfric entered the receiving room with freshly laundered towels in his hands. With all the work he was doing, he was gaining a new appreciation for his own servants. It took great effort to keep a household running smoothly. He would never have fully appreciated that without performing the menial tasks himself.

He also appreciated the constant duties, which kept his mind from thoughts of his recent confinement and torture. Sleep was elusive, his dreams tormented him. Hard work was the only thing that distracted him.

Catching a flash of jeweled color out of the corner of his

eye, Wulf turned his head to catch the departure of his lovely brunette keeper.

In truth, work wasn't the *only* distraction. He was fascinated by the woman who'd stood like a wanton angel before the healing chamber.

He always seemed to be one step behind her. It didn't help that she was avoiding him. In the last three days, he'd caught only fleeting glimpses of her scantily clad figure. Brief, tantalizing glimpses. After hovering near death, the way she brought his senses to life was a miracle he wanted to explore.

But Wulf tempered his impatience. Their time would come. He would have escaped already if he didn't know that for a certainty.

Looking around the room, he noticed all of the other men engaged in various tasks. He approached the one closest to him, the one who seemed the least wary. They all looked alike to Wulf—tall, blond, and possessed of lean lengths of muscle so different from his own bulk.

He couldn't comprehend why these men chose to be *mästares*. With their good looks, they could have any woman they wanted. Why they chose to dedicate their lives to one woman they had to share among them was beyond his understanding.

"*Mästare.*"

"Yes, Your Highness?"

Wulf snorted, finding it amusing when they called him by his title, as if he were not toiling alongside them. Their forced respect was *her* doing, he was certain. Some of the *mästares* bore him a barely restrained hatred and he could well understand. It was a sad fact that several of them must have lost a friend or loved one during the Confrontations. While he had not been the instigator of that war, he had fought without mercy, doing whatever was necessary to protect his people. Of course, the citizens of Sari would not see it that way. "I have some questions to ask you."

"Certainly. And my name is Dalen."

Wulfric nodded. "Dalen, what do you know about the mistress of this household?"

"I know everything about Mistress Sapphire."

Arching a disbelieving brow, Wulf tested her name silently. *Sapphire.*

"Truly," Dalen insisted. "It's in her best interests to have us understand her. The more we know about her, the better we can serve her needs."

"A man such as you could have his own needs met."

"Your reputation with women precedes you, Your Highness. You think I should have many women rather than just one."

"The thought had occurred to me," Wulf agreed dryly.

"A hundred women couldn't give me the prestige I receive from being in the service of Mistress Sapphire. Her value increases mine, which in turn increases my family's."

"What makes her so important?"

"She is the king's *karisette.*"

"The *king*?" Wulf's gut knotted.

"Makes your position quite interesting, doesn't it? I'm certain the king has no knowledge of your presence here."

"Someone will turn me in." Wulfric looked around the room with renewed alertness. "Some of these *mästares* would pay dearly to see my capture."

"When I first learned of your identity, I intended to give you up. My older brother was almost killed during the Confrontations. General Erikson saved his life. If he hadn't . . ." Dalen tensed, the thought visibly taking root before he shook it off. "The other *mästares* and I swore to serve the Mistress. She may be the king's *karisette*, but she is our first responsibility and turning you in would endanger her."

"What the hell is a *karisette*?" Wulf snapped, suspecting from the way the word was said that he wouldn't like its meaning.

Dalen lowered his voice. "The king's love."

"A concubine?"

"More than a concubine. His Majesty is in love with her."

Wulf's jaw tensed. His angel belonged to his greatest enemy.

"The Mistress is something of a national celebrity," Dalen explained. "Her value to the king is well known to the people of Sari, which makes my position as her *mästare* a prosperous one."

"If he loves her, why send her here? Why not keep her in the palace, where access would be more convenient?"

Owing to the bitter relations and ever-present threat of war between their countries, Wulf had learned all there was to know about the Sarian Army and the king's family, but he had left interest in the king's concubines to others. Now he had a very strong interest in a royal concubine, one who'd brought him back to life just from the sight of her. It had been a very long time since he'd felt such attraction to a woman. So long, he couldn't recall it.

"You know the king has no children, Your Highness, and Sari needs an heir. All royal offspring must be made naturally. The king must spill his seed directly into the queen. Assisted inseminations are not allowed, as they are for the general population."

"It is the same in D'Ashier."

"The king was unable to perform his duty to the queen with Mistress Sapphire in the palace. So he sent her away."

Wulf wasn't confused exactly, the story was quite clear, but the king's motivation eluded him. "Did he send all of his women away?"

Dalen shook his head. "From her first night in the palace five years ago, the king has only had Mistress Sapphire in his bed. A year after she joined the *seraglio*, His Majesty realized the desire he once had for his other concubines would not be returning and he offered to end their contracts. A few accepted his offer, the rest stayed. The *mästares* in the palace service the remaining women, since the king does not call for them. Therefore, whether those *mätresses* stayed or left meant nothing to him, but the Mistress had to go. Having her close at hand made his duty to the queen impossible."

Wulf grew very still. "Your king kept Sapphire in his bed exclusively? For *five years*? With no break?"

"I see by your expression," Dalen grinned, "that you have never been in love."

It was beyond Wulfric's imaginings to picture the same woman in his bed over a five-year span. If he wanted longevity in a bedmate, he'd marry. As it was, he was blessedly unattached.

"So," Dalen continued, "maybe now you can see why the Mistress has been gifted with this palace and all of us *mästares*. It's no coincidence that we were all selected based on our physical resemblance to the king."

Very clever of the monarch, conceded Wulf, to keep constant reminders of himself all around his former lover.

But the king had only imitations to give Sapphire.

Wulf was here in the flesh.

Chapter 3

As Wulf walked the length of corridor that framed the center courtyard, hot air coursed over his sweat-dampened skin. He relished the heat, accustomed to it from long months spent in the desert protecting and strengthening the borders of D'Ashier. Attired in a *mästare*'s uniform, he was clad only in a loose pair of linen drawstring pants that hung low on his hips. His chest and feet were bare. He moved toward Sapphire's office with his customary bold gait, a stride that proclaimed without a word that he controlled all things around him.

The cool tiles felt wonderful against the soles of his feet. Apparently Sapphire shunned technology whenever she could comfortably do so. He liked that about her. He'd had his share of pampered, indolent women. The thought of an earthy lover made his pulse race.

And now, finally, he was moments away from seeing her again, face to face. Wulf's palms itched at the thought.

The first time he'd seen her, he had been rousing from near death. In the days since, he'd almost managed to convince himself that she couldn't be as breathtaking as he remembered. He was hopeful those first moments of renewed life and consciousness in the healing chamber had simply caused a temporary susceptibility. Perhaps any woman would have been especially appealing.

His mouth curved in a self-deprecating smile. Obviously he hadn't convinced himself of the ordinariness of her charms, because he could have escaped at any time, yet here he was. The efforts Sapphire had taken to detain him were impressive and intriguing, displaying a knowledge of imprisonment he would have thought beyond a concubine's sphere of study. Still, he was confident he could slip away with a little effort . . . if he weren't trapped here as surely as if he were chained. No matter how vital it was that he return to D'Ashier, he couldn't leave without knowing what the consequences would be for her.

And if she wanted him as much now as she had before, he intended to celebrate his rebirth in her bed.

Wulf paused on the threshold of her open-walled office. As he caught sight of her, his body hardened with need. He hadn't been mistaken or delusional. Sapphire was stunning. Small-boned and petite, she stood on a short step reaching for a book. When she turned to face him, her smile tightened his chest.

"How are you feeling?" she queried in a raspy voice.

Dressed in an almost transparent shift, she robbed him of speech. The sight of her lush curves sent heat flaring across his skin.

Full, firm breasts swayed unfettered over rounded hips, and jeweled rings sparkled from luxuriously long nipples. Her waist was not small—in fact, she had a slight womanly roundness to her belly—but it looked tiny in relation to the voluptuousness of her figure.

Her hair was waist-length and a lovely shiny brown color like the pelt of a hosen fox. Her face, while not classically beautiful, was arresting with intelligent brown eyes, full lips, and a determined jaw. Beneath the shimmering sheer fabric of her gown, her skin was creamy and completely hairless—the hair most likely lasered off permanently.

Wulf's mouth was as dry as the desert outside. Sapphire possessed something much more attractive than physical beauty—she radiated confidence. She aroused because it was clear she hungered for the pleasures of life and she was determined to pursue those pleasures. He sensed she was a kindred spirit, a primitive creature like himself in a world that had long ago evolved and been tamed.

As she stepped down to sit at her desk, her smile widened, and a sudden realization burned through Wulf's mind. When he was in her presence, his focus narrowed until he was aware only of her. When she'd stood in front of the healing chamber, he had ceased to feel the excruciating pain of his wounds or his profound exhaustion. He could only watch her, ache for her as she rubbed herself against the glass and stared at him with open admiration and desire. The way she'd looked at him had made him feel powerful and virile at a time when he was helpless and disgusted by his own weakness.

He *wanted* her. She made him feel both carnal and possessive. His body craved hers on some base level. He wondered if his recent ordeal had changed him in some way, made him vulnerable, as he hadn't been previously.

"Well, Prince Wulfric? How are you?"

A ripple of pleasure coursed through him at the sound of her throaty voice. "Mistress," he answered, the word rolling off his tongue in a way that said *he* was in *her* service only because he chose to be, and not because she forced him. "I'm feeling much improved."

Her dark eyes sparkled. "I'm happy to hear that. The Guardian says you asked for permission to speak with me. You have it. Speak."

He started in surprise at her tone, but didn't show it. Authority had slipped over her like a monarch's robes. Wulf noted her self-possession and her ease in command. There was more to this concubine than met the eye. He was determined to discover as much as he could about her before he left.

"I'm curious as to the state of my present circumstances." He kept his face impassive, not wanting to betray his confidence that he could leave her at will. It was obvious Sapphire had nothing to do with his capture. The *mästares* had told him of her surprise at discovering him in her home and she made no effort to question him or torment him as would someone who had a malicious intent. That left many questions unanswered. "Am I to be ransomed?"

"You didn't have to see me to ask that question. Guardian, will you answer?"

"There is no ransom, Prince Wulfric. Your countrymen believe you to be dead."

Wulf didn't even blink. After his failure to check in, search parties would have discovered the remains of his patrol. Despite that evidence, the palace would know he was alive. Deep inside the flesh of his right buttock was a nanotach—a chip powered by his cellular energy that conveyed his location.

To avoid war, his father would allow him a reasonable amount of time to escape. After that, fighting would begin. D'Ashier needed him. He had work to do. The assault against his patrol had succeeded owing to careful planning. No one would dedicate that amount of effort for mere sport. What had been the original intent of the ambush? Ransom? Information? And how did the plans change so greatly that he was now in the care of the king's favorite concubine?

The Guardian misunderstood his silence.

"Be forewarned if you think to end the Mistress's life for your freedom. With her training, you may find an unexpected result."

Sapphire studied him with a penetrating gaze, as if she hoped to see his intentions from the outside.

"I don't want to kill you," he assured her. "If I did, I would have done so by now."

Wulf tensed a moment too late. What occurred next transpired so quickly he couldn't be certain later what happened. He remembered only that she sprang from her chair and flew across the desk in one fluid movement. Her smaller body hit his with enough force to knock him to the floor. The teasing prick of pain at his neck warned him that she held a blade in her hand. With a flick of her wrist, he would bleed to death.

For a moment, horrifying memories of his ambush made his heart race desperately. His chest lifted and fell in near panicked rhythm. He could smell the cave and taste his own blood. He inhaled sharply—

—and the scent of Draxian lilies permeated his senses. *Her* scent.

The warmth and softness of her body was a salve. He was soothed, just from the feel of her, his fear and confusion gone as quickly as they'd come. Still he was shocked, staring up at her with wide eyes. It took years of training for a woman of her slight build to better a man of his size. Sapphire wouldn't have managed it without the element of surprise. But that was not the point. The point was she *had* bettered him. She was no easy target and she wanted him to know that. He was impressed.

Then his admiration flared into something hotter as the press of her curves onto his body burned into his consciousness. Suddenly, he was more than impressed, he was aroused.

Her breasts, so full and soft, were against his chest with only her transparent shift between them. Her legs, lithe and obviously powerful, were tangled with his. Gripping her waist with one hand, he watched her lips part and her pupils dilate. His cock swelled against her thigh. Her hair surrounded them in fragrant silk and he wrapped his fist into it, pulling her closer. Moistening his lips, Wulf longed for her to kiss him, his gaze riveted to her lush mouth.

Every nerve ending in his body was alert, every muscle tense. Every breath pushed his chest into those beautiful tits.

"Kiss me," he ordered.

The knife at his neck wavered. "I won't."

"Why?"

"You know why," she whispered.

"I know I almost died a few days ago and woke instead to the sight of you." Wulfric lifted his head and nuzzled his nose against hers. "Kindness, a gentle soul—none of that would have revived me the way your desire did. You've no notion of what I owe you for that."

Sapphire sighed, her free hand brushing briefly across his cheek. "Then don't ask this of me."

It was the regret in her tone and that fleeting caress that moved him. He didn't have time to woo her properly, but he knew when it was wiser to retreat than press a shaky advantage. It took tremendous willpower to release her, but Wulf managed it.

When Sapphire slid off him and returned to her seat behind the desk, his disappointment was acute. He sprang from the floor and landed on the pads of his feet with the grace of a cat.

His stay with the lovely Sapphire was limited by necessity. Fortunately, the desire he felt was mutual. With that on his side, his rushed seduction just might succeed.

Needing a distraction from his erection, Wulf asked, "How did I end up here?"

"You were a gift." Her low voice betrayed her response to him.

"A *gift*?" He scowled. He was not an object to be passed around.

A laugh escaped before she covered her mouth.

Heat coiled inside him at the seductive sound. He almost didn't care why he was here. It was worth it to experience the things she made him feel.

"I believe you're to be my punishment, Your Highness."

"Punishment? For what?"

She gave an offhand shrug. "It was another time. Another life. It's of no consequence now. The fact remains that you've been given to me, and we must make the best of the situation."

"You could release me," he purred in the silky smooth voice that never failed to get him what he wanted from women.

She surprised him by agreeing. "It would be wise to do so

and really, I have no other choice. You can't stay here. Unfortunately for both of us, I'm reluctant to let you go."

"Why?"

"You're magnificent. The handsomest man I've ever seen." She stared at him with clear admiration. "I enjoy looking at you."

Wulf had never realized how arousing honesty could be. All of his concubines were practiced, even jaded. Sapphire's reluctant appreciation was far more flattering. He could give her no gifts, promise her no boons, yet she still wanted him.

He walked toward her, allowing her to see his hunger. "I give you leave to do more than look. In fact, I encourage you to do so."

Her eyes widened. "*You* give *me* leave?"

The Guardian interrupted. "*Mistress, the general has arrived.*"

Wulfric froze in mid-stride, his body instinctually flexing in preparation for battle. He watched as Sapphire rose from her chair, and the Guardian's words came back to haunt him—*With her training, you may find an unexpected result.*

After the surprise attack of a moment ago, he quickly comprehended how foolish he was to have stayed. Sapphire did indeed move with a warrior's grace; he'd simply been too enamored to notice. She was concubine to the King of Sari and received visits from generals. He was in a hell of a position, completely at the mercy of his enemies.

"Who the hell are you?" he demanded, noting the apprehension that passed over her features.

"Go to your room." She shooed him off with a wave of her hand. "And don't show yourself until you're told to do so."

"I have the right to know what's planned for me."

"Planned for you?"

"Yes. Where is the general taking me?"

She grasped his meaning. "Wulf, you're not going anywhere. I want you to hide."

For a moment he stood motionless, his heart pounding. "You're protecting me."

Sapphire glanced at the wall behind her. The Guardian obligingly projected an image of the general striding toward her front door. The man's face was downcast, hidden from view. "Go, Your Highness," she urged. "Please. We can discuss this later."

"Why are you doing this?" Wulf crossed his arms over his chest.

She groaned. "Hell if I know. Stay then, if you're so eager for my father's hospitality over mine."

"Your father?" How much worse could this get?

"Yes." Her dark gaze locked with his. "The choice is yours, but make it quickly."

"You want me to hide so that I can stay."

"I don't know what I want. Other than for you to hide yourself as I asked."

Wulf found her irresistible—her honesty, strength, and beauty. Something was building between them; something she felt, too, or she wouldn't be so concerned for him. He shouldn't trust her, but he did.

Without a word, he turned and left, seeking the isolation of his room and the chance staying here would allow him to get to know her better.

As the door to his chamber slid closed behind him, an unfamiliar restlessness clawed at him. He was not a man to run from a challenge, and he chafed at allowing another person to protect him.

"What the hell is going on out there?"

In response to his inquiry, the Guardian projected a view of Sapphire and her father against the bare wall, complete with sound.

"Thank you."

He'd found an ally.

Wulfric watched as Sapphire was wrapped in an affectionate embrace. When her father stepped back and his face was revealed, the air rushed from Wulf's lungs.

No wonder the *mästares* wouldn't tell anyone about his presence in Sari—they were protecting the daughter of their national hero.

Sapphire's father was none other than General Grave Erikson, the highest-ranking officer in the Sarian Army.

Chapter 4

Sapphire waved her father into an oversized chaise, then she took the seat next to him, relishing the opportunity to have his undivided attention. She smiled into brown eyes identical to her own and asked, "How is Mom?"

Grave Erikson looked dashing in his uniform of sapphire sleeveless tunic and matching loose trousers. His long, sable hair was tied back at the nape, revealing a face of austere handsomeness and quiet strength. With a glaive-hilt strapped to his muscular thigh, her father radiated a danger that caused his enemies to run in fear and filled Sapphire's heart with pride. "She's well. Lovely as always. She plans to visit as soon as she can."

"I'm surprised you came without her."

"Work brought me out this way." He held out his hand, palm up, revealing a large man's ring nestled there. "A souvenir for you."

Picking up the offering, Sapphire admired the massive talgorite gem, its vibrant red color distinctive and singularly beautiful. It was also exceptionally valuable, its size sufficient to power a deep-space *skeide* through several lightspeed jumps. "What's this symbol imbedded in the stone?"

"The royal shield of D'Ashier."

She swallowed hard, knowing how brutally Wulf was forced

to part with the item. Her fist closed around it protectively. "How did you get this?"

"Talgorite is too valuable to use for jewelry, for the most part. When the ring hit the black market, word spread and a vice officer picked it up. He recognized the shield, and the ring made its way up the chain to me."

"Did you find out why the royal family parted from it?"

"The fence admitted to working with a mercenary group that attacked the Crown Prince of D'Ashier's patrol last week. I knew of it, of course, because we'd intercepted transmissions from the search party that was sent to locate the prince's group."

"Did they kill him?" Sapphire shoved aside the guilt she felt at deceiving her father.

"That's the most interesting part. The fence says they tortured Prince Wulfric and sold him. Unfortunately, the man was not privy to any internal discussion in the merc group. The lack of information is frustrating. Obviously Wulfric never made it to either the Sarian or D'Ashier palaces, so where the hell is he? Who would be able to afford him, and why would they want him? I wonder if he's received medical care for his injuries or if he's been taken off-world."

Sapphire studied her father. "You seem . . . upset."

A *mästare* entered the room and laid out trays of sweet-meats, fruits, and cheeses. The ale the servant poured was cold and slushy, instantly frosting the glasses.

Grave waited until the servant departed before continuing. "I'm a warrior, not a politician. I could care less about the trade agreements and Interstellar Council squabbles that keep us at odds with D'Ashier. I care about men and honor. Prince Wulfric is a brave man and an excellent warrior. To be ambushed, tortured, and sold . . . It's cowardly and dishonorable. I would have preferred a more fitting end for a man such as him."

"You think he's dead?"

"I hope he's not, but odds aren't in his favor at this point."

"You sound as if you like him."

Grave shrugged. "I admire him. I fought against him hand to hand during the Confrontations. He was young then, but he had fire and an air of command I admired. His tactical plans were well thought out, he never moved rashly or responded in haste. His first concern was always for the well-being of his men, and he never allowed his desire for victory to goad him into actions that would needlessly cost lives."

"But it's *you* who walked away triumphant and a national hero from those battles," she reminded him proudly.

"We won, but only by the skin of our teeth. If the weather hadn't changed and that sandstorm blown in, the outcome could have been very different."

"You've never told me that before!"

"We've never talked about Prince Wulfric before." Grave reached for a piece of melon and popped it into his mouth.

"Let's talk about him now." Leaning against the curved arm of the chaise, Sapphire met her father's gaze with a challenging smile. "Tell me everything you know."

He eyed her speculatively. "Why the sudden interest in Wulfric?"

"You've never been defeated, now you tell me it almost happened once. I'm curious about the man who is such a match for you."

"Some other time. Maybe." He downed the contents of his mug in one gulp.

"Are you still investigating what happened to the prince?"

"Persistent as ever, I see." His indulgent expression turned serious. "Yes, I'm investigating. *Quietly.* I've notified the palace, but the king and queen both felt it was best to leave this matter to me and not involve the Interstellar Council."

"I want to know what you discover, Daddy."

"Why?"

"Maybe I'll venture into investigations or bounty hunting. Maybe I'm just curious."

"And maybe you just don't want to tell me your reasons."
Grave chuckled. "But I'll keep you posted anyway. Now I want
to talk about you. Word has spread about your retirement. Have
you made any plans for your future?"

"I think I'm going to spend a little time doing nothing. I want
to eat all the foods I couldn't in the palace and wear clothes in
all the colors I've missed. I'd like to see what's been happening
outside of the palace walls, and reorient myself to society." She
smiled. "Then, I'll figure out what to do with myself."

Setting his hand atop hers, he gave an encouraging squeeze.
"I think it's wise that you're taking time to find your bearings,
instead of leaping without knowing where you're going. Do
you have an idea of where your other interests lie?"

"Not yet. Maybe I'll make use of my training. Or teach. I
haven't decided yet."

"You were always good with stratagems. I could send over
training plans and you can help assemble some manuals."

"Truly?"

"Yes, truly." He gave her an affectionate smile. "It'll be a good
excuse for me to stop by more often. I was rarely able to see
you when you were in the palace."

Sapphire threw her arms around her father's neck, upsetting
his empty mug, but he didn't mind, as evidenced by the crushing embrace he returned.

"Now show me around this palace of yours," he said with
a laugh. "So I can brag about it to anyone who will listen."

It was much later when Wulfric was summoned to Sapphire's office.

"I believe this is yours." She leaned over the desk, and set his
signet ring on the edge. Her demeanor was distant and rushed.

He moved slowly to retrieve the ring, betraying none of
his relief. "Thank you," he murmured. Now his freedom
was assured.

She spun her chair to the side and waved him away in a dismissive gesture. She seemed distracted, lost in thought.

Wulf knew he should leave. Not just the room as she had indicated, but the entire country. The ring she returned to him was by itself just a ring and even close examination would reveal nothing suspicious. But when the talgorite was in contact with his body, it worked in conjunction with the nanotach. Together, they could transfer him instantly to his palace in D'Ashier and back to this place if he chose, as long as the signal wasn't blocked.

In the blink of an eye, this could all be over. One or more of his concubines could assuage the lust that weighed heavily between his legs. He'd been on patrol too long. He was a man of a healthy sexual appetite and his powerful desire for Sapphire was due only to his long abstinence. Surely, that was the only reason . . .

"I want you," he said before he could stop himself.

Sapphire tensed visibly at the sound of his voice, low and throbbing with desire. He watched her closely, noting the exact moment her eyes softened and her lips parted in response to his hunger. They had an undeniable affinity, despite the many things that stood between them.

"I should release you," she whispered.

"You should, but you won't. You've gone to too much trouble to keep me."

"You need a woman." She looked away. "All the *mästares* do. I've arranged for some of the fourth-year Sensual Arts students to visit a few days a week. They will arrive this evening. I think you'll be pleased. They're—"

"I don't want someone else. I want *you*."

Resignation crossed her lovely features. "That's not going to happen."

"Being inside you is all I can think about." And when he was thinking about her, he wasn't thinking about the cave. No other woman could do that. Maybe later, but not now.

"Sex between us would only complicate matters, Wulf, not make them easier. If you started thinking with your head rather than your cock, you'd admit I'm right."

"You're an insolent creature." Something he wouldn't have thought he'd find arousing. But did.

"And you're not ruler here. If you want to command, go home."

Wulfric drew air deep into his lungs. No one ever spoke to him as she did. She had no fear and refused to display the respect that was due a man of his station. All that fire and passion . . . He wanted to sink into it and forget everything else.

As he strode toward her, Sapphire remained still, relaxed in her chair.

"One time will never be enough," she warned softly.

He stopped.

"Already, you no longer desire other women. Do you really believe that will change once you've bedded me?"

"You're vain," he said without heat. "Don't confuse me with your besotted king."

"That would be impossible." She laughed and the throaty sound rippled down his spine. "I'm not speaking out of vanity, and you know it. You think I don't feel the attraction between us? If you're even half as good in bed as you look, I'll want more. And I'm not without skills of my own. You would enjoy me immensely. You suspect how good it could be, that's why the thought of other women is so unappealing. When was the last time you desired a woman who wasn't interchangeable with another?"

His cock hardened further. Her bold challenge excited him. "Never," he admitted. Staring at her, he felt as if she was some new, previously undiscovered species. "Do you ever not say exactly what's on your mind?"

"I've spent the last five years never saying what I thought. I didn't like it and vowed never to do it again."

His smile was predatory. "Then allow me to be as honest with you. Unless you refuse me outright, I *will* have you."

"You have another life to return to."

"I'd say let's hurry, but I have no intention of doing that." She rubbed at the space between her brows. "This is crazy."

"Isn't it?" He was glad that it was, and grateful that his heart raced and his stomach was clenched tight in anticipation. *He was alive.* A miracle in itself and he wanted to celebrate that with her.

"Arrogant bastard." She glared at him.

Wulf moved around the desk and growled when she spread her legs, revealing her glistening sex beneath the short hem of her dress. She was as ready as he was. He reached for the drawstring at his waist.

"No."

His fingers stilled.

She pointed to the floor at her feet. "On your knees, Prince Wulfric. If you're so eager, you may pleasure me with your mouth."

Frozen mid-step, he stared at her. Sapphire was going to fight him every step of the way. He searched her face, judging the strength of her resolve. He groaned inwardly at the obstinate set of her jaw and the defiant gleam in her eyes.

The prince in him was affronted at being ordered to forgo his own pleasure to service hers. But the part of him that was pure primitive male smelled her arousal and knew it was his to take. The two sides battled for only a moment.

A war of wills—it was a new and highly intriguing situation for him, a man who'd never had his will challenged in his lifetime.

After years of war and months on patrol, Wulf knew how to deny his baser needs, but he seemed unable to do so now. His ego chafed at the loss of control; his body ignored it in favor of the animal attraction that flowed thick and hot through his veins.

He decided then to use all of his considerable skill, charm, and physical attributes to make Sapphire burn as he did.

Lifting his gaze from between her legs, Wulf met her dark eyes with a raised brow. "So intimate an introduction should be preceded by a kiss, don't you think?"

Her face clouded with uncertainty for just a moment before she hid her emotions behind a cool mask of indifference. She rose from her chair with a mysterious smile.

"What a lovely idea." Her tone set him on edge. He was left wondering if he'd won the engagement or lost it.

They moved toward each other, every step increasing the sharp awareness between them. When she reached him, she placed her palms against the rippled ridges of his abdomen, then slid them slowly around to caress the corded length of his back.

Her touch was electric, her scent intoxicating. In the days since the ambush, he'd avoided any contact with the other *mästares*, making a wide berth when passing to avoid even a fleeting contact. The thought of anyone touching his skin made his stomach knot, but Sapphire's touch was like warm silk—healing and soothing.

He drew her to him, holding his breath as her full breasts flattened against his chest and the heavy weight of his erection pressed into the softness of her belly. His nostrils filled with the scent of Draxian lilies and he buried his face in her hair to catch more of it.

Despite the many hours he'd spent looking forward to this moment, Wulf still wasn't prepared. A shiver moved down his spine and coursed the length of his cock. He stared at her upturned face and knew in his gut that his next move was pure madness. Still, unable to do otherwise, he lowered his head and took her mouth, groaning.

The instant her lips softened under his, raw need flooded his senses in a rush so powerful he was almost dizzy with it. Sapphire moved with him, giving as good as she got, her tongue gliding along his, stroking against his. Her head tilted to take more, her lush body surging into him with a hunger he knew because he ached with it.

Shuddering at the fervor of her response, Wulf hugged her closer. He cupped her nape and gripped her waist, mantling her, sheltering her body with the size and power of his own.

It was heady, the combination of her obvious skill and his own. He had a dozen women at his palace who were more beautiful, and every bit as knowledgeable, yet no woman in his memory had ever aroused him as Sapphire did. Her kiss alone rivaled his most heated coupling. He could kiss her for days. Everywhere.

Wulf realized she had been far wiser than he.

Once wouldn't be enough.

He groaned, knowing it was true, knowing they didn't have near enough time to slake this depth of craving.

With shaking hands, he pressed her back into her seat and dropped to his knees, spreading her thighs wide with his hands. His mouth watered at the sight of her, slick with desire, swollen and pouting for the touch of his tongue.

"You're wet." His voice was so low he hardly recognized it.

She whimpered as he drew closer, then gasped as he licked upward through the soft hairless folds.

Her head fell back on a breathy sigh. "Oh Wulf . . ."

His jaw tightened with the effort to remain where he was instead of rising to his feet, freeing his cock, and sliding into her. She'd welcome him, he knew. She would cry out and relish every deep thrust. But he needed her to give herself freely. He needed her to be hungry for him, famished, and with her spread out like a feast, he had everything he needed at his disposal.

Kneeling, he pulled her chair closer and planned her seduction with military precision.

★ ★ ★

Sapphire waited breathlessly, every muscle tense with anticipation as Wulf pulled her closer and arranged her to his liking. That he took such care with the preparations told her he intended to pleasure her for some time. The thought made her shiver. The last five years had been spent with a man who cared only for his own needs. To have a lover so completely consumed with the pursuit of her enjoyment was unbearably arousing.

He hooked her knees over his forearms and cupped her hips in his hands. "I hope you're comfortable." His breath blew intimately across her sex. "You won't be moving for a while."

"This is a bad idea," she whispered.

"It feels damn good to me."

Then he plunged his tongue into her.

Sapphire arched upward, panting, her short nails digging crescents into the arms of her chair.

Wulf groaned, the vibration moving up her torso and tightening her nipples. He nuzzled against her with his lips, the silky strands of his hair caressing her inner thighs. His grip was firm, his fingers kneading, his mouth gentle as his tongue glided without haste through the evidence of her desire to stroke over her clitoris.

"Wulf . . ." Her hips rocked upward to match his rhythm. She bit her lower lip to stem the cries that would betray her need. This man was a seducer. If he knew how rarely she'd been serviced like this, he would use it against her and weaken her further.

With a low growl, he stroked his tongue into her, then withdrew, repeating the gentle rhythmic fucking until sweat covered her skin and dampened her hair. Her entire body tingled, her breathing grew more labored, while the ache deep inside coiled to near pain. He was methodical, thorough, licking into every groove and crevasse, nipping lightly with his teeth, suckling teasingly on the hard knot of her clitoris. She'd never been taken with such patience and obvious enjoyment on the part of her lover.

Her pussy rippled around his tongue, and unable to bear another moment of the torment, she begged him, "Don't tease."

Pulling back, Wulf spread her with the fingers of one hand. "Are you not enjoying yourself?" The other hand released her hip and two long fingers pushed into her.

"N–no . . ." A shudder shook her frame. Her hands cupped her breasts, her fingers pinching her painfully tight nipples. ". . . no more."

"No?" He rubbed inside her, caressing the slick walls of her sex with practiced fingertips. "I'll have to try harder." Wulf lowered his head and fluttered his tongue over her clit.

She could not have prepared for this—the slow, determined ravishment of her body. It was beyond her experience. "Please . . . make me come . . ."

Forming a circle with his lips, Wulf sucked her off as he fucked her with his fingers. Sapphire came in a spreading, blossoming climax, one that built with every pull of his mouth and every pump of his hand until one orgasm flowed into another.

It was devastating. Unlike the pleasure she attained by her own efforts, this was wrung from her with relentless skill. Yet Wulf was not unaffected. She felt his powerful body quaking beneath her legs as she pleaded with him to stop and attempted to push him away, but he was intent on some goal she couldn't understand.

She cried brokenly, writhing under the onslaught.

Only when her hands fell to her sides and her legs hung limp over his shoulders did he desist and rest his cheek against her thigh with a breathless chuckle of masculine triumph.

As her senses drifted back into awareness, Sapphire resigned herself to the truth.

She was in deep trouble.

★ ★ ★

"You may rise, Wulf." Sapphire's voice was so passion-hoarse it only worsened his predicament.

"I don't think I can." His dick was so hard, he couldn't move. But he managed a smile, satisfied that he'd pleased her so well.

Sapphire's desire simmered just below the surface, sadly un-tapped, if his guess was correct. When was the last time a man had loved her body just for the satisfaction gained from her re-sponse? He wished he had weeks to do so. He could easily imagine days spent with her in his bed, reveling in her scent and the feel of her curves, her lush body arching and writhing beneath his own.

She cooed, the sound coursing over his skin like a tactile caress. "Let me help you with that."

Tucking her legs in, Sapphire set the soles of her feet to his shoulders and kicked gently, thrusting him backward to the floor. Languid only a moment ago, she was now able to strad-dle him with impressive speed, her hands caressing his chest before any remnant feelings of helplessness took hold.

"I'm so glad you were spared and restored," she whispered, untying his drawstring before tugging his pants past his hips. "Perfection such as yours should not be marred."

As he stared up into her lovely, passion-flushed features, Wulf's throat clenched tight with gratitude. Sapphire wasn't coddling him, she was instead quite rough with him, but every time she pushed him, he gained a little confidence. And every time she gazed at him with such heat, the chill of his ordeal melted a little more.

She circled his cock with confident fingers, angled him into position, then drenched the swollen head in the liquid heat of her mouth.

"Oh hell." He gasped, his back arching, his balls drawing up painfully tight. "Don't make me come too quickly."

Lifting her gaze, her eyes twinkled wickedly and he knew he would receive no mercy from her. "You taste as delicious as you look." Her tongue licked the drop of semen that beaded on the tip, then traced the length of a thick vein in a sinuous caress. "What a magnificent cock you have."

She drew back, and the admiration in her dark eyes gave him such pleasure he hardened further. Curving both hands around his dick, Sapphire squeezed. "How big will it get? I can barely hold you."

"Your hands are tiny." He was burning up. His body was tense and hard all over, his skin damp with sweat.

"It feels marvelous," she breathed. "The skin is so soft."

"Put it inside you," he groaned as she stroked him. "It feels much better that way."

She shook her head, the silky strands of her hair drifting over his hips. The fingertips of one hand trailed over his rippling stomach, and he quivered under her touch. "I've never seen anything as good looking as your body."

Wulf cupped her head gently. He didn't pull her toward him, just massaged her scalp with the convulsive twitching of his fingertips. Holding her, even so distantly, was a wonder he marveled at.

"That feels good," she purred, her eyes drifting shut.

He wanted to tell her that he would always make her feel good, that giving her pleasure was now a primary focus of his, but he could no longer speak. He was so close, on the edge . . .

She took him in her mouth again, using her hands to caress the length of his cock that wouldn't fit inside her. She sucked him with strong, greedy tugs, killing him. With stunning ferocity, his orgasm was upon him, his back bowing upward, his semen spurting thick and hot into her working mouth. His shout of release was sharp and tormented, his body straining and jerking with the violent force of his climax.

Only moments could have passed, but it seemed like hours before his body sank lax into the floor, incapable of movement.

Sapphire continued her ministrations with a gentle lapping of her tongue, cleaning his seed from his cock as he panted and fought for sanity.

Wulf could only lie there, sprawled and dazed. His body had responded to her touch with the same speed and forceful passion with which hers had responded to him. He knew with resigned horror that she'd been correct. Despite the orgasm that wrung him out, he still wanted her. More than he had before. Wanted to pull her close, hold her tight, wrap his body around hers. Then he wanted to fuck her properly. Hard, deep, and long. He wanted to watch the pleasure take her, brand her. He wanted to see her face, lost in the moment. Lost in him.

The lover of his enemy. The daughter of his greatest adversary.

He would have to forget this intimacy and her. He refused to start a war over a concubine.

Sapphire's long hair caressed his thighs as she continued licking his cock with soft purrs of pleasure. His eyes slid closed.

No war.

Chapter 5

Sapphire relaxed on the divan in the receiving room after supper, but her mind was far from languid. After studying the plans to her palace with a well-trained eye, she had plotted out every means of escape, then set in place steps to prevent them.

There was only one reason to take such measures. There was only one person who would even consider leaving, let alone wish to and she'd told him that he was free to leave at any time he wished. Her actions were irrational at best, but then she hadn't been thinking clearly since she first saw him.

If she had any sense at all, she would force him to go. His presence in her household imperiled them both.

She'd scrupulously avoided speaking with him the last two days, but he was often on her mind. Every time she thought of him, she remembered the feel of his mouth between her thighs and the taste of him flowing down her throat. Every time she overheard him talking, her body vibrated with need. His voice was rich, dark, and commanding. It suited him perfectly and drove her crazy. He had only to speak and her insides melted.

If it were just his striking looks and sexual skill that drew her, she would be able to resist him. But the bemused glimpses that followed her everywhere made her weak in the knees.

The way his head tilted when she gave an order, as if every word that passed her lips was of the utmost importance to him, made her stomach flutter. The way his fists clenched at his sides when she emerged from the bathing pool made her nipples hard. The way—

"May I suggest, again, that you ring him?" the Guardian asked.

"Not an option."

"In my estimation, your precautions are pointless. Prince Wulfric is well versed in our technology. Instead of contriving to detain him, you should be wondering why he has not left of his own free will. He is more than capable of doing so."

"I know." Sapphire had spent the last couple of nights tossing and turning, trying to reason out why he remained with her. She didn't have the strength to send him away. Apparently, Wulfric didn't have the sense or the strength to leave. Instead, he waited. For her.

Every time the Sensual Arts students came, he retired to his chamber, the only one of her *mästares* who did not indulge in their carnal skills. She knew because she watched, wanting to know if he would partake and feeling relief when he didn't.

Swearing, she flung herself off the bed and headed down the hallway. "Guardian, ready the holo-room." She was so anxious to burn off her frustration, she didn't even notice the emerald gaze that followed her.

"Where would you like to go? Crystal Springs? The Laruvian Rain Forest?"

"Did you download my holo-programs from the palace?"

"Of course."

"Then set up the Valarian Mines."

There was a weighted pause before the computer responded. *"Mistress, I have reviewed that program extensively. It has none of the fail-safes required by most holo-programs. The Valarian trolls are unrestrained."*

Sapphire smiled grimly. "I know."

"It is dangerous," the Guardian insisted. *"Even for a warrior with your level of training."*

"Precisely."

Wulfric sat with the other *mästares* and replayed in his mind the sway of Sapphire's hips as she stalked off, her lush form radiating suppressed violence. He was intrigued by the repeated references to Sapphire's training. Training that would apparently help her fight off dangerous trolls. After witnessing her agility firsthand, he was burning with curiosity about that aspect of her. His need to know kept him here, restrained as if he was ringed.

"Why am I here?" he wondered aloud.

"It is only a guess," Dalen answered. "But I assume the queen arranged for you to be here as a punishment."

"Punishment for whom? Sapphire or me?"

Dalen shrugged. "I'm not sure. How could the queen have foreseen how miserable you and the Mistress would make each other?"

Wulf snorted. "How did she know we wouldn't kill each other?" The thought of Sapphire injured affected him strongly. He was as protective of his captor as she had been of him, a reaction that confounded him.

"That might have been Her Majesty's intent."

Wulf held Dalen's gaze to drive home his sincerity. "I would never physically hurt the Mistress. Not even to secure my freedom."

"I believe you, Your Highness, but even if you wanted to, you'd find it very difficult to hurt her. She's too well trained."

"Because of her father."

"Yes. She was taught by the general himself."

"The Mistress requires a towel in the healing chamber, Prince Wulfric," the Guardian called out.

Wulf grabbed a couple towels from the cart by the arched doorway. "I'm on my way."

As he left the receiving room, he began whistling. At this particular moment, he didn't mind being a servant. A person had to be naked in the healing chamber. He was about to get his first unobstructed view of Sapphire's naked body.

He waited at the door for one of the guardsmen to approach and disengage the lock. Wulf's prints were banned from all of the lock pads in the palace to prevent his escape. Pointless, but he was flattered by the effort. He would leave soon, regardless. One night—one *full* night—with Sapphire and he would be able to leave without looking back.

The door slid open and he stepped inside. He froze when he saw Sapphire in the healing chamber. Her perfect body was marred with an assortment of cuts and bruises that were fading quickly. As he approached, she looked up with a fierce gaze and jerked her chin toward the exit in silent dismissal.

He stood stiffly for a moment, his hands fisting in the towels at the sight of her so abused. He had to force himself to retreat as she'd ordered. The healing chamber opened with a hiss of released air pressure just as he turned to leave. From the periphery of his vision, he caught sight of Sapphire stumbling. With a warrior's quick reflex, he dropped the towels and spun on his heel, catching her before she hit the tiled floor. She was unconscious.

Cradling her in his arms, Wulfric left the room, heading down the hallway to her bedchamber. The day was ending, the center courtyard bathed in shadows as darkness began to fall.

"Guardian." Worry was evident in his voice. "Open the door to Sapphire's quarters."

The doors retracted as he neared. A guard attempted to follow him inside, but the Guardian prevented the intrusion by sealing the room with unusual haste. Wulf smiled grimly. "Thank you."

"My pleasure."

"How are her vitals?" He laid her down on her bed. The

drapes slid closed and simulated candlelight illuminated the space.

"Vitals are stable. She is simply exhausted."

He sat beside Sapphire on the bed and brushed her dark hair away from her forehead. "What the hell happened to her?"

In answer, the computer projected a recording of the holo-room on a bare wall beside him. He watched, appalled, as Sapphire fought a brutal battle with at least ten Valarian trolls. They were called trolls because of their short stature, but in truth they were evenly matched to the petite courtesan.

Wulfric was astonished by both her skill and his reaction to it. She was good. Very good. She could easily best most men and she neutralized over half the trolls before they gained the upper hand, dragging her to the ground. He winced as she was subjected to violent kicks and vicious blows. Suddenly the holo-program disengaged and Sapphire lay alone on the floor. Struggling to her feet, she cursed at the Guardian for aborting the program even as she clutched at bruised ribs.

The projection ended.

"Okay." Wulf's voice was carefully controlled. "Explain to me what that was all about. And while you're at it, relay her bio for me, as well."

"I can share public records, Your Highness."

"That's fine." Wulf arranged himself on the bed beside Sapphire, turning her gently to her side, then spooning behind her. He enjoyed the feel of her softness and appreciated the opportunity to hold her, despite the circumstances. Burying his face in the curve of her neck, he listened as the Guardian began to speak.

"Katie Erikson was born on—"

"You lost me already."

"The woman in your arms."

He smiled. "Go on."

If the Guardian could have sounded smug, she would have. *"Her given name is Katie. Katie Erikson. Daughter of General Grave Erikson and his wife, Sasha."*

"Katie." The name rolled off his tongue. What a sweet, girlish name for such a fierce woman. He wondered what she'd been like as a child and listened attentively as the Guardian told him.

Looking over Katie's shoulder at the wall, Wulf studied the scenes projected there. Over the course of the next hour, he was regaled with a litany of her accomplishments. He saw her graduate from primary, secondary, and the Sensual Arts School. He watched recordings of training sessions with her father and televised royal events where she had been in attendance, standing just behind the Sarian monarchs.

He was intrigued by the deference King Gunther had shown to his favorite concubine and the resulting notoriety that esteem had given her with the people of Sari. Curious as to how that had affected the queen, he employed a keen eye and several replays to catch the carefully veiled hostility Her Majesty displayed toward her rival in unguarded moments.

When he had finished riffling through all the data and the Guardian fell silent, Wulf realized that everything he'd just learned only whet his appetite to discover the individual behind the life. He still had no idea who Katie was, only what she was capable of. It wasn't enough.

Wulfric refused to put a name to why he cared. Until now, he'd preferred to know little about the women he slept with. He maintained his distance because clingy, dependent females were an annoyance he had no time to deal with. A quick, mutually enjoyable tumble in bed was all the entanglement he needed or wanted.

"Wulf . . ."

He tensed at the sound of Katie's sleep-soft sigh. She wiggled her body more firmly into his embrace, her bare back pressed as closely as possible to his bare chest.

"Katie?" he queried in a gentle whisper, refusing to call her by a possessive appellation given to her by another man.

"She's not awake," the Guardian informed him in the subdued evening volume. *"And she's cold."*

Careful not to wake her, Wulf reached down and pulled the velvet duvet over them, then drew her back into his embrace. After a few moments, when Katie had settled more firmly, he called out to the computer, "Does she always talk in her sleep?"

"If you call the mention of your name 'talking,' then yes, she does that fairly often of late."

Wulf couldn't restrain his triumphant smile. It was good to know he wasn't the only one with torrid dreams.

"She has taken great pains to keep you here."

"I know."

"But it would be more logical for you to leave."

His smile vanished. "Yes. I shouldn't be here."

"Yet here you are."

"I could give her more than the king has given her." The moment the words were said, he wished he could take them back. He shouldn't say such things, or even consider them.

"The only thing she ever wanted from the king was her independence."

"Independence . . ." Wulf wanted to own her. Possess her. Have her at his beck and call. He could imagine sparring on the practice field and returning to her drenched in sweat and filled with aggression. He wanted to take her like that. Rough, gritty, raw sex. A base, primitive claiming.

As he drifted to sleep holding the love of his enemy while deep in hostile territory, he pondered his responses to all he had learned. When Katie slipped a silken leg between his own with a pleasured sigh, he knew, despite the danger, that he'd never felt as safe or relaxed in his life—simply from the act of holding her. There was a constant, vibrating anxiousness inside him that was soothed by her proximity. He hadn't realized it was there until it was gone.

Addiction. Katie was the fix that eased his restlessness.

A dangerous thought solidified in his mind, unbidden and astonishing: How much more content would he feel with her in *his* bed, in *his* country?

Chapter 6

"You allowed him to spend the night in my bed?" Sapphire asked, incredulous.

"The prince was concerned for you and wanted to assure himself that you were well."

"Like hell he did. That's what I have you for." She buried her face in her hands. "Damn you."

"It is my primary programming to ensure your happiness."

She lifted her head. "I should upgrade you for this."

"There is no Guardian system of greater capability. I am a prototype, uniquely designed to serve only you."

"Giving an enemy such intimate access to me is dangerous!"

"On its face, I would agree. However, his vital signs and deportment tell me differently. He cares for you. He cared for you last night when you were unwell."

"You don't understand human behavior, Guardian." Sapphire brushed the hair back from her face. "I'm valuable to him because I'm protecting him and because fucking me also fucks the king and my father."

"You are not being truthful."

"You are being a pain in the ass."

"My programming is such that I am able to seek your happiness, even while you seek to sabotage it."

"We'll deal with your programming in a minute," Sapphire snapped. "First, tell me how I'm supposed to deal with him now."

"He was pleased to spend the night with you."

"I'm sure he was. Where is he now?"

"Unpacking the household goods that just arrived."

"When His Highness is finished, I want him taken to the coordinates I specify. If he follows the instructions I leave with you, he should be able to cross the border without getting killed."

"Should he approach you with any questions he might have?"

"No. I'm leaving for the day. Arrange my transportation into the city."

"Mistress, may I suggest—"

"No." Sapphire held up her hand. "You have caused enough mischief. I can manage this part on my own."

Sapphire surveyed the assemblage at the governor's residence with an indifferent eye. Once she'd enjoyed such lively events, but that had changed over the years. Her value to the king had created a barrier around her that few could breach without incurring his wrath. She was sorry to realize that she still felt lonely in a crowd. She was tired of being alone, and exhausted from wearing a façade so carefully crafted no one saw the woman beneath it.

Dignitaries, wealthy entrepreneurs, even the governor himself had approached her to come out of retirement. The sums of money offered for her services had been staggering, but she was far from flattered. The career of a concubine was a revered position requiring years of training and dedication. Depending on how wisely she selected her contracts, she could attain much power and privilege. There was no doubt in anyone's mind that Sapphire was at the top of her game, but she couldn't find much satisfaction in the notoriety. Not now that she'd experienced what it was like to enjoy the attentions of a giving, attentive lover.

"You look bored."

She turned with a smile at the sound of her father's voice. "I didn't know you were back in town!"

"I arrived this evening." Grave Erikson cut a suave figure in his military dress uniform of dark blue jacket and slim trousers. "I went to your home and your Guardian told me I might find you here."

"Is this a social visit or business related?"

"Both. You wanted updates on the investigation into Prince Wulfric's disappearance. Or have you lost interest?"

"No." Her heart raced. "What have you learned?"

"Not too much, to be truthful, but it was a good excuse to visit you."

"Dad!" Sapphire laughed. She adored her father for all his many facets. He was strong and powerful, yet infinitely loving and blessed with the ability to find the silver lining in every cloud.

"Let's take a stroll through the governor's conservatory and I'll tell you what little I know."

He offered his arm, then led her easily through the crush. The masses parted quickly for their revered war hero and his equally famous daughter. "I still haven't determined where the prince was taken after he was sold."

"Have you found out who hired the mercs to attack him?"

"No. I tracked down the go-between, but he communicates only through videoless comm-link." Grave glanced down at her. "I had assumed the prince was attacked in an effort to kill or ransom him, but apparently that was not the case. He was to be delivered to someone here in Sari. The torture was merely for the merc's amusement."

They had almost killed him, the fools. The memory of Wulfric's horrifying network of injuries would haunt her forever. It was a testament to his resilience that he remained proud and unbroken after such abuse. His will to survive was strong and admirable.

Aching with the knowledge that he would be gone when she went home, Sapphire pushed him from her mind. The only future contact she would have with him would be through news reports in the media. Look, but don't touch or covet. In the brief time she'd known him, he had become an ever-present specter in her thoughts. Her body was attuned to his on a deep level. He had only to look at her and she became aroused, hungry. She knew he was thinking of all the ways he could please her, which was entirely removed from the king's weighty expectation for how she would please him.

Quite simply, she would miss Wulf, but keeping him had not been an option.

"Who in Sari would wish to purchase Wulfric?" she wondered aloud.

"*Wulfric,* is it now?"

She purposely ignored the query, schooling her expression into bland lines. "I'm as intrigued as you are. I'd like to join your investigation."

Grave laughed. "Getting restless already?"

"I've been restless the last few years. I'm ready for change and a little excitement."

He clasped her hand in his large one and squeezed. "Well, I'd love to have you. How about we start on Firstday?"

"Why don't we start tonight?" The thought of returning to her home and finding Wulf gone was depressing. Her father's company would provide a welcome distraction. "You're staying with me, right? We can drink until we're silly."

He gave a regretful shake of his head. "I wish I could, but the king is making an appearance tonight. He spends more time away from the palace since you left. Now that I've been seen, I will have to stay in my quarters or he may use me as an excuse to visit you. Considering his mood lately, I don't think that would be wise."

"Poor Daddy." Lifting to her tiptoes, Sapphire kissed his cheek. "I'm going home before he arrives. We'll talk more on Firstday."

"I'll be there bright and early, sweetheart."

"I love you."

Despite the crowd around them, he caught her close and squeezed her tight. "I love you, too."

It was well after midnight by the time Sapphire returned to her home. The interior was dimly lit and quiet, with most of her *mästares* either out for the evening, as she'd suggested, or in bed. She went straight to her bedroom, striding quickly over the threshold as the doors retracted, then slid closed again behind her.

"Keep the lights off," she ordered, when they didn't come on immediately.

Trained to be comfortable with moving in the darkness, Sapphire advanced easily through the space, setting her jewelry on the vanity before slipping out of her dress. The garment pooled at her feet and she kicked it away before starting toward the comfort of her bed.

She was mere steps away when a rustle of sound stilled her. Paused in mid-stride, she waited, alert and wary.

"Your clothes reek of men's cologne." Wulf's deep voice rumbled across the space between them.

He was directly behind her. If she hadn't been distracted by melancholy, she would have felt his presence sooner. His fury radiated like a heat wave.

She shifted away silently, knowing that when she spoke, he would be able to pinpoint her position. "You're not supposed to be here," she whispered.

"We have unfinished business." His tone was icy and originated from a different location in the room.

He was circling her.

Sapphire moved toward the bed, her intent to place the massive piece of furniture between them. "We have nothing."

Wulf tackled her from behind, twisting before they hit the bed to take the brunt of the impact. Surprised by the assault, she was easily overpowered. He rolled over her, pinning her arms above her head and her writhing body beneath his.

"Guardian!" She arched upward, attempting to dislodge him.

There was no reply. The only sound in the room was the harshness of their combined breathing.

"She can't help you," Wulf murmured. "I disengaged her alarm and her control of this room. She can't send for help and no one can get in."

"She'll find a way to notify the guards."

"I don't think so. She likes me. Who do you think let me in here to begin with?"

Sapphire refused to believe him, struggling against his grasp until she realized he was as naked as she was. She moaned as the minutes continued to pass without any sound from the Guardian. Wulf's skin was on fire against hers, his cock thick and hard against her thigh. "Let me go."

"Who were you with?"

"That's none of your damn business." She increased her efforts to buck him off.

Trapping both of her wrists in one of his hands, Wulf reached between her legs with the other. Her belly clenched as he parted her and stroked through the lips of her sex. He dropped his forehead to hers with a harsh exhale.

The tension drained from his frame and his body relaxed against hers. "You're untouched."

"You're insane."

He continued to tease her with his fingertips. Her blood heated from his touch, but her rage burned hotter.

"You'll regret this," she snapped.

He brushed tender kisses across her eyelids. "I'm sorry if I frightened you."

"You can't do this, Wulf. *We* can't do this."

His lips continued to move featherlight across her face. "Do you have any idea what I've gone through these last hours waiting for you?" He licked the corner of her mouth. "Or perhaps you know? Perhaps you felt the same every time the Sensual Arts students came?"

"Now who's vain?"

"You watched to see if I took one of them to bed," he purred, his lips slipping along her clenched jaw.

"I did not."

"Yes." His velvety voice curled around her in the darkness. "You did."

His tongue thrust into her ear and she shivered beneath him. Her body betrayed her by melting into his hand. He growled softly and stroked the slickness of her desire up to her clitoris, where he rubbed with perfectly gauged pressure. She whimpered, her senses inundated with the scent of his skin. Wulf was so hot. A fully aroused and determined male animal. And he was skillfully building her lust to match his.

"I waited for you," he whispered. "I was fit to kill, thinking you'd turned to someone else."

"Why would I go out for sex? I have thirteen virile men right here." She deliberately left him out of the number.

He nudged her legs wider. Two fingers thrust inside her, sinking knuckles deep in one fierce glide, contradicting her without words. "Who were you with?"

"W—what . . . ?" She couldn't think.

He chuckled and she could picture the smug look on his handsome face. The man was too arrogant; a trait that turned her on. She wanted to be pissed at him, not creaming all over his hand.

"Why didn't you leave?" she asked with a tortured groan as he fucked her with steady, rhythmic plunges. She was so damn hot for him she was soaking his fingers. She could hear how wet she was and knew it was driving him crazy. His cock thickened and throbbed insistently against her thigh.

"I won't leave until I have you, Katie. I can't."

The sound of her name on his lips undid her, coaxing a lone tear to slip past her lashes and down her temple.

Wulf slipped a third finger inside her, stretching her to fit him, stroking her clenching inner walls with tender skill. His mouth pressed kisses along her breasts, his lips parting to surround a hard, aching nipple and its tiny ring.

"Stop." She writhed beneath the relentless lashing of his tongue. He teased her nipple, nipping it with his teeth, before suckling her with long, drawing pulls.

He spoke against her skin. "I couldn't stop touching you now even if the entire Sarian Army was outside the door."

Sapphire moaned, seduced by his desire for her. "Hurry, then. Finish this."

His laugh was a richly triumphant sound that swelled in the darkness. "I won't rush this. I want you to give yourself completely. Nothing held back."

"We don't have time."

"Act as if we do."

"For one night?"

"For tonight. Then I'll go."

Sapphire closed her eyes. "Alright."

Her hands were released and his weight left her. Taking advantage of the freedom, she rolled from the bed and darted to the window. A flash of light mellowed into the steady glow of a real candle. She blinked, her eyes adjusting to the sudden illumination.

"Where did you get that?" she asked, surprised.

Wulf smiled and her breath caught. "From Dalen. He claims women find real candlelight arousing. Do you?"

He stood within the circle of the golden glow, magnificent in his nakedness. He was flushed with heat and rock hard, his gaze dark and possessive. He had no right to look at her that way, but she liked it.

"I've risked my life to keep you," she said.

"I've risked mine to stay." He raked her from head to toe. "How stunning you are."

Wulf's voice dropped even lower and his thick cock swelled further. "I love how you force me to fight for you every step of the way."

"Tomorrow, you have to leave."

"I don't want to think about tomorrow." He approached.

"We have to think about it. It's only a few hours away."

He held his hand out to her. "So let's not waste any more time."

"You take this too lightly."

"I've neglected my responsibilities to my people to be with you," he retorted. "An attempt has been made on my life, and as the days pass, the trail to the assassins grows colder. I don't take this lightly. I don't *want* to want you. But you gave me life when I was hoping for death and you made me want it. There's nothing light about this."

She took a step toward him, drawn to his passion and raw honesty.

Wulf reached her and wrapped his arms around her, lifting her feet from the floor. His mouth claimed hers with an ardor that broke what little resistance she had left.

Her arms slipped around him, pulling him tightly against her. She stroked his back, her fingertips kneading the hard muscle beneath the satiny skin. His groan rumbled against her lips, and before she registered movement, he was pressing her down into the bed. She cupped the firm flesh of his buttocks and urged him closer, cradling him in the apex of her thighs.

Despite her desire, Sapphire felt like crying. Through the heat that clawed at her, reason prodded, demanding her attention. She thought of her king, her father, her freedom—torn between her loyalty and the realization of a dark fantasy she'd never known she had.

Rolling, she took Wulf under her, keeping her mouth joined with his. His hands reached for her but she stopped them, lacing her fingers with his and pinning them to the mattress.

"Let me touch you," he said hoarsely.

"No." She managed a seductive smile. She needed control, not just of herself but of this encounter. Her livelihood was the satiation of carnal desire. If she focused on the mechanics, perhaps she could reduce this overabundance of feeling to something manageable. "You wanted me to give myself to you."

Her lips moved across his face. She kissed his eyebrows and eyelids, then the tip of his nose and his chin. When she nipped at his throat, she felt his erection jerk between her legs. She rubbed her wet pussy along the satiny length until he groaned, then she stilled, teasing him with the damp heat of her desire.

"Don't play with me," he growled. "I've waited long enough."

Sapphire rose slightly, leaning over him until her breasts pressed into his chest. She slid down until the broad head of his cock was lodged at the slitted entrance to her body. She quivered at the feel of him. He was big and hot and hard.

Slowly, she pressed downward, taking the first thick inch with a sharp exhale. Impatient, he bucked upward and she gasped as he fed more of his cock into her.

Wulf froze. "Am I hurting you?" His voice was lust-thickened. "You're so tight. I want to fuck you until you fit me like a glove."

She ground herself onto him, biting her lip to keep from crying out as he thrust insistently, working deep into her. The sensation of being stretched to the limit refocused her, reminded her to keep this sexual. Physical. Nothing more.

He cursed. "Relax. Let me in."

Sapphire released his hands, sat upright, and closed her eyes.

She gave herself up to him, letting him shift her, move her, work her onto him until he was as deep as he could go.

A desperate whimper escaped her, then another. Wulf's breath hissed out between clenched teeth. "Yes," he growled, gripping her hips, pumping her up and down on his cock. "That's it . . . keep doing that, Katie . . . keep making those hot little sounds . . ."

The rough carnality of his words made her slicker, and the ride became easier. She concentrated on the tempo and her own breathing, finding his rhythm and matching it. Stroke for stroke. He increased the pace, swiveling his lean hips and thrusting high and hard. Their breathing grew more labored, the need more urgent. She moved faster, settling into an erotic pounding rhythm.

"Look at me."

Sapphire tilted her head back and kept her eyes squeezed shut.

His fingers on her thighs gripped her painfully, halting her movements.

"Are you *working*?" he snarled.

Lightning quick, Wulf wrenched her to the bed and pinned her beneath him, thrusting balls deep. She gasped, startled into looking at him.

"You thought I wouldn't notice?" His fist wrapped in her long hair, arching her neck to his ardent mouth. "When every part of me is focused on you, you thought I wouldn't notice that you were holding back? Sex is sex. I can get that anywhere. It's *you* I want. All of you. That was the deal."

"You're getting what you wanted."

"Not yet. But I will." Wulf began to fuck her with long, deep plunges. "I can ride you all night . . . until you give me what I want."

She tried to close herself off, but he wouldn't allow it, driving hard and fast into the very heart of her, breaking the concentration she needed to separate mind and body. She panicked, panting harshly, her heart racing until she was dizzy. Struggling to get away, she found herself trapped by her restrained hair and Wulf's pounding cock.

He couldn't last. Not like this.

Sucking in air like a swimmer too long under water, Sapphire changed tactics, spreading her thighs wider so that he could plunge deeper. His skin was slick with sweat, his lungs heaving for breath. He rose above her, trapping her gaze with his.

With a slow, seductive smile, he hit the end of her and began to grind. "Oh no, Katie. I won't come that easily."

He pulled back, tugging his cock from her greedy depths, then screwing back into her. It burned her, that deliberate thrust, flushing her skin and knotting her womb.

"It feels good, doesn't it?" His voice was deeply sexual. "I love how you squeeze me. You're so soft and slick. I want to come more than I want to breathe. But I can wait."

"Don't."

"Yes." Wulf continued the seductively slow plunge and retreat, watching her. Studying her reactions, repeating movements that made her crazed for him.

She had no defense against his sexual siege. Her body adjusted to him, then welcomed him. She had never felt such pleasure. His cock filled every crevasse inside her as if it were made for her. He rocked his hips and she couldn't stifle her moan. The friction was irresistible, urging her to work with him. As she thrashed beneath him, his hands moved over her, gentle and soothing.

"Shh." He gathered her closer. "Don't fight it. Let go."

"Wulf . . ."

"Feel how deep you can take me?" His tone was reverent and tender. "What a perfect fit you are for me? You were made for me, Katie."

Detachment was impossible. If he'd focused on the sex, she would have as well. But he made the sex a part of a larger whole and she wasn't strong enough to resist the connection.

Cupping a breast in his free hand, he plumped it, then lifted it to receive the attentions of his mouth. The moist heat of his breath burned across the straining nipple. "When you're in my bed, these jewels will be talgorites."

The royal stone of D'Ashier.

"One night," she insisted, tightening in anticipation of her coming orgasm, her hips lifting eagerly to meet his.

His voice came slurred with desire. "You've been mine from the moment we first saw each other. When we're lying in *my* bed, in *my* palace, and I'm buried deep inside you, you'll know just how completely you belong to me."

Wulf's possessiveness curled around her as surely as his body did.

"Damn you, Wulf. You can't—"

He increased his pace. "You're so wet . . . so hot . . . I'm the last man who'll ever touch you."

She moaned, focused solely on the simmering tension inside her. All of her skill and training fled her mind. She could only feel Wulfric moving within her, over her, so handsome he stole her breath and reason. She arched up, pressing herself against him. "Please . . ."

Releasing her hair, he rose above her, shoving his arms beneath her legs and opening her fully to his possessive drives. "That's it, Katie," he urged. "Don't hold back . . ."

Wulf plunged deep. It was almost painful but not quite. He was so skilled, he knew where she was most sensitive. He rubbed the flared head of his cock over and over the spot, deliberately driving her out of her mind.

Sweat dripped from him onto her, branding her with his scent. Wulf growled low in his throat, an animal sound of pure pleasure as he rode her. She gripped his clenching thighs, digging her nails into the rock-hard surface, her entire being consumed by a lust so fierce it scared her.

She arched like a bow as her climax rocked her. Her pussy convulsed around him, milking him, rippling along his plunging cock. He held her captive with his gaze, watching her come apart with tangible masculine satisfaction, flooding her greedy body with violent spurts of white hot semen.

"Katie," he gasped. "Katie . . ."

Shuddering, he wrapped himself around her and buried his damp face in her neck.

As Wulf pulled free of Katie's body, she whimpered in her sleep. He understood the loss she felt because he felt it as keenly. His response was disturbing. He'd never felt the desire to linger in a woman once his physical needs were met. What would be the point?

With Katie, the point was simple—it was an undeniable claim. She couldn't belong to anyone else when his body was inside hers.

Frustrated by the emotional remnants of the encounter, Wulf stood with the intent to reengage the Guardian, but his legs faltered beneath him. She'd sapped his energy and will to leave. He had never climaxed so hard in his life.

He looked at her now, still spread on her back, lost in sleep. Impatient, he waited for the strength to return to his limbs so he could dress and return to his life in D'Ashier.

She turned, curling onto her side, unconsciously seeking his warmth. Her sun-kissed skin was flushed from his ardor, her hair tangled all around her. She sighed his name.

"Katie." Without thought, his hand extended toward her.

Even now, he wanted her. Wanted to hold her close and share the warmth she was seeking.

Clenching his outstretched hand into a fist, Wulf pushed to his feet and retrieved his pants. He drew them on, tied the drawstring, and refused to look at the bed as he twisted the face of his signet ring. Instantly he stood on the transfer pad of his palace in D'Ashier.

His eyes burned, but he told himself it was caused by exhaustion and the relief of being home.

Chapter 7

Sapphire awoke and reached her arms over her head, her legs stiffening in a full body stretch. She winced at the soreness that plagued various parts of her body, but her mouth curved in a feline smile. Wulf had been a dominant lover, but his touch was so gentle, his focus so completely on her pleasure, that she relished the experience.

Turning her head to the side, she expected to find Wulf beside her, but he wasn't there. Frowning, Sapphire lifted her head to search the shadows of the room.

"Guardian?"

"Yes, Mistress?"

"Glad to have you back. Open the drapes." The gold velvet parted, letting sunlight drench the room. She blinked, hurrying her blurry eyes in their adjustment to the brightness.

"Wulf?"

There was no reply.

"His Highness is no longer in the residence."

Wulf had left, just as he'd promised.

Sapphire swung her legs over the side of the bed and paused a moment to collect her thoughts. She would have to relegate Wulf to a distant corner of her memory. They'd shared a stolen moment and indulged in temporary pleasures. Now, it was time to move on.

Easier said than done, she realized as her eyes began to sting. She held on to the edge of the mattress as she dropped gingerly to her feet. The tightness in her chest made breathing difficult, and she forced herself to inhale deeply and exhale slowly.

"*Should I send for a* mästare?"

"No. I'm fine."

A moment later the doors to her room slid open. Rapidly becoming accustomed to a computer that did whatever it wanted, Sapphire reached for a sheet to cover herself. "I told you—"

"Good morning, Sleepyhead."

She paused at the sound of the familiar, deeply commanding voice and stared at the man who filled the doorway.

Wulf's smile weakened her knees. "I was going to feed you breakfast in bed."

Relief flooded her and Sapphire found herself sinking to the floor.

He was kneeling before her in an instant, lifting her chin with gentle fingertips. "Are you crying?"

She shook her head violently and scrubbed at her eyes.

His grin turned roguish. "You missed me."

"You weren't gone long enough to miss you."

Scooping her up in his arms, he draped her in the red silk robe waiting on the dresser and headed out to the atrium courtyard. "Liar."

"Arrogant bastard."

"Ah, Katie, I love the way you talk to me."

"Because you're too used to having women kissing your—"

He cut her off with a quick, hard kiss.

Turning away, she buried her face in his neck to hide her smile and breathed in the scent of his skin. "You broke your word."

"I said I would leave today and I will, but the day is still young. We have hours left." He nuzzled his cheek against her hair. "Now open the door."

She raised her head and saw they were standing in front of the healing room. The lock pad disengaged with a wave of her hand. "Why are we here?"

His emerald gaze was hot; the intimate timbre of his voice was hotter. "Because you have to be sore after last night."

As he lowered her to her feet, heat suffused her cheeks. She, the most famous courtesan in Sari, was blushing. It was an outward sign of how deeply intimate their lovemaking had been.

Sapphire felt like a new woman, when she exited the healing chamber moments later. Wulfric waited with an out-stretched hand, and when she accepted it, he led her out to the courtyard.

"Let's bathe together," he suggested when they passed the bubbling outdoor pool. "Then we'll spend the rest of the day in bed."

"Is this an exercise in making our parting as difficult as possible?" She descended the steps and sank into the hot, steaming water.

He reached for the drawstring of his pants. "Will it be difficult for you?"

Sapphire was contemplating the best way to answer when Dalen came running through the courtyard, startling them both. Without a word, he grabbed Wulfric's arm and started to drag him away.

"What are you doing?" Wulf asked, remaining rooted.

"Come, Your Highness." Dalen's face was grave. "We must hide you. Now!"

"Mistress. Forgive me," the Guardian said in hushed evening tones.

Instantly apprehensive, Sapphire looked at Wulf. "Go. Hide yourself."

The anxiety in her tone prodded Wulfric to move. He

allowed Dalen to pull him behind a thick patch of vegetation. Then, Dalen pivoted and ran a few feet away to prostrate by the pool.

Moving on instinct, Sapphire leaped from the pool and folded into a low bow. There were only two people for whom such deference would be paid. Neither was someone she wished to see.

Not now.

"Karisette."

Her eyes squeezed shut at the sound of the king's voice.

"I told your Guardian to keep my arrival a surprise. I knew you would be as pleased to see me as I am to see you. Rise. I've missed you."

Stunned, she stood and met his gaze. "Welcome, my king."

Wulf watched through the cover of man-sized fern fronds as the King of Sari approached Katie with covetous eyes. Two dozen royal guards entered behind the monarch and spread out to encircle the atrium, their deep blue uniforms embellished with gold threads that glimmered in the sunlight.

The six royal guards who lived with Katie wore silver thread—apparently, the queen's guards. An interesting development.

As Wulf watched Katie become enfolded in the arms of the king, envious fury filled him. Earlier that morning, when he'd returned to his own palace, he had intended never to see her again. But the thought of her naked in bed, her skin scented of his sweat and flushed by his passion, had been irresistible. Just a few more hours, he'd thought. More time with her would dull the most biting edge of his craving.

Now, watching her with her former lover and burning with jealousy, he knew he'd deluded himself. He couldn't leave her in the grip of another man. Not when it would be so easy to claim her, to make her irrevocably his, to have her near at hand whenever he felt the need to touch her.

He'd been truthful when he told the Guardian that he could give Katie more than the king had—in bed and out. She would want for nothing as his concubine and she would be restored to the position she'd recently lost, a position she had trained years for. Of course, there was the matter of logistics and familial ties . . . But he would benefit there, as well.

Katie's throaty voice drifted to him, and Wulf clenched his fists. Her beautiful curves were bared to the king's ravenous gaze. Regardless of the contingent of guards around her, Wulf was dangerously goaded to leap from his hiding spot and cover her, shielding her from any other eyes but his own.

"My king, what brings you to me?" she asked.

"My heart." The monarch dropped to his knees and wrapped his arms around Katie's hips, burying his face in the tautness of her stomach as if she were the ruler and he the servant.

Wulf's reaction to the sight was not what he would have expected. Instead of seeing the king's affection as a vulnerability, he saw it as a threat.

Katie's fingers drifted into the king's tousled blond hair. She crooned so softly Wulf couldn't hear what she said.

The king urged her down, and when she sank to her knees, the monarch pushed her onto her back and climbed over her.

Wulf lunged forward, but was restrained by a desperate grip.

He'd been so focused on the scene before him, he'd failed to notice Dalen moving stealthily into position behind him. The guards, too, were riveted by the unfolding drama.

The *mästare* shook his head and mouthed, *They'll kill you.*

Wulf was prepared to take the risk regardless, but he was arrested by Katie's outraged cry.

The king, equally stunned, was easily thrown from her.

"You must return to your queen now, Your Majesty." Leaping to her feet, Katie backed away, her arms wrapped around her naked body.

"You think I haven't tried?" He rose to his feet in a ripple of sapphire blue robes and seething frustration. "I've tried everything—total darkness, your perfume and bath oil, aphrodisiacs. Nothing works. She has no passion, no fire, and she arouses none in me." He held his hand out to her beseechingly. "I ache for *you*."

The rigidness of her shoulders softened. "I'm sorry."

"Come to me," the king ordered.

She shook her head.

"I am the king."

"With a duty to your people."

"What of your duty to me? I have loved you to the exclusion of everyone else for the last five years. You belong to me, Sapphire."

"I was contracted to you. You never owned me."

The king's gaze narrowed. "Our contract is void. You must come to me of your own free will. Come now."

"No."

"You *deny* me?"

"Yes," Katie said simply.

"You love me," he stated. "You're angry with me for setting you aside."

"How could I love you, my king? You belong to one woman and are in love with another, and I am neither of them."

"It will never be over between us." The king began to pace with a powerful, agitated stride. "If I must court you anew, I will. If I must bend you"—he jabbed a finger in her direction— "I will. Whatever it takes, Sapphire."

Katie dipped her head in an elegant acknowledgment of his threat. "You will do as you wish, Your Majesty."

He glared at her for a long, tension-filled moment, then spun in a flurry of robes and stormed away, the guardsmen filing out behind him.

A moment later, the Guardian advised, *"His Majesty has departed, Mistress."*

Dalen released Wulf just as Katie sank to the ground.

Wulf went to her. "If you hadn't stopped him, I would have."

Dropping to his haunches beside her, he tried to pull her into his arms, but she recoiled. He frowned. "Don't be afraid. No one will take you against your will."

She didn't meet his gaze when she spoke. "Go home, Your Highness. The Guardian has the information you'll need to cross the border safely and she will arrange your transportation."

Wulf yanked her toward him. "Talk to me."

"I'm no longer in the mood to take you to bed," she said without inflection. "You should go."

He tensed, insulted. "Don't punish me for another man's faults."

Katie opened her mouth to argue and he took it, gripping her by the elbows and lifting her to meet him halfway.

For endless moments she hung motionless in his arms, her lips unmoving beneath his. He changed tactics, revealing his need in soft, deliberate licks. Soft, coaxing sounds rumbled from his throat. He rubbed his furred chest against the softness of her breasts until her nipples peaked hard, and strained for his touch. He obliged, lifting one hand to cup the full flesh, his thumb and forefinger tugging the taut point in just the way she liked.

Katie surrendered. She opened her mouth to him with a growl of hunger, sharing a passion so potent it enslaved kings and princes alike. Wulf's tongue swept inside and tangled with hers.

His hands cupped her buttocks and pulled her into his lap. She whimpered. He tore his lips from hers, pressed her to the ground, and settled between her spread thighs.

Wulf gazed down at her flushed features and sad eyes, and asked, "How can you send me away after last night?"

"You act as if there's a choice, as if there's an option for us to be together. You know there isn't."

"I know I want more. So do you." He suckled and nipped along the column of her throat. Rolling his hips, he urged the hard length of his cock between the damp lips of her pussy.

He didn't want her thinking right now. *He* didn't want to think right now. It was impossible to want something this badly and not have it.

"The time when we could've walked away has passed, Katie."

"You would give up your kingdom and your freedom for sex?" she argued in a husky voice. "You're not the man I thought you were."

Wulf lifted his head to meet her gaze. "I wouldn't give up D'Ashier for my life. But you . . . Nothing you have is truly yours, not even your body. The king can come for you at any time. You'll never be free as long as you stay here."

Katie snorted. "Don't act as if life with you would be better. I wouldn't be free with you either. You would treat me just as he does. You are no different."

"I am entirely different, because you crave me and what I can do to your body. I see the way you look at me, I feel the way you touch me." His mouth lowered to her ear. "I promised I'd leave today. And so I shall."

His tongue swirled around the shell of her ear. "But I'm taking you with me."

"My father would hunt you down," Sapphire snapped, "and finish what the mercs started. The king would use my abduction to incite a call to arms. All hell would break loose—"

"If they knew where you were," he murmured, "you might have a point."

Wulf's hands moved together at the side of her neck and suddenly the ground beneath her back was cold. Startled, her head jerked to the side, her wide eyes taking in her surroundings. She was pinned beneath him on a transfer pad; her atrium and the familiar surroundings of her home were gone. Panicked, she noted the shield on the wall and recognized the same crest that embellished Wulf's signet ring—the D'Ashier royal family crest.

"I'm going to kick your ass," she bit out.

Wulfric shielded her with his body until a servant came forward bearing a thick talgorite-red velvet robe, then he rose and covered her. Gaining a seated position, Sapphire clutched the rich material to her breasts. Royal guardsmen dressed in red and gold uniforms lined the walls of the transfer room. As they prostrated themselves respectfully, she realized that Wulfric's return had been expected, as evidenced by the ready availability of the royal garment she was draped in.

"What the hell have you done?" she breathed.

He extended his hand to her. Sapphire ignored it, jumping to her feet and deliberately leaving the robe on the floor.

Stepping in front of her, Wulf blocked her nakedness from the guards behind him. He kicked up the robe with his bare foot, caught it in his hand, and held it out to her. "Cover yourself."

Her chin lifted. "No."

He moved so quickly, she had no time to avoid him. Within the space of a gasp, Wulfric had her swaddled in his royal robes and tossed over his shoulder.

"Damn you, Wulf." She struggled to free her arms. "You're starting to piss me off!"

He ignored her. Moving toward the exit, he barked orders en route. "Send a platoon to the return coordinates. I've adjusted the Guardian system to allow transfers from this pad's signature, so you'll have to instigate the engagement from here. Collect the servants and guards, and bring them to D'Ashier. Retrieve the home's computer chip—undamaged. Nothing and no one that would betray my recent presence in Sari can be left behind."

Sapphire screamed in frustration. "Put. Me. Down. Before I hurt you."

Wulfric's voice rose to drown out hers.

She bit him.

He swatted her buttocks with his free hand. "Stop that."

"You *know* you can't do this, you arrogant ass!"

She felt laughter rumble through him and saw the shocked expressions on the faces of his men. She glared at them.

"Tell the king I have returned." He strode toward the door. "But I am not to be disturbed until tomorrow."

Wulf cupped her backside possessively. "I'll be busy a while."

Wulf's long-legged stride ate up the seemingly endless length of white stone hallway with ease. The guards stationed at various intervals bowed at the waist as he passed, their eyes wide as they stared at Katie squirming and swearing loudly over his shoulder. She had the vocabulary of a hardened soldier and she didn't hesitate to use it. He'd never been so verbally abused in his life. Coming from Katie, he found he enjoyed it immensely.

The doors to his *seraglio* slid open when he approached. He entered to a chorus of eager greetings and sighs at his half-dressed state. As his concubines rushed toward him, he kept them at bay by holding up the hand not currently caressing Katie's buttocks.

"Your Royal Highness."

He turned to the elderly woman prostrated just to the right of him.

"Sabine." He greeted his chamberlain with a smile. Once, she had been his father's concubine. Now retired, she served Wulf by maintaining order in his harem. "You may rise."

"Who is that you have there?" she asked, rising gracefully to her feet.

As he started toward the large rectangular pool that dominated the center of the room, she fell into step beside him. Three fountains broke up the tranquil surface of the water, the splashing sounds mingling with the melodious voices of his concubines and the sounds of birds chirping in the various cages that decorated the perimeter. The humid air was redolent with lush hothouse flowers, various perfumes, and luxurious bath oils. Jewel-encrusted doors lined the walls, each portal leading to the private quarters of a concubine. Drenched in the sunlight pouring from the massive skylight above, the expensive and precious gems winked and flashed to glorious effect.

He slid Katie from his shoulder, careful to keep his hold on her while maintaining her confinement within his robes. "Sabine, this is Katie."

"Sapphire," Katie corrected testily.

Grinning, he told Sabine, "She needs a bath and suitable garments. I want her body jewelry changed from sapphires to talgorite. I prefer her hair down. When she's ready, bring her to my rooms."

Sabine was eying the disheveled Katie appraisingly when the import of his words registered. Her gaze darted to meet his. *"Y-your* rooms, Your Highness?"

"That's what I said." With a flourish, he yanked the voluminous fabric of his robe from Katie, causing her to twirl outward from the enveloping folds.

She recovered her footing several feet away and glared at him. "Afraid to do it yourself, Wulf? We both know I can take you."

His concubines gasped at her insubordination and her use of his given name, but he laughed.

"Yes. I'm quite taken." His tone was a husky murmur, his gaze riveted by the sight of her bare body.

Enamored of her beauty, Wulfric watched her gaze roam. Her dark eyes paused briefly on each of the women surrounding the pool, all of whom eyed her back with curiosity and/or suspicion. Her expression grew taut, her hands fisting at her sides. It was only then that he registered his error in bringing her *here*. To the *seraglio*. Distracted by lust, he'd considered only the fastest way to get her ready for the long hours of sex he intended for them to enjoy.

He opened his mouth to reassure her, but before he could speak, Katie spun on her heel and fled.

Chapter 8

"Guards!" Sabine sounded the alarm before Wulf could react. The doors slid open and four guardsmen charged into the room.

"Lock the door," he roared as Katie leaped through the air to attack the nearest soldier. Naked as she was, the man was stunned and vulnerable to her assault. She kicked him dead center in the chest, knocking him flat on his back, then turned to engage the others.

Wulf raced after her.

"Don't touch her!" Fear roughened his voice. Images of her injuries from the holo-room knotted his stomach. "Hurt her at your peril."

Katie's head turned at the proximity of his voice. Her grim expression betrayed her determination to find another way out.

Almost there . . .

He was a hair's breadth away from catching her when she darted out of his reach and deserted the locked exit. He cursed. She backtracked into the room, heading toward the opposite side of the pool. Squeals and screams rent the air as startled concubines scattered out of her way. The birds in their cages cried out their alarm, their wings flapping frantically and littering the air with feathers.

She rounded the corner of the pool. Wulf vaulted diagonally across the small gap, his body stretched out as he flew over the water. He caught her, twisting in midair to absorb the impact when they crashed onto the marble floor and slid several feet.

"Let me go." She struggled against him. He rolled, pinning her beneath him.

Their chests heaved together; his heart raced with the excitement of the chase. The scent of Draxian lilies filled his nostrils and relief at holding her after her frantic attempt at flight heated his blood. As Katie's naked breasts pressed to his skin, his focus altered. Desire for her acted like a potent drug in his veins, making his entire body hot and hard.

Wulf lifted his head. "Everyone, *out!*"

His mind distantly registered the sounds of footsteps fading and doors slamming shut, but his focus was on the woman in his arms.

Taking her mouth, Wulf groaned his pleasure when she returned his kiss with equal fervor. He loved Katie's body, so strong and lithe. She could fight and injure him—she had the knowledge and stamina—but she touched him with tenderness. She was toned by years of combat training, yet still soft, with generous curves and valleys that fit perfectly against him.

Katie began to struggle again, even as her tongue swirled greedily in his mouth. She didn't want to want him, but couldn't resist. That affinity stoked his lust to a fever pitch.

Wulf broke the kiss and buried his face in her throat. "Don't fight me," he murmured against her flushed, scented skin. "I'll make it good for you."

Gasping, she arched into him. "Release me."

"I can't." He grabbed her wrists, and pinned her arms above her head. He drew a taut nipple into his mouth, teasing it with his tongue before suckling her with hard, deep pulls.

"Oh!" Katie twisted in an effort to deter him "No . . ."

Wulf moved to her other breast, nipping the hard peak with his teeth before soothing the sting with gentle licks.

"Stop wriggling," he rumbled, then he curled his tongue around the straining point of her breast.

Katie tried to buck him off but the movement only forced her legs to spread. His hips dipped between her thighs, settling perfectly into place because she was made for him.

"Wulf. No."

"Remember last night?" he crooned. "How good it was?" His hips swiveled against hers, rubbing his rock-hard cock against her clitoris. "We were meant for this . . . you and I."

As he rocked into her, massaging her pussy with the hard length of his dick, she moaned, "Give me the top."

Wulf growled, remembering the way he'd felt last night when she plied her trade. "Why? So you can work?"

Holding her wrists with one hand, he reached between them to loosen his drawstring. His wrist rubbed against her and she hissed in pleasure.

"Isn't that why you stole me?" she challenged. "Isn't that why I'm here in your *seraglio* with all your other women? To work?"

Rough and impatient, he shoved his waistband down and his cock sprang free. With a deft twist, he pulled her over him, his legs kicking until he was freed from his pants. "It was a mistake," he said gruffly. "I wasn't thinking."

"You're not thinking now." She gasped as he positioned his dick between her petal-soft folds and pushed into the tight, plush clasp of her pussy.

She held herself aloft with her hands on his chest, the slick walls of her sex sucking on the head of his cock.

He forced himself to wait. "Your choice, Katie. You said you could take me. Do it."

Katie's lithe thighs were defined by the effort required to keep herself above him. The sight of her bared, toned body was so erotic it made Wulf perspire. It was such a provocative and tantalizing view. He couldn't imagine ever growing tired of it.

"Will this satisfy you, Your Highness?" With a practiced

swivel of her hips, she took him to the root, the denuded lips of her pussy kissing the base of his shaft. "Is this what you wanted?"

Wulf's breath hissed out between clenched teeth. His fingers dug into the slick marble beneath him but found no purchase.

Her hands lifted to slide into her hair, thrusting her breasts forward wantonly. With narrowed eyes, Katie licked her lips and rose, stroking his cock in a heated, intimate embrace.

"Katie," he groaned, lost in her. "You are so beautiful."

She began to dance then, her seductress's body undulating over and around him, her hips rolling and lowering, her arms manipulating her hair into a graceful curtain of dark silk.

"Is this what you had in mind?" she purred, riding him with breathtaking skill and schooled elegance. "To steal your enemy's lover and fuck her in your *seraglio*? To take his prized courtesan and add her to your stable as just one of many?"

"What?" he choked, as she rippled her inner muscles along the length of his throbbing dick, stealing his wits.

"Are you thinking of him now?" Katie goaded, her throaty voice roughened by passion. "Wishing he could see you? Wishing he was watching me give to you what I wouldn't give to him?"

With a growl of fury, Wulf tugged her flat against him and twisted, taking her under him again. "The king has nothing to do with this. *Nothing!"*

"You lie." Her eyes glistened, and the sight made his chest tight. "Why else would you bring me *here?* To be with all of *them!"*

"Because I'm an idiot." He pressed the words into her throat with fierce kisses. "I lost the ability to think clearly the moment I saw you."

"Wulf . . ." Her voice broke.

The wealth of emotion between them made him dizzy, but he welcomed it. He was alive. His heart beat strongly in his chest. His lungs breathed in air. And in his arms lay a beautiful, desirable woman he admired. A woman who felt as he did—reckless and out of control.

He laced his fingers with hers and pulled their arms over her head. "Let me make it good for you."

"It's too good," she whispered, her hands squeezing his.

His chest flexed against hers as he returned her grip. "It is. And it's between us. No one else."

She hugged him deep inside her, caressing him with those maddening little muscles. He dropped his head next to hers. "I don't want to hold back, Katie. I want to ride you hard and deep."

Her tongue delved into his ear, making him tremble. "Do it. Burn this out."

With a grunt of pure lust, he wrapped himself around her and began to thrust. Wild, he drove into her with a singular madness, his buttocks clenching and releasing in rapid rhythm as he propelled himself as far into the heart of her as he could go.

It wasn't enough. He wondered if it would ever be enough, if he would get deep enough . . .

Katie sobbed and cried out his name, rising to meet every downstroke. Scratching and clawing at his sweat-slick back. Trying to crawl into him, even as he was trying to pound into her.

The pleasure built, rising like a swelling tide until it spilled from his lips.

"Katie . . . yes, like that . . . you're so tight . . . so hot . . . so fucking good . . ."

Snarls and savage groans rose in volume around them. Distantly, Wulf realized it was he who was making those abandoned sounds of pleasure but he couldn't stop, didn't want to stop.

His climax was wrapping around his spine and fisting his balls. He wanted to slow down, make it last, but there was no way. Not with her begging him as she was, pleading with him to fuck her harder and deeper. His knees were bruised from the stone floor, but the pain anchored him to the present, to this moment, to this woman. The woman who'd wanted him when he'd wanted to die.

Gritting his teeth, Wulf tried to will away the unbelievable pleasure. But Katie screamed his name, climaxing with a torrent of sound, her body clenching around him in exquisite inner convulsions. She dragged him with her into orgasm, yanking him under. He succumbed with an exultant shout of masculine triumph. He came violently, his tormented cock jerking with every thick spurt, his jaw clenched tightly as he emptied his lust into the quivering depths of her.

Shuddering with the devastating force of his release, Wulf fought to pull air into his lungs. Katie's greedy body continued to grip him in aftershocks that stole his sanity. He pressed tender, grateful kisses along the side of her face and neck. Releasing her hands, he hugged her, then curled them both on their sides.

How had this obsession consumed him so quickly? Why did it have to be focused on this woman, a woman never meant for him? His mind was too fogged to think. His embrace tightened.

Katie was tucked into the crook of his shoulder, and Wulf knew by the extremity of her relaxation that she was asleep. He left her only for the length of time necessary to stand and draw up his pants. Then he lifted her into his arms.

"Guardian, send for Sabine." He carried Katie toward the exit. Within a moment, he heard a door open behind him.

"Yes, Your Highness?" Sabine asked.

Wulf paused and faced his chamberlain. As she straightened from a low bow, he noted the high flush on her cheeks and wondered at it. Then he remembered the abandon with which he'd taken Katie and his own face heated with unfamiliar embarrassment. Everyone would have heard them. Sabine eyed the sleeping Katie with new respect.

"I will call for you when she wakes," he said. "You will attend to her in my chambers."

He started to walk away.

"Y-you're taking her with you?" Sabine was incredulous. "It will only take a moment to prepare a room for her."

He shook his head. Like Katie, he was exhausted, and all he wanted was his own bed and Katie curled up beside him. "That will be all, Sabine."

"I apologize for being unprepared, Your Highness." The chamberlain hurried after him. "Her room will be ready shortly."

"No need to apologize. And you misunderstand. She will share my rooms."

Wulf didn't have to turn around to know Sabine was dumbfounded. He felt the same. He likened the feeling to blunt force trauma to the head, which was dangerous, considering how he'd need sound reasoning to explain his actions to his father.

Stealing the King of Sari's prized concubine for ransom was one thing. It meant returning her was intended and a war unlikely.

Intending to keep her, despite all the risks, was another circumstance altogether.

Warmth and comfort were the first two things to register in Sapphire's mind when she returned to consciousness. Keeping her eyes closed, she relished those sensations before she was bombarded with others—the feel of a man's hard leg between her thighs, a thickly muscled pectoral beneath her cheek, warm lips pressed to her crown, and Wulf's scent clinging to her skin.

She opened her eyes and saw totally unfamiliar surroundings. A large red velvet canopy loomed overhead with matching drapes tied to each of four bedposts. An inlaid seating area scattered with multi-colored pillows was several feet away. Beyond that was a massive bank of windows that were nearly the size of transport bay doors.

Curious, Sapphire disentangled from Wulf's embrace despite his sleepy protests, and walked to the windows to take in the view. Set high atop a mountain, the D'Ashier royal palace overlooked the thriving cities below. The sun was setting, bathing the vista spread out before her in a reddish golden glow.

She jumped when Wulf's warm arms surrounded her from behind. His chin came to rest atop her head with a silent exhale.

"It's breathtaking," she whispered in awe.

His embrace tightened. "I was thinking the same thing about you."

Sapphire leaned into him, then winced at the bruising she felt in her right buttock. She remembered their encounter on the tiled floor by the pool, and reached for the spot. Wulf brushed her fingers aside.

"Let me," he murmured, knowing exactly where to rub to soothe the ache.

"You can't keep me a prisoner here."

He groaned, as if he were dealing with a difficult child. "It doesn't have to be like that."

"What else can it be like? My father is the General of the Sarian Army. I have been a concubine to the King of Sari—*your enemy*—for the last five years, and he's reluctant to forget me. When they discover that I've been taken against my will . . ."

Wulf turned her to face him. "Why does it have to be against your will? Stay with me by your own choice, and your father would become your advocate. Without the general's full support, the king would have difficulty acting."

His emerald eyes glittered in the shadows created by the setting sun. "I can make you happy. I can give you things you never knew you wanted."

Sapphire's heart stopped, then raced. "What are you of-fering?"

"A place in my life, in my bed. I will spoil you, shower you with gifts, take you places you've always wanted to see."

"For how long?"

"For as long as it pleases both of us." He cradled her cheek in the palm of his hand. His thumb brushed across her skin.

"It would never work."

"I saw the way your father is with you," Wulf went on. "He won't risk you."

"The king doesn't need my father's approval."

She slipped free of his embrace and moved back toward the bed. It wasn't what he said, but what he didn't say. "You have many beautiful women who you can enjoy with far less risk. Instead you imperil an entire nation for temporary pleasure."

He was silent behind her.

She waited, but as the moment drew out, Katie looked over her shoulder. She kept her facial expression carefully neutral.

Wulfric stared at her, then ran a hand through his dark hair. "What do you want me to say?" He looked away. "That my cock is overruling my reason? I told you it's more than that. This isn't easy for me."

"I know."

Just as she knew that she couldn't stay. She would have to leave—*soon*—before the direness of the situation escalated. Wulf had given her a week of his time in Sari. She might be able to manage a week in D'Ashier. Then she would go, before her desire for Wulf turned into something deeper and more painful to lose.

"I'm hungry," she said. "And I want a bath. Then I want to see my *mästares*."

"So you'll stay?" Wulf came to her and searched her face.

"For a time."

"How long is that?"

"As long as it pleases both of us."

She moved away, creating the necessary distance between them by walking through an archway into a private bath beyond. The massive room was stunning, the walls covered in jeweled tiles. Fountains sprayed a steady stream of warmed water into the bathing pool. Bubbling jets pulsed from the depths, releasing a subtle fragrance into the humid air. The ceiling was made of low emissive glass, revealing the night sky above them, while simulated candlelight shimmered along the colorful walls.

It was a voluptuary's paradise; therefore, it suited Wulfric perfectly. He had a ravenous appetite for life and lived on the extreme end of every spectrum. He was wild and unrestrained, which both lured and repelled her. What would it be like to tame such a man? She doubted it was possible or that she would like the result if it was.

Stepping into the warm water, Sapphire dove beneath the surface and swam to the opposite side. When she came up for air, she noted Wulfric's frown. He slipped into the water. She waited until he neared, then she moved willingly into his arms.

"Katie . . ."

She silenced the inevitable questions with a kiss, tilting her head to better seal her mouth over his. Her tongue caressed his before she caught him between her lips and sucked.

When he moved to pin her to the edge, she slipped under the water and went to the semi-submerged ledge where various bath oils and soaps waited in fluted glass bottles. As she reached for a container that was less full than the others, she felt Wulf's hands glide over her hips.

"I can bind you to my bed and keep you," he threatened.

Pouring the liquid into her hand, Sapphire tossed an arched look over her shoulder. "If you make me a prisoner, I'll deny you and fight you. Never doubt it."

She built up the richly scented lather, then turned and

worked it over his chest. He watched her with dark, hooded eyes. "I can hold you without chains."

"Will you enslave me with this magnificent body?" She caressed his deeply bronzed skin with soap-slippery hands.

"Can you be enslaved?"

"Why would you want such a thing?" Her fingertips stroked over his broad shoulders and down his well-defined arms. She admired the hard ripples of his abdomen, then stepped around him to wash the corded length of his back. The skin of her palms tingled and burned from touching him. The force of the attraction shortened her breath. It was insanity, but she couldn't fight it. "Isn't my desire and admiration enough?"

As she kneaded his muscles, he groaned, his head tilting back. "No."

Soaping her hands again, she ran them through his hair, massaging his scalp with her fingertips. "Would you prefer I wail and wring my hands over you while you're away? Then cling to you when you return because you've been gone too long? You don't strike me as the type of man who'd appreciate drama from a lover."

Wulf turned and caught her, tugging her beneath the water and pressing his mouth to hers. With a powerful lunge, he propelled them upward, breaking the surface with an explosive splash. She sputtered and pushed her wet hair out of her eyes. He chuckled before kissing her again. "I risk a war for you. I want more than your desire in return. A little drama wouldn't hurt."

"I didn't ask for this." Sapphire wrapped her arms around his shoulders, which pushed her breasts against him. His gaze darkened.

"I didn't ask for this either." He reached down to wrap her legs around his hips. "I don't have time for obsessions."

"You need a foreign princess with excellent political connections." Her voice was low and raspy, an audible sign of how it affected her to cling to his big, naked body.

"Someday." Wulf thrust one hand into her wet hair and arched her neck. "But right now, it's you I want. And I won't be satisfied until you want me the same way."

"What makes you think I don't?"

"You'd leave, if you could."

"Not for lack of wanting you."

"Prove it." His smile made her toes curl.

Sapphire smiled back. Straightening her legs, she once again stood on the pool floor. "Let me finish washing you."

"More work?"

She linked her fingers with his and drew him to the shallow steps. "I'm not working. I'm touching you because I'll take any excuse to do so."

"You don't need an excuse. You don't even have to ask."

With gentle urging, she maneuvered Wulf into sitting on the shallow first step. She began to wash his legs, kneading the muscles of his calves and thighs. She worked her way up to the eager jut of his cock and paused. He was hard and thick, as if he hadn't just screwed her into exhaustion mere hours ago. It looked delicious. Her mouth watered at the remembered feel of him sliding over her tongue.

"Katie . . ." The way he said her name made her shiver. His voice—always dark and deep—was laced with a sensual threat. "Keep looking at me like that and I'll give you what you're asking for, right here on this step."

She finished washing him quickly, understanding by the high flush on his cheekbones and the fists clenched at his sides that he was close to following through. Delicious as the thought was, Sapphire had something else in mind. She rinsed off the soap with handfuls of water splashed over his hips.

Wulf was nearly prone, his body taut, his eyes heavy-lidded but alert. He presented such an erotic sight, spread out before her, his chiseled features austerely handsome.

She bent her head and took his cock in her mouth.

He bowed upward with a grunt, his hands thrusting into her hair to urge her closer. She suckled deeply, keeping the thick head trapped between the moist heat of her tongue and the curved roof of her mouth. Gripping the base of his cock with one hand, she cupped his scrotum with the other, rolling the twin balls with gentle fingers. She moaned when he swelled and throbbed with the beat of his heart.

Wulf began panting harshly, his fingers flexing against her scalp. "Temptress . . . that hot little mouth . . ."

He held her head still and bucked his hips, fucking through her suctioning lips. Then, suddenly, he pushed her away, slipping into the water with a vicious curse.

"Wulf?" Her mouth tingled in frustrated longing. Her blood was heated and pumping fast with her hunger.

The glance he shot her was furious. "You want to reduce this to nothing but sex."

"It can't be anything more than that."

"It can be whatever we make it." He collected a jar from the shelf and swam toward her, his jaw set mutinously.

Wulf clearly hadn't heard the word "no" often enough.

"Why do you want it to be?" she asked. "You said it was my desire for you in the healing room that caught your interest. Desire leads to sex."

Wulf halted before her. He removed the lid of the container in his hand, releasing the scent of Draxian lilies.

"It was your desire that revived me," he corrected. "But it was the blade at my throat that first fascinated me, and the way you hid me from your father."

"Moments of insanity." Against her will, her hand lifted and came to rest lightly on his hip. The rumble of approval that rose from his chest made her fingertips knead restlessly into his firm flesh. The urge to press herself against him was difficult to resist.

"Yes. And the moments continued, stringing together, turning into days of madness where I thought of nothing but you, and you thought of nothing but me."

"Given time, we would forget."

"Before I left for my last patrol"—he soaped his hands—
"I asked Sabine to select four of my concubines. I was unde-
cided, so I made no decision at all."

The images that filled Sapphire's mind made her jealous.

"I remember they possessed different colored hair," he
continued, "but when I walked into the *seraglio* today, I couldn't
remember who they were. If all the women were lined up
before me, I doubt I could pick them out. As pleasant as the
debauchery was, it was forgettable."

He cupped her aching breasts in both hands and squeezed.
Sapphire's breath caught.

"But you . . ." He smiled. "I know you have a birthmark
on your hip and a freckle on your shoulder. I know the way
you smell, the way you feel. You are unique to me. Vivid. I
want you for more than sex. I want to do more with you than
fuck you."

She watched him, riveted, as he caressed her in progressively
smaller circles. When he reached her nipples and plucked them
into stiff points, a low moan of pleasure escaped her.

"I want to learn more about you," he murmured. "The
outside and the inside."

He washed her body slowly with the same attention she'd
paid to his. As blissful languor weighted her limbs, he reached
between her legs and rubbed her swollen flesh, cleansing her.
Teasing her. Making her grip his shoulders to keep from falling.

There was nothing beyond her ability to withstand—
except a tender Wulfric. Did he know what he was doing to
her? Was he doing it deliberately?

"Rinse," he ordered.

When she emerged from the water, he was waiting for her.

"Come here." His tone was coaxing. Gripping her waist,
he lifted her onto the edge of the pool, leaving her legs dangling in the water. He parted her knees.

She knew what he intended. Her eager pussy welcomed
his attentions with a rush of slick moisture. Her breathing

grew shallow; her heart raced. Wulf smiled wickedly, knowing damn well what he did to her. She notched her heel at the back of his calf and tugged him closer.

He sat on the steps and spread the lips of her sex with his thumb and forefinger. "You want me."

"Some parts of me do."

His smile widened. "I won't rest until every part of you does." He rubbed her with his fingertips in a leisurely back-and-forth glide. "Look how slick you are. Insatiable."

"Wulf . . ." She mewled as he bent his head to her pussy and gifted it with a lover's kiss, pushing his tongue inside her. Stroking. Tormenting.

"I want to know you here." He licked her again, his verdant eyes lit with primitive masculine need. "I want to memorize the taste and feel of you." He drew her clitoris into his mouth and suckled, fluttering over the tight bed of nerves with rapid flicks of his tongue.

Her legs began to shake. Sapphire cupped his nape and pulled him closer. He tilted his head and fucked her with his tongue, his thick, wet hair tickling her inner thighs. Her body was on fire, her hips rocking and straining for the orgasm he deliberately kept out of reach.

It was all so new to her—the seduction, the lack of control, the gift of doing nothing but accepting the attentions he doled out so freely. She watched him with narrowed eyes, enamored of the sight of so handsome a man—an enemy prince—servicing her so intimately. Wulf growled his pleasure and the savage sound freed the knotted tension in her womb. It burst in an intense, shattering release. She cried out, her chest tight with emotion. Gratitude. Longing.

"Beautiful," he praised, his tongue gentling her down from the last tremors of her orgasm.

"Stop," she begged, too sensitive to bear his expert lashing. Instead, he started over, working her quivering flesh until she climaxed more fiercely than before. Then he began again. And again.

"Please." She pushed him away. "No more."

He studied her intently, his lips swollen and glistening. "Are you satisfied for now? Ready to enjoy a meal and conversation?"

Sapphire smiled. "I'm ready for a nap."

Wulf gripped the ledge of the pool and levered himself out of the water. He stood over her, dripping, fisting the heavy length of his cock. His hand pumped hard and fast, milking the engorged shaft she coveted. Semen beaded on the tip before spurting thickly across the tile. As he finished, Wulf's chest heaved. Then he smiled wryly. "I haven't done that in years."

"You didn't have to do it now." She was willing, even if overly satisfied. She would have taken him gladly and he knew it. He was making a startling point—he intended to give as much as he took.

"Yes, I did." He bent and rinsed his hands in the water. Sapphire slid in, washing again before exiting the pool by way of the stairs.

Wulf was waiting for her there, extending his hand to help her out, then pressing his lips to her forehead in a quick, hard kiss. He laced his fingers with hers and led her to the far corner, where a drying grate waited. As the warm air spun around them, he pulled her close. Sapphire urged him even closer, so that no air intruded between them.

He was tender, his strength held in check, his large hands caressing the length of her spine with such reverence. Tears leaked from beneath her closed eyelids, but the heated air whisked the evidence away.

When they were dry, he dressed them both in his robes and led her out to his bedchamber.

"Food and wine," he told the palace Guardian. Then he proceeded to order a meal she would have ordered herself; a feast of all her favorite foods. He'd paid attention, she realized, and took pains to remember. Or perhaps it was easy? Perhaps it was just a matter of being highly alert, as one would expect a warrior prince to be.

"As you wish, Your Highness."

And so they ate a light meal of various sweetmeats, fruit, and cheeses before Wulf ordered Sabine to join them.

"Rise, Sabine," he instructed after she had proffered a box and prostrated before him.

The chamberlain rose. "I brought clothes for the new concubine. I also brought talgorite, Your Highness, and this," she held out a long, thick golden chain with a cylindrical charm on the end of it, "as you specified."

Wulf extended his open hand and Sabine draped the necklace across the palm. He turned to Sapphire and drew it over her head, then arranged it around her neck.

"Your Guardian's chip," he explained.

Lifting the charm from where it rested between her breasts, Sapphire looked at it, admiring the shield of the royal family of D'Ashier engraved in the gold. She shot Wulf a quizzical glance.

He shrugged. "I have a soft spot for that Guardian."

Sabine bowed. "The king respects your wish for privacy, Your Highness, but he urges you to meet with him at your earliest convenience."

"Tomorrow."

"Go see him," Sapphire urged. "He must have been worried sick about you."

He raised a sardonic brow, but an easy smile curled the corners of his mouth. "You've forgotten where you are, Katie. I don't take orders here. I give them."

"Not to me you don't, Your Royal Arrogance."

"Is that so?" He leaped across the bed, catching her in his arms. She squealed, then dissolved into peals of laughter when he tickled her.

"Stop!" She smacked at him. "Oh, stop it . . . Please, Wulf."

He laughed. "Begging. I love it."

"And you call *me* 'insatiable'?"

"I'm exhausted from keeping up with you."

Locking one leg around his, Sapphire twisted and gained the top. She straddled his hips and he allowed her to pin his hands to his stomach. "You probably have a lot of things to take care of, having been gone for so long."

"Nothing that can't wait until morning. After tonight, I'll be very busy. You won't see much of me during the day." While his tone was light, his expression wasn't.

"Perhaps your father has new information about the attack against you."

"If he needed me urgently, he'd say so."

"You aren't the type of man who ignores duty for pleasure, yet you keep doing it for me."

Wulfric frowned. "There's too much I can't explain. I need time to think before I see him."

"And you can think around me?" she teased. "I'm envious. I can't think at all around you."

Pulling her hand to his mouth, he kissed the back. The look he gave her was rife with promise. "Fine, I'll go."

"Good." She brushed his hair back from his forehead, then slid off him. "I'll see you when you return."

"You'd better be here."

"Where would I go?" Sapphire batted her eyelashes with mock innocence. His gaze narrowed.

Wulf rolled from the bed, shrugged out of his black bathrobe, and slipped into the dark red robe Sabine held out for him. He moved to the armoire and entered the code that released a secure drawer containing his crown—an understated golden circlet liberally encrusted with talgorite. When he turned to her with his royal robes billowing behind him and his black hair shining in the simulated candlelight, her heart lodged in her throat. His lean waist was cinched with a golden clasp, leaving a V-shaped opening that revealed his powerful chest and sun-dark skin.

"You take my breath away." Her mouth curved wistfully and she sheltered her racing heart with her hand. Wulfric was the embodiment of every fantasy prince she'd ever imagined— except Wulfric was more sexual and far more dangerous. The determination with which he pursued their attraction was both endearing and devastating.

He stilled. His emerald gaze arrested her with its roiling emotions. Desire. Confusion. She knew exactly how he felt.

"For the rest of my life," she said, "I'll remember you looking just as you do right now."

Wulf spoke hoarsely. "How the hell am I supposed to leave when you look at me like that?"

"I just wanted you to know what the sight of you does to me."

He stared at her for so long, she began to doubt that he would go. Finally, he turned and departed without another word.

Sighing inwardly, Sapphire turned her attention to Sabine with a smile, wanting very much to find a friend in this foreign place. The chamberlain approached her hesitantly.

"Let's see what you have there." Sapphire gestured to the box of stones, then patted the mattress next to her. "Sit with me. You can help me pick."

"I cannot," Sabine replied. "It's forbidden to touch His Highness's bed."

"I see." Sapphire frowned, considering. For security reasons that made perfect sense. It also made the exception given to her more puzzling. Did Wulf really discount her political connections? "You regard me strangely. Tell me, Sabine. Is Prince Wulfric acting in ways you find unusual?"

"That would be putting it mildly," Sabine answered dryly. "If I were a more fanciful woman, I might think a completely different man had returned to us."

"Could you tell me what it is about his behavior that's out of character?"

A smile tugged at Sabine's mouth. "To begin with, there is a bedroom set aside for his use of the concubines. Yet you are in his rooms, in his bed. And he means for you to stay here. That is the most shocking circumstance to me."

"I see." Sapphire hid the pleasure she found in the knowledge that she was special and separate from his other women.

The chamberlain continued. "It's equally odd that he allows you to talk to him the way you do—to call him by his given name and to argue with him." Sabine lifted the lid of the box and revealed a dazzling array of jewels. "You are special to him. If you maneuver well, you could achieve great power. I can help you."

Sapphire admired the woman's cunning. A great chamberlain knew how to position herself and the women beneath her to best advantage. But Sapphire wouldn't be staying long enough to need the assistance.

A week. No more. And even that, she knew, was long enough to ensure that she wouldn't leave unscathed.

Chapter 9

"Wulfric." Anders, the King of D'Ashier, greeted his son with obvious joy.

"Father." Wulf dropped to one knee and kissed the back of the hand extended to him.

"Thank you for finding time for me in your busy schedule," the king teased dryly. "Between mercenaries and beautiful naked women, I'm certain meeting with your father is a great imposition."

Wulf laughed while his father pulled him to his feet and gripped him in a backslapping embrace. The king wasn't as tall, but he was equally muscular, giving the monarch a stocky and barrel-chested build.

"I spoke with you earlier," Wulf reminded his father, "when I returned the first time. I expected that meeting would allay the most pressing of your concerns until the morning."

"You spoke with me for thirty minutes and only about the ambush," Anders complained. "Nothing about your whereabouts or activities since. You were agitated and clearly distracted. Then you left and came back with a beautiful captive."

"Katie isn't a captive."

Anders sank into a pile of multicolored silk pillows and gestured for Wulf to do the same. Above them, a domed ceiling painted with a mural of many suns supported a single massive chandelier. Simulated candlelight lit the curved seating area and caused the strands of silver that accented the king's raven hair to gleam. Despite the massive size of the royal private sitting room, a feeling of intimacy was achieved by the liberal use of colors and the fur rugs that warmed the stone floors.

"She's a wildcat by all accounts," Anders said, adjusting the train of his talgorite red robes. "And you thought I wouldn't be eaten up by curiosity? You don't know me at all, if you thought I could wait until morning."

"A wildcat." Wulf smiled as he sat. "That's an apt description." He could still feel the dig of her nails in the skin of his back and buttocks.

"Sabine tells me you've created a furor with your performance in your *seraglio* today. The other concubines are eager for similar attention from you. You'll be a very busy man trying to keep up with the demand. How I envy you that!"

Wulf winced, still embarrassed that so raw an encounter had also been so public. "I'll make arrangements for them when I return to my rooms."

Anders's brows rose. "Arrangements? Like a schedule? Or did your captive exhaust you? Give it a day or two, son. You're young, you'll recover quickly."

"Recovery time isn't a problem." Just thinking of Katie made him hard and ready. The way she responded to him, as if she'd been made for him . . . He couldn't get enough.

"I, too, have had my favorites." Anders tossed his arm over a pillow and settled more comfortably. "Sabine was one of them. It's heady while it lasts. Enjoy."

"I am." Wulf bent forward, setting his forearms on his thighs. "Perhaps you can understand why I was reluctant to leave her."

Anders sat in contemplative silence for a moment. "Who is she? Where did you find her?"

"I don't know where to start. And frankly, it doesn't matter how I present the information, you're not going to like it."

"Start where you left off," his father suggested. "Tell me what happened to you. Were you able to gather some useful information while you were in Sari?"

Taking a deep breath, Wulf started his tale with the moment he came to consciousness in the healing chamber and ended with him sitting in the king's private sitting room. When he finished, he braced for his father's reaction, which he expected to be nothing less than explosive. He wasn't wrong.

"You're a genius!" Anders leaped to his feet. "This is fantastic. We've got them by the balls now. Erikson's daughter and Gunther's favorite concubine—"

"*Former* concubine."

"No wonder you're enjoying her so much." His father laughed and rubbed his hands together.

Wulf stood. "It isn't like that."

Anders went still. His gaze narrowed. "Think with your other brain. She's leverage and a hot fuck. Don't lose sight of who she is."

Wulf couldn't lose sight of it. Her history made her into the woman she was. A woman he respected and found fascinating.

His father scowled. "You can't keep her, Wulfric. Erikson will come for her eventually, if we don't ransom her within a reasonable period of time. And he'll have the backing of the king, if that idiot is as in love with her as you say."

"Not if she wants to stay." Katie hadn't said so outright, but he would make her want to. He was determined.

Standing with arms akimbo, Anders lip curled scornfully, a bitter nasty smile that caused Wulf to clench his fists. "What the hell does she have between her legs? To get both you and Gunther panting after . . ." He paused. Discovery lit his eyes. "She's a *spy*."

"No, damn it!"

"Think, Wulfric! She's been sleeping with the King of Sari for *five years*! She must care for him."

"She was contracted."

"Bullshit. Your imprisonment doesn't make sense any other way. Why the hell were you sent to her instead of the palace dungeon? Why did her Guardian allow you to watch her meeting with Erikson? Concubines don't have combat training. Why is she so knowledgeable?" Anders drove his point home with a stab of his finger. "She's a fucking assassin or a spy, that's why!"

Wulf stood stiffly, his heart hammering. "Katie didn't want to come. You know that. I brought her here against her will."

"You don't know whether you're coming or going! First, you say she wants to stay. Then, you say she didn't want to come. Which is it?" The king snorted. "It's the oldest female wile in history—play hard to get. You can have any woman you want, Wulfric. The fact that she's the only woman who denies you makes possessing her irresistible. But that denial melts when you fuck her, doesn't it? It's all for show."

"You accuse me of confusion? While you suggest she doesn't want me, then say she does . . . all in the same breath?"

"No matter how you look at it," Anders retorted, "her motives are suspect."

Sinking into the pillows, Wulf buried his head in his hands. His skin broke out in a sweat and his chest tightened, making it hard for him to breathe. The suspicious circumstances surrounding his introduction to the beautiful Sapphire were unavoidable, but he'd done a damn good job of avoiding them anyway. He had been so grateful for her attentions after the horrors of his captivity.

Everything his father said could very well be true. He'd known Katie such a short time, how could he discern the truth behind her motives?

"Wulfric." The king lowered to his haunches before him. "I've never seen you like this over a woman. Maybe they put an aphrodisiac in the healing chamber air. Maybe she's wearing it in her perfume or lotion."

Wulf exhaled harshly. "I'll take care of her. I'll uncover her true intentions."

"Maybe we should give her to your brother. He can—"

"No." Wulf's tone left no room for argument. "Duncan is still a boy, barely a man. He couldn't manage her." Wulf stood, suddenly weary. "She's mine. Whether she's my lover or my mistake is a determination I'm more than capable of making on my own."

The king straightened. "I'm worried about you."

"Don't be." Wulf looked straight into eyes the same color as his own. "My first love is D'Ashier. Always has been. Always will be."

Still, the possibility of Katie's duplicity caused a piercing pain in his chest.

He bowed. "I'll see you in the morning."

"Yes." The king looked grim. "I'll be waiting."

The sight that greeted Wulfric when he returned to his room hit him like a physical blow. His gut clenched and his breath shortened. Katie waited on his bed, her body adorned with glittering red talgorite. Her beautiful features illuminated from within when she saw him.

Whatever they had between them couldn't be a complete lie. There had to be some truth to it. When he was inside her, her response to him was real and heartfelt. He knew it.

Sabine exited the bathing chamber and lowered to the floor upon seeing him. "Your Highness."

His eyes never left Katie.

"You look unwell." Katie frowned. "What happened?"

She rose from the bed and came toward him. The red diaphanous gown she wore shimmered and wafted over lush curves, teasing him with tantalizing glimpses of the creamy flesh beneath.

The perfect weapon, if that's what she was.

"Rise, Sabine," he said gruffly. "Prepare a room for Sapphire with the other concubines. She'll join you shortly."

Wulf heard the doors slide shut behind the departing chamberlain. Something inside him closed along with them.

Katie stopped in front of him. "You called me Sapphire." She seemed to wait for an explanation, but there was a knowing look in her dark eyes. "You don't want to send me away. I can see it on your face."

"I have an early day tomorrow."

She shook her head. "That's not what this is about, is it? Something your father said upset you."

He couldn't stop himself from embracing her. His head ached. He didn't know what or whom to believe, and until he knew with certainty, he had an obligation to the Crown to protect himself and his people.

Turning Katie roughly away from him, Wulfric positioned her prone on the bed.

"What are you doing?" she asked, her voice huskier than usual.

Wulf bent over her, his lips to her ear. "Tell me, Katie. Why would a career concubine study combat techniques? You have the skills of an assassin." He pushed her gown up around her waist and slipped his hand between her legs. The feel of her, so warm and soft, aroused him further. His cock grew heavy. Ready.

"I—I . . . My father insisted I learn to protect myself." She gasped as he parted her sweet pussy and circled her clitoris with the pad of his index finger. "In secondary school there was a young man . . . umm . . . that feels good."

"Keep talking," he ordered, gritting his teeth as she slicked his fingers. As Katie's skin heated, the scent of alluring, willing woman filled his nostrils and made him crazy. She didn't need to wear an aphrodisiac; she was one. Whenever he touched her, he felt wild and out of control. If he trusted her completely, he would revel in the potency of the animal attraction between them. As it was, he felt as if he was drowning. He'd be damned if he would drown alone.

"He walked me home one day. He tried . . ."

Wulf pushed two fingers inside her, biting back a growl at the feel of tight yet plush tissues. He began fucking her in an unhurried rhythm determined to reduce her to the same base craving he suffered. In and out. He hooked his fingers and rubbed across the sweet spot inside her.

"Oh . . ." Katie moaned and writhed in a way that made him perspire from the effort of holding back. "I can't think when you touch me."

Wulf watched her rest her cheek against his velvet coverlet and close her eyes. Even now, divided as he was, he wanted her as much as he wanted to breathe. And he would have her. He would take her like this, facedown, so that she wouldn't be able to see what she did to him.

"He tried to take liberties . . ." Her hips were swirling against his hand in tight little circles, taking what she needed, making her pussy ripple hungrily along his fingers. "But my father c–came . . . h–home in time. No permanent damage was done, but a–afterward I wanted to know how to defend myself."

"You took it to the extreme," he growled. "You're trained to kill. Not just one opponent, but several."

"I do nothing in half measure." Irritation strengthened her voice. "Neither do you."

"Aren't you loyal in half measure? Betraying your father and king to protect me."

Opening her eyes, Katie lifted her head and glared at him over her shoulder. "Something was said to you tonight to make you angry with me. If it's a fight you want, face me directly. If you want to fuck, get on with it. Either way, get to the point."

Snarling with confusion and frustration, Wulf unclasped his robe with deft fingers. The two overlapping halves parted, and he took his cock in hand. Without a word, he thrust hard into her.

She cried out as he filled her in a violent surge, the force of his entry pushing her flat on the bed.

"Have you always driven men mad?" he asked harshly. "Am I just one of many who lose their minds around you?" He raised her knees to the mattress edge and held her hips immobile, restraining her from pulling away. He began to drive into her, shafting her rough and fast.

"Yes," she snapped. "Is that what you want me to say? That you mean nothing to me? That I'm just screwing you in every way I can?"

Katie was hot and tight, so extremely tight Wulf thought he might die of the pleasure. No man could live through endless lust like this. He fucked her like a man possessed because he felt as if he was, trying to crawl into her so he could see her motives and ascertain the truth about her feelings for him.

"You lie," he gasped. "You care."

Her helpless cries spurred him like whiplashes. He rode her with deep, long strokes, growling each time he hit the end of her. It was unbelievable, the coiling ecstasy that wrapped around his spine and burned through his blood. He loved making love to her. He craved the closeness, the feeling of connection he felt only with Katie.

She was fisting the bedclothes and thrusting back at him, fucking him as hard as he was taking her. Her pussy gripped his cock in delicious, rhythmic pulses that took him to the knife edge of climax. He reached beneath her and teased her clitoris, relishing the way she whimpered his name. He timed his thrusts to the movements of his fingers.

"Wulf . . . it's so good . . . so good . . ."

He wrapped his straining body around hers.

"Katie," he whispered, wishing he'd never gone to see his father, wishing he had stayed in the room with her, ignorant of outside prejudices and the doubts they created.

This was real.

He felt her stiffen, then her pussy contracted around his pumping cock. He stilled at the deepest point of her, allowing her body to milk him into orgasm. He shuddered against her back, erupting inside her with a pained groan of pleasure. The pulses were endless and destructive, each spurt of semen followed by a shudder that rocked his entire frame.

Wulf followed her down to the bed, then turned them both onto their sides. Cupped together, their bodies were still joined.

As his erratic breathing slowed, he noted how her fingers laced with his and held their joined hands over her racing heart. He drew her against his chest, his plans to send her to the concubines' quarters abandoned in favor of staying deep inside her. Connected.

If she was the traitor his father thought her to be, Wulf risked his life every time he slept with her. She could kill him when he was most vulnerable. His death would send D'Ashier into chaos, and since he was the head of the country's military forces, his loss could create a momentary vulnerability easily exploited by his enemy.

Strangely the possible threat to his life didn't frighten him, at least not enough to send her away. Yes, there was no denying that their meeting had been improbably coincidental, but she hadn't killed him yet.

"If you send me to Sabine," Katie whispered fiercely, "I'll never forgive you."

In answer, he nudged deeper inside her and cupped a full breast in their joined hands.

When they'd lain together in her bed in Sari, he'd thought having her here in his palace and his bed would ease the sensation of being minion to a ticking clock. But instead of the permanence he'd thought to feel, he felt a yawning chasm widening between them.

He held her tighter and knew he would have to keep her until he no longer craved her. Nothing would stand in his way.

Not even her.

Chapter 10

Sapphire sat up in bed with a start, her sleep-fogged mind attempting to discern what had awoken her. She pushed her hair out of her eyes with impatient fingers and was startled to see a man standing before the doors; his legs spread wide and meaty arms crossing an impossibly broad chest.

He was massive, his height easily nearing seven feet tall, his shoulders possessing gigantic breadth and tapering to a narrow waist and thighs the diameter of tree trunks. His skin and eyes were as dark as night, his head was bald, and large gold hoops adorned his earlobes.

She eyed his bright red vest with its liberal weave of gold thread and medals. Smiling, she said, "You must be Captain of the Palace Guard."

Momentary surprise lit the man's eyes before he answered in a deep, rumbling voice, "I am."

"Good morning, Captain."

He bowed, arms still crossed. "My name is Clarke, Mistress."

"That's unusual. I like it." She gave him a bright smile. The corners of his dark lips twitched.

Wanting to start the day with an exploration of Wulf's home, Sapphire ran a hand over the fine fabric of her red gown. She wondered if Wulf had noticed her decision to dress in his colors. He might have been too agitated. His father had instilled some doubt in him about her, which she'd expected, considering who she was.

Much as she hated the new tension between them and the desperate edge it had added to their lovemaking, Sapphire knew it was important for Wulf to face the facts—they were together on stolen time.

Regardless, she would always treasure Wulf for following his heart last night. He'd planned to send her away. Instead, he had wrapped himself around her and never let go. A vague memory of a tender kiss before he departed this morning left her defenseless. Heartache was inevitable but worth it. She'd experienced her grand passion and felt it returned. Wishing for the impossible—more time, and less impediments— would only detract from what they did have.

As she slid out of bed, she returned her attention to the captain. "Is there something I can do for you, Clarke?" Seeing the inquiring lift of his brow, she elaborated. "Why are you here?"

"His Highness, Prince Wulfric, ordered me to accompany you today."

With a contemplative nod, she walked into the bathing chamber and washed quickly, emerging a few minutes later attired in a long white robe. "I need to dress. What should I wear?"

Clarke frowned. "My orders are to follow you wherever you wish to go."

So . . . Wulf thought she might flee. Her mouth curved wryly.

"Poor captain," she lamented on Clarke's behalf. "What a miserable assignment."

She laughed at the captain's ready nod of agreement and was delighted at his answering smile. Perhaps she could make another ally. Security and military stratagems were two of her interests. It would be fascinating to study those aspects of the D'Ashier royal palace—and ascertain ways to escape. Of course, she would have to be careful in her curiosity . . .

"What would you normally be doing today?"

"Overseeing the training of my men."

"Excellent." She rubbed her hands together. "I love training. What do you think about *me* following *you* wherever you
go today?"

Clarke hesitated.

"I don't have anywhere to go. I don't particularly relish the
idea of spending all day in this room, do you?" At his answering look of discomfort, she smiled. "That's settled, then. I'll
see if I can find a *dammr*-suit in the mass of clothes Sabine
brought me last evening."

Unfortunately, there weren't any practical garments among
the lovely gowns that were set aside for her use. It took almost
an hour to locate a *dammr*-suit in her size, but the delay was
fortuitous. By the time she was suitably dressed, the captain
was positive that he had no wish to take part in female activities. Whatever doubts he'd harbored about her accompani-
ment were set aside.

As they traversed the arched stone corridors, Sapphire
jogged to keep up with Clarke's massive stride. She was
warmed up and limber by the time they joined his men on
the training field, which was located in a large, open-air courtyard.

The captain was quickly in his element, overseeing the dis-
bursement of the guards into several groups, each focused on
a specific area of combat training. One group practiced with
glaives, another with bio-filter masks, and another with fire
readiness. The group that most interested her, though, was the
one engaged in hand-to-hand combat. She watched them
carefully, noting their strengths and their weaknesses.

She turned to Clarke. "Which of these men are directly responsible for the protection of Prince Wulfric?"

"The men wearing red and black stripes."

"I have something to show you that you might find interesting. Would you call them over to us, please?"

Eyeing her curiously, Clarke did as she requested. Soon, twenty men stood in a semicircle around them. With her chin lifted and shoulders back, she asked, "Did any of you fight in the Confrontations?"

Five men stepped forward, and she took note of the special braiding on their uniforms that the other men lacked.

Walking the length of the gauntlet, Sapphire inspected each man carefully. "I suppose at least one or two of you lost your glaive when you riposted like this . . ."

She reached the last man, grabbed his weapon, and engaged the blade. Lunging forward gracefully, she demonstrated the complicated footwork/attack combination common to the D'Ashier military force.

"It happens to the best of men," one of the guards said, somewhat defensively.

"True. But I can show you how to make it happen less often. Anyone care to demonstrate with me?"

After a brief hesitation, Clarke nodded his approval, and one of the five guardsmen engaged his blade and faced her. Sapphire bowed at the waist, then attacked. The man parried with restraint at first, then with more vigor as he recognized her skill. Within moments, she knocked his glaive from his hands using a technique she and her father had perfected.

"Damn," he muttered, wide-eyed as the blade disengaged and the hilt skidded to a halt a few feet away.

Wulf's guards began to speak excitedly.

"*. . . just like that . . .*"

"*. . . happened to me . . .*"

She faced them. "Since you protect Prince Wulfric, I'd like to show you not only how to do what I just did, but how to avoid having it happen to you."

Training Wulf's men in the style of her father wasn't the most loyal thing she could do, but since she intended to learn how Wulfric transferred them from her palace without a pad, she told herself that it was only fair. The knowledge she imparted wouldn't put Sarian troops at any more risk than before, but it

would make successfully attacking Wulfric harder. As guilty as
her offer to train them made her feel, she was decided. She
would acquire valuable information from her lover, but she
would also leave a valuable piece of herself behind.

Clarke scowled down at her. "Where did you learn how
to do that?"

"Never ask a woman her secrets." Retrieving the fallen
glaive, Sapphire returned it to the guardsman she'd separated
it from.

As the captain internally debated whether to accept her
offer or not, the silence lengthened.

Sapphire shrugged and turned away. "If you decide to accept
my offer, I'll be over there relaxing in the shade."

"Mistress?"

She glanced over her shoulder. "Yes?"

Clarke tossed her his glaive. She spun neatly on her booted
heel and caught it.

"Great." She offered him a wide smile. The thought of re-
inforcing Wulf's protection filled her with joy. Perhaps her
knowledge might save his life. It eased her melancholy and
guilt to think of it.

She threw herself into the training with vigor.

As Wulf strode down the stone corridor in search of his
father, his mood was grim.

He'd spent the day catching up on everything that had been
neglected in his absence, but his heart wasn't in the task. Katie
lingered in the back of his mind, a sensual puzzle he needed to
solve. His concentration eluded him. Four of the men responsible for the attack against him had been captured and were
being interrogated. He hoped that soon he would have enough
information to resolve the mystery surrounding his ambush
and subsequent "gifting" to Katie.

Rounding a corner, Wulf stepped out onto the semicir-
cular balcony that overlooked the central courtyard of the

training barracks. His father stood at the railing, his back rigid.

Flanked by stairs on either side and covered with a canopy, the landing was shielded from the heat of the setting sun, which bathed the guardsmen below in a reddish light. Wulf joined Anders at the edge and looked down, attempting to discern what bothered the king.

"What is it, Father?"

Then he saw her.

Katie was crouched within a circle of palace guardsmen, preparing to spar with one of his personal guards.

"What the hell is she doing?" Wulf barked, tensing at the sight of her in danger, real or otherwise.

His father turned to him, revealing features distorted by fury. "She's sabotaging us from the inside! She's been down there all day, retraining the men on the use of glaives. Now she's going over hand-to-hand combat. She'll be the death of us all. Her father will come for her and our men will be useless, retrained by that bitch to fail."

The guard lunged for Katie and they collided in a tangle of *dammr*-suit-clad limbs. The surrounding guardsmen scrambled out of the way as the two rolling bodies grappled furiously in the center.

"*Halt!*" Wulf's voice echoed through the courtyard.

Everyone froze and looked toward the balcony, except for the two oblivious fighters in the center of activity.

Wulf lunged toward the stairs, racing to end the confrontation before Katie was injured. A dark form darting across the lawn caught the periphery of his vision. His steps faltered as his brother, Duncan, rushed toward the crowd. Charging through the guardsmen, the prince yanked Katie free of the fight by the scruff of her *dammr*-suit and viciously backhanded her across the face before Wulf perceived the threat.

"*No.*"

Filled with bloodlust, Wulf charged down the balcony steps

and across the grass, tackling his brother. Katie fell to the ground.

Wulf drew his arm back and struck hard. The blow was followed by another, then another, both fists raining down in a barrage delivered too swiftly to be repelled.

"Wulfric!" his father roared. "Cease!"

But he didn't, too enraged to heed the command. A multitude of arms restrained him, yanking him from his prone brother despite his substantial resistance. Duncan cowered in the face of his fury, but the sight of a crumpled and wounded Katie stemmed any hope of mercy.

Wulf shrugged free of those who held him back. "You have no right to touch what's mine!"

The king gripped him by the shoulder with bruising force. "What the hell is the matter with you? The woman refused to heed a direct order. Discipline was necessary and appropriate."

"She couldn't hear me and you damn well know that."

He twisted free of his father's grasp and moved to kneel beside Katie. With a gentle grip on her chin, he angled her face to ascertain the extent of her injury. Her right eye was swelling shut and her cheekbone was discoloring, but not one tear fell.

The fierce look Wulf shot Duncan's retreating back promised retribution. His brother was heading toward the healing rooms, a route the young man would find familiar, if he ever thought to touch Katie again.

Assisting her to her feet, Wulf tucked her protectively into his side. His gaze burned over their audience. "No one is to discipline this woman but me. Do I make myself clear?"

The king's lip curled. "And what do you consider a suitable punishment? Fucking her into submission?"

Wulf turned away in disgust and gestured to the captain of the palace guard. "Take her to a healing chamber."

It pained him to part with her now, but he had no choice. His insubordination to the king had to be addressed and Katie needed medical attention immediately.

As the captain led her away, Katie said nothing to anyone.

Anders ran both hands through his hair. "Do you realize what you've done, Wulfric? You've undermined the authority of your king and your brother in order to defend the enemy."

"She's not the enemy."

"Would you feel differently if I told you she deliberately selected *your* personal guardsmen to retrain? She's a serpent waiting to strike. Ransom her or send her to a detention facility. That's a royal command." Anders marched away.

Wulf was left alone in the center of the courtyard, struggling with a riot of emotions he had no clue how to deal with. The last few weeks of his life had changed him in ways he could never have prepared for. He'd almost died, then found himself in the arms of a beautiful woman. The life he'd regained was irrevocably altered by his affection for her.

"Katie." Irrational though it was, he wanted her promise that she would stay with him. He could manage the worst of days, if she soothed his nights.

He headed toward the medical wing of the barracks with rapid, impatient strides. Turning a corner, he walked directly into Duncan, who emerged from a healing room.

"Wulfric, damn it." Duncan stumbled before regaining his footing. "What the hell was that all about?"

Wulf inhaled a calming breath before responding. "Don't ever touch her again. Do you understand?"

"Father said she's the enemy!"

"She is a woman first and foremost. I won't tolerate the beating of women. And regardless of who she is, she's *mine*. I will see to her."

The corners of Duncan's lips dipped petulantly. "You didn't have to beat me half to death to make your point."

"I lost my temper, but I won't apologize for it. You were wrong to strike her."

Lifting his gaze, Wulf looked over Duncan's shoulder at the next healing room, where the captain stood guard at the door. His brow furrowed. As he attempted to pass, Duncan blocked him.

"In lieu of an apology," his brother said, "how about a boon?"

Wulf returned his attention to Duncan. "What kind of boon?"

"I'd like to purchase some contracts of my own and have my own *seraglio*."

"Fine," Wulf agreed gruffly. "You're old enough now."

"Can we go to the trader's in Akton tomorrow?"

"No. I have too much that needs to be attended to. But you may visit my concubines and see if any of them would have you. You may begin your own *seraglio* with whichever ones are willing. I will release them from their contracts."

Duncan's face was almost comical in its astonishment. "Are you jesting?"

"You'd be doing me a favor."

The next door slid open. Katie stepped out, attired in a white robe. Her gaze locked with his, devoid of any emotion. Then she turned, heading rapidly away from him. Clarke obediently fell into step beside her.

Wulf brushed his brother aside. "Katie."

Her pace quickened.

"Discipline, brother." Duncan's tone was snide. "The prisoner doesn't seem to know who's in charge around here. Her insubordination could be contagious, if you're not careful."

Katie pivoted abruptly and stalked back toward them. "Run, boy." Her voice was filled with soft venom. "Before I finish what your brother started."

Duncan stumbled backward a few steps. Wulf shoved him aside to intercept her. "Go, Duncan. Now."

With a steely grip on her arm, Wulf jerked Katie away from danger, dragging her in the opposite direction. "You forget yourself," he said curtly.

"Excuse me?" She gaped at him.

"He is a prince of D'Ashier."

She stopped and ripped free from his grip. "I don't care if he's the king! He's nothing to me."

Wulf pinned her to the wall. His hand wrapped her neck, careful to be gentle, but needing to drive his point home. His mouth dropped to her ear so they would not be overheard.

"You must obey," he ordered in a furious whisper. "You must be courteous. You must show respect. For your own safety."

"I will not. I am not a slave or a prisoner." She attempted to push him away, but he held tight.

"Your position here is perilous. Your connection to your father and the King of Sari makes you suspect."

She began to struggle against him in earnest. Her robe fell open, exposing her nakedness to his gaze. The sight of talgorite adorning Katie's nipple and navel rings heated his blood. He pressed the heated length of his body against her, remembering the sight of her outside the healing chamber that first day. And last night, when she'd worn red. *His* color.

As his cock swelled against her belly, she froze.

"Let me go." She looked at him with luminous dark eyes. "Send me home."

He waved Clarke's towering presence away.

Her throaty voice throbbed with emotion. "You know we've run out of time."

"We can't be out of time. I still want you."

"You can't always have the things you want, Wulf." Katie began to struggle anew, her lush body writhing against his aching cock.

Inhaling deeply, he attempted to calm the need that clawed at him. Instead, he found his nostrils filling with the scent of her skin. Cleansed of the fragrance of Draxian lilies by the healing chamber, she was still uniquely appealing to him.

"Katie, stop. I'm not . . . myself. I'll fuck you against the wall, if you don't stop rubbing against me."

She pushed against his shoulders. "You can't keep me here against my will. I'll find a way to go home."

His heart thundered in response to her words.

"I'll make you want to stay." His tongue rimmed the shell of her ear. He reached between them and pushed down the waistband of his trousers, freeing his dick. It bobbed between them, straining and so hard it hurt. "I'll make you burn as I do."

Sapphire's gaze was riveted by the sight of Wulf's penis, so thick and long, thrusting brutally upward between them. He was so blatant in his desire, baring himself shamelessly out in the open air.

As Wulf's free hand drifted beneath her robe and cupped her hip, she gasped in both fear and pleasure. His sensual threat hung in the air between them, causing her to shiver. It made him doubly dangerous that he knew how much she desired him and didn't hesitate to use it against her.

"What the hell are you doing?" Her chin lifted.

His smile didn't reach his eyes. "My father thinks you're a spy or an assassin."

"I don't care what he thinks."

"I do." His tone had an edge that stilled her. "And yet I've defied him, embarrassed my brother, and placed D'Ashier in jeopardy. For you. Yet you don't seem to feel as I do. You remind me often that it's easy for you to throw me aside."

Sapphire was unable to move with Wulf's hand at her throat, his leg between hers, and his body pinning hers to the wall. She cursed and bit his ear hard enough to draw blood, but he held her fast. "What do you want from me?" she demanded. "My love? My devotion? Knowing that we must part and that it would kill me to do so if you meant more to me than you do right now?"

"Yes," he growled. "For all that I've risked for you."

He released her throat. Slipping his hands around the back of her thighs, he lifted her up—

"Wulf!"

—and with a tortured groan, dropped her onto his rampant cock.

Sapphire moaned as the thick head forced its way through tissues not yet ready for him. She was moist, but not wet. He held her to the wall and pumped his hips, working his way into her, fighting for every burning inch he claimed.

"You're hurting me," she whispered.

Wulf froze.

Her hands drifted to his shoulders and felt the thick muscles clenching beneath her palms. She arched against the intrusion of his body into hers, pressing her breasts into his chest.

Shaking, he pressed his damp forehead to hers. "You're *destroying* me. You give me no quarter. You could stay or go. You don't care."

"I can't."

"You won't let me in."

"If I didn't care, things would be different. They must be this way because I do care."

"I am unmanned by my lack of control with you," he snarled, his tone filled with self-disgust. "I almost killed my brother for hurting you, then I do worse. Trying to get inside you the only way you let me."

"I forgive you." Sapphire cupped his nape and pressed her temple to his. He held her with effortless strength, poised with only half of his cock throbbing inside her. "You almost died. I was the first thing you saw afterward and—"

His grip on her waist tightened. "You understand nothing,

if you think *this*"—he punctuated the word with a flex of his cock,—"is gratitude. I wish it was. I could gift you with jewels and other trinkets, and be done with you. I could have left you as you asked and considered your freedom recompense for your hospitality."

With shaking hands, Sapphire turned his head toward her. She could feel his teeth gritting through his cheeks. His pupils were dilated; the emerald green mere rims around the black center. His large frame shook against her, belying his claim that he lacked control. He was in rut, yet managed to hold himself at bay.

His gaze was fever-bright when he said, "I have never wanted to be anyone other than who I am. Until now."

"I would never change you. *Never.* I adore all that you are, just the way you are."

You won't let me in . . .

Reaching between them with one hand, Sapphire began to rub her clitoris with slow, gentle circles of her fingertips.

"Katie . . . ?"

"I want you in me."

His breath caught, then he lowered his head to her breast. His tongue curled around a jeweled nipple and stroked the underside. He aroused her swiftly, with breathtaking expertise. She became hotter. Slicker. Enabling her pussy to slide over his cock like a custom made glove. He seated to the hilt inside her and the tension left him in a harsh exhale that puffed hotly over her damp breast.

For her, the sense that she'd connected to the interlocking half that made her whole was profound. The sensation was becoming as necessary as breathing. Too swiftly. Too frightening.

She hadn't known. No one had told her that sex could give more than physical pleasure. She'd thought the enjoyment would be greater and the need more acute, but there'd been no way to prepare for the feeling of oneness that came from making love to a man on an emotional level.

Sapphire knew it was the same for Wulf—a voluptuary so locked into his role as crown prince that only the prospect of death had freed him.

"I knew it would come to this," she breathed, balanced on the point between physical pleasure and emotional pain. "I knew we would be forced to choose between the rest of our lives and each other. And I knew how we would both decide. I tried to be strong . . ."

"I love your strength." He kissed her, long and slow, a melding of lips and tongue that made her pussy clench around his hardness in hunger. Breathing harshly, he spoke against her mouth, "But I need to know that you have a soft spot for me."

Locking her ankles at the small of Wulf's back, Sapphire lifted up, tightening her inner muscles so that she hugged the length of his cock from root to tip.

He groaned. Sweat dotted his brow. "Take me. I've already taken too much from you."

She lowered back onto him, hissing with pleasure at the feel of him gliding endlessly into her. "I like it when you take me."

When she was with him, she could be a creature of passion. No thought or calculation. It was a sort of freedom she had never known and had already grown addicted to.

Leaning back against the wall, her arms fell away from him, knowing his strength was such that he could bear her weight with ease. She opened herself to him in every way, showing him with her eyes and defenseless posture that she was his. If only for now.

Wulf began to fuck her. First, with short and shallow digs. Then, with greater force and speed, his arms straining in time with his hips, pulling her down as his cock tunneled up.

It was savage and wild, and she loved it. All of it. From the hasty and desperate beginning to this rampaging drive to the finish.

Rocking her hips, Wulf ground her onto him, his thick cock-head so deep in her that her toes curled and cramped. He stroked over and over the spot deep inside her that made her insensate with pleasure, made cries spill from her lips that only spurred him further.

"The sounds you make," he growled. "I hear them even when you're not with me."

The smell of his skin, musky and exotic, intoxicated her, as did the feel of his waistband rubbing rhythmically against her inner thighs. She moaned, her eyes closing.

"I'm coming," she gasped, everything tightening up inside her. The tension broke in a violent pulsing climax. Her pussy clasped at Wulf's thrusting cock and rippled along its length, milking the thick shaft in ecstatic clenches.

Wulf cursed and crushed her to the wall, his chest heaving against hers as he pumped his semen into her in hard, fast spurts. It was delicious. Decadent. The feel of him erupting inside her with such ferocity.

Rubbing his sweat-slick forehead against her, he panted, "I am crazed for you like a youth with his first woman."

"I wish I was your first," she breathed. "Your only."

A half smile uplifted one corner of his mouth. "I'm grateful for the experience I have, or I would doubt my ability to please you."

"You please me too well." Her hands covered his where he held her hips. "I always want more."

His features grew solemn, losing all levity and taking on a bleakness that constricted her chest. "How much time can you spare with me?"

"A week. Maybe. If I can speak with my father and allay his concerns."

Wulf nodded. "Will you give me that?"

"If I can." Sapphire pressed her lips to his brow. "If I could, I would stay with you until you tired of me."

"Or you tired of me."

"I doubt that's possible."

His smile was grimly determined. "I have a few days. I intend to make it impossible."

Chapter 11

Sapphire stared at the smear of blood that marred Wulf's bed, and a painful knot formed in her stomach.

Her courses had started. On time, as usual.

You knew this was coming. But forewarned didn't mean forearmed.

She wouldn't be able to accommodate Wulfric tonight or for the last few days before she left. She knew from Sabine and her own personal experience that Wulf was a man of voracious sexual appetite. A few days ago—before the horrid scene with Prince Duncan in the courtyard—she might have believed Wulf would want her with him anyway, that he would be willing to spend their last days together without sex. Now, she didn't know what to believe.

He no longer kissed her, no longer cuddled her, no longer smiled. Their lovemaking was as passionate as ever and at times she felt as if she'd reached him, touched him. His eyes would glitter down at her in the semidarkness and she would imagine longing there. Yearning. Her lips would part in hunger for the taste of him, the feel of him drinking her in as if he'd never have enough.

Then he would retreat and become the distracted prince she didn't know at all. A reserved stranger who wasn't cold, but wasn't warm either. Distancing himself emotionally before he had to physically.

Moving into the bathing chamber, Sapphire went through her morning ablutions by habit. Then she traversed the long stone hallway to the *seraglio,* where she spent her daylight hours for her safety. The sounds of various conversations and women's laughter were familiar to her after the five years she'd spent in service to the King of Sari. Reading or talking with the concubines helped to shorten the hours while Wulf was occupied.

Today, however, Sapphire wished time would stand still. The other women came to her, smiling tentatively, trying to draw her into conversation, but her gloomy mood soon drove them away. She couldn't eat or lose herself in a book. She could think of nothing but the moment Wulf would return and the choice he would be presented with. Would he call a concubine to serve the needs she couldn't? Perhaps he would send her home early? She couldn't fight the hope that he would emerge from his isolated shell and return to being the man who set her blood on fire. A man willing to fight for her and claim her, despite the costs.

"Mistress."

Turning her head, she watched Sabine approach.

"It's time to prepare you," the chamberlain said.

Releasing her pent-up breath in a rush, Sapphire blurted out, "My courses have begun."

"Oh . . ." Sabine frowned. "I see."

"I thought you might," Sapphire muttered bitterly.

"Well . . ." the chamberlain began hesitantly. "Under usual circumstances—"

"Under usual circumstances, you wouldn't send a concubine to His Highness who was unable to perform her duties."

Sabine offered an encouraging smile. "This is a different situation, Mistress."

"We don't know that. I would prefer that we follow protocol."

"You want to provoke him." Sabine took a seat on the padded chaise opposite her.

"Perhaps. It would be a relief to see some fire in him." She rubbed at her stinging eyes. "He's distracted to the point where I think he sometimes forgets I'm here. I feel like a piece of furniture. He refuses to discuss anything personal. He—"

"Calls for you every night and keeps you with him until morning," Sabine interjected dryly.

"Because the sex is fantastic. It's certainly not for our sparkling conversation. He only talks about military maneuvers. Last night I fell asleep before he even came to bed."

"And you slept until morning?" Sabine asked with a teasing smile.

"Well, no, but that proves my point. If I can't service him, what use will I be? We did nothing else. We ate. He worked at his desk. I slept. Aside from the sex, I served no other purpose."

Wulf had shut her out, as he'd once accused her of doing to him. He shared his body freely, but everything else was locked away.

"His distance is bad enough. I refuse to be rejected . . ." Sapphire shuddered.

"Mistress, I suggest—"

"I'm sorry, Sabine," she said with quiet authority. "His Highness told you to obey me in all things. Please do as I ask. Follow protocol."

Sabine stood and bowed. "As you wish." She gestured for a willowy redhead to follow her.

An hour later, Sapphire watched as the flame-haired concubine followed two of Wulf's guards out of the *seraglio*. It was obvious the woman had slept with Wulf before; her eager anticipation was evident in the lightness of her steps. She was lovely, tall and slender with a wide mouth and a ready smile.

Sapphire turned away, her stomach roiling. She began to circle the pool restlessly. Clarke fell in step beside her.

"I think this was a bad idea," he grumbled. "Idiotic and ill-conceived."

"I have to know."

"It's a woman's wile, designed to drive men insane. It will only lead to trouble."

She stopped abruptly. "You think I like this? I *hate* this. I hate that I care. I hate that my chest is so tight I can't think straight for lack of air. I hate that he made me care." Her hands clenched into fists at her sides. "I *hate* this."

His dark eyes softened. "Then why?"

In her mind's eye Sapphire saw Wulf pulling the redhead into his arms. Gifting the woman with one of the devastating kisses he no longer gave to her. Caressing the length of the concubine's slender frame with his skilled hands . . .

She shook. How long had the concubine been gone? Too long . . . far too long . . .

The doors to the *seraglio* slid open. She pivoted. As Wulfric entered the room with concubine in tow, Sapphire reached for the support of Clarke's massive arm. Pausing just inside the threshold, Wulf gripped the redhead's shoulders and pressed a swift kiss to her forehead. Then he urged her toward a waiting Sabine.

Sapphire's hand lifted to her chest. The sight of Wulfric kissing the concubine was painful, despite the chasteness of the gesture. Needing a moment to collect herself before facing him, she spun blindly away, darting toward the room Sabine had readied for her use. She didn't get far. Wulf overtook her, stepping nimbly into her path. He was casually attired in loose trousers and sleeveless tunic, the latent power of his body visible in every line of his tall form.

"So," he drawled, his gaze burning. "I can fuck her, but kissing her upsets you?"

Her chin lifted.

Catching her by the waist, he tugged her closer, his biceps flexing with the movement. "From the very beginning, Katie, I have most admired your honesty. Why start playing games now?"

She stared at the golden expanse of his chest revealed by the V of his tunic. "My—" She sighed. "I'm menstruating."

A muscle in his jaw ticced. "I see."

"Do you?"

"Yes." Wulf lifted her chin with his finger and studied her. "Did I pass the test?"

She jerked her head to the side, her face heating.

"Is this where I tell you how wrong you are?" he asked hoarsely. "Where I allay your concerns with protestations of my undying affection?"

"You're cruel to tease." She glanced at him, unable to resist. The sight of him made all they risked worth it.

His mouth curved in a tender smile for the first time in days. "It worked. You have my undivided attention."

Sapphire's breath caught. "I do?"

"When I was told the concubines' annex room had been prepared, I was surprised, but thought maybe you meant to role-play or tease me in some way. I was aroused by the mere thought. I can't tell you how disappointed I was to find another woman there. A cold shower would have been kinder."

The rigid tension in her shoulders released. She sagged into his strength, clinging to his beloved body.

He held her firmly against him. "Sweet Katie. I would kill any man who touched you. Don't you feel the same possessiveness toward me?"

"Yes . . ." She buried her face in the crisp hair of his chest. "But you've been so distracted. I assumed your feelings had changed. I'd hoped you would prove me wrong. I should have asked, but—"

"Shh," he soothed, his hands molding her curves into him. "Yes, you should have asked. But then you're menstruating, which seems to mess with women's minds."

Sapphire gave a mock growl. He laughed.

"You haven't smiled at me in days," she noted. "I'd almost forgotten what it does to me."

"I'm under a great deal of stress." The lines of strain that had begun to bracket his mouth in recent days deepened.

"But you don't share any of it with me."

"I don't want to burden our time with it."

She snorted. "Every moment is spent keeping me distant with talk of stratagems and—"

His head dropped to hers, his hot, open mouth covering her lips and silencing her effectively. His hands cupped her shoulder blades, pressing her breasts into his chest, as his tongue swept inside with teasing flicks. She surged into him, holding his lean hips to keep from losing herself in his unexpected display of passion.

An hour without a kiss from him was too long. The last two days had been torture.

He pulled away with a groan.

"I am not keeping you distant," he denied gruffly, resting his forehead against hers. "I speak of military matters, because you're so adept at them. I admire your reasoning and respect your viewpoints. I discuss those things with you because I want to show you how much I value your knowledge."

"Liar. You're shutting me out. Now, kiss me again."

A faint smile teased the corner of his mouth. "You won't let me save myself, will you?"

"Save yourself for what? Another woman? No, I won't. I gave myself to you completely for a week. It's not fair when you won't give me anything of yourself in return."

"Save myself *from you*," he corrected with a resigned exhale. "It's not lack of interest that affects me. It's too much interest."

"Wulf." She wrinkled her nose. "We're acting like idiots."

"Right. Let's go. I want to be alone with you. We have so little time." He laced his fingers with hers and led her back to his rooms.

As the doors to his bedchamber slid open, Sapphire's eyes were immediately drawn to the mass of maps and notes that littered Wulf's desk.

"If you want to show respect for my opinions, tell me what's troubling you," she challenged.

He settled into the sunken seating area and pulled her backward to recline against his chest. His hands stroked the length of her arms; his fingers teased the centers of her palms. "The four mercenaries we have in custody had little information of any importance. They could only say that I was captured for a different purpose, then traded for their leader when he was apprehended by a Sarian patrol. Interesting, but not really helpful."

She heaved out a frustrated breath. "I can't stand this uncertainty. I worry about what will happen to you when I leave."

He nuzzled against her neck. "My personal guards are now the envy of the entire palace unit. You trained them well. You continue to protect me, just as you've done since we met."

"Why would the mercenaries go to so much trouble to capture you, then relinquish you so easily?" Sapphire turned in his lap to face him. "You would think they might sacrifice their leader in order to claim whatever reward there was for you."

Wulf retained his hold on her hand. "Unless he was the only one who knew what my value was, and who would pay it."

"Ransom from your father? Talgorite maybe?" D'Ashier held the distinction of having the largest deposit of the stone anywhere.

"Yes. Anyone who uses talgorite as a power source would have motive."

"That opens endless possibilities." She could feel the weight of weariness that descended upon him and knew she would do everything in her power to help him discover the truth. When she left the Sarian palace, she'd wanted a purpose. She had one now, something to occupy her after she returned home.

"It does." His voice rose. "Guardian. I'm starved."

"I will see to it, Your Highness."

A few moments later, several attendants arrived bearing platters of food and chilled wine. Wulf fed Sapphire her dinner by hand, his long fingers bringing tempting morsels of her favorite foods to her mouth. She memorized the sight of him, his gaze focused with singular attention on her lips, so intent on serving her and making her happy. The earlier incident with the concubine seemed to have worked in refocusing Wulf on how little time they had. Not enough time to waste even a moment on lack of communication, doubts, or juvenile tests of affection.

Moments like these, fleeting though they were, gave her a tiny glimpse of the life they could have had, if only they were different people. Her warrior lover was her perfect counterpart, so like her, yet different enough to keep her enthralled. He continued to surprise her, yet he remained familiar and comfortable.

She was madly in love with the impossible man. The food he fed her with such tender eroticism could have been tasteless for all the attention she paid to it, arrested as she was by the panicked beating of her heart.

Later, Wulf tucked her into his bed, his body curling behind her, the heavy weight of his erection wedged in the valley of her buttocks. He held her close, with no space between them, burying his face in the curve of her neck and quickly falling asleep.

She stayed awake for hours, afraid to sleep and miss a moment of it.

Chapter 12

Sapphire sat on the edge of the pool in the *seraglio,* her bare feet moving restlessly in the warm water. Her week with Wulfric ended tomorrow, which created a sense of urgency that drove her crazy. She was so distressed, her courses had ended early. A small blessing, but one she appreciated.

"You're unhappy," Clarke said.

She looked at him. It had taken her a great deal of wheedling and cajoling before the reserved Captain of the Guard had agreed to join her by the pool rather than stand at attention behind her. Once resigned to her wishes, he had rolled up the legs of his uniform trousers and sat, his thick calves plunged halfway into the water.

"I am," she agreed.

"Are you homesick?"

She laughed softly. "I haven't been away long enough to be homesick, but then I don't really have a home to return to. My father travels extensively and my mother is tenured at the Sensual Arts School, a position that takes up much of her time. The home I live in is more the king's than mine, and I realize now that I can't ever return there. I'm not sure it would be wise for me to live in Sari at all."

Clarke's gaze was sympathetic. "Maybe you could find a way to make this your home."

"I couldn't be happy here. The king suspects me of malicious intent and Wulfric's solution is to lock me away to keep me safe." Kicking the water, Sapphire watched the fluid beads arc into one of the three fountains. "I can't spend my days waiting on his pleasure. I just left that life. Gratefully. I don't want it back."

The captain was silent.

"And what would happen to me when he marries?" she continued. "I couldn't bear to share him with another woman." She remembered the icy demeanor and deep bitterness that encapsulated the beautiful Queen Brenna in an aloof shell. Sapphire would never allow that to happen to herself. She refused.

"His Highness is a fool," Clarke growled.

"Clarke!" She glanced around, making sure his treasonous statement hadn't been overheard.

"He's burying his head in the sand. One day he'll look up and realize what he's lost. By then, it will be too late."

"There's no help for it. I knew from the moment I discovered his identity that we were doomed. He knew it as well. The end was as assured as the beginning."

Clarke shook his head. "I don't believe that. I think things can be changed to suit a purpose."

"You are just as obstinate as Prince Wulfric." Sapphire placed her hand over his. "In case I don't have the chance again, I want to tell you how much I've come to like you, Clarke. You're a good man, one anyone would be lucky to call a friend."

He grunted and a flush spread across his dark skin. "Consider yourself lucky then."

The doors to the *seraglio* slid open, and they both turned their heads to see who entered. Prince Duncan swaggered in. Sapphire eyed him cautiously. The young prince came to Wulf's concubines' quarters daily, luring those who were interested to move to his wing of the palace.

Through him, Sapphire glimpsed a younger Wulfric. Duncan had similar dark hair and green eyes, and was just as tall as his brother. But at nineteen years old, he was still boyishly built. He lacked Wulfric's broad shoulders and muscular physique, and his chest was almost hairless.

Her mouth curved wryly. According to the women who'd moved to his *seraglio,* what he lacked in experience he made up for in youthful vigor. And apparently, he was kind to them and charming, something hard for Sapphire to understand because he always stared at her with malice. As he was doing now.

Duncan approached her. Both she and the captain tensed.

"Come with me," the young prince ordered her.

She looked at Clarke.

Duncan hauled her up, catching her close when her wet feet slipped on the tile. "Don't look at him. He can't stop me."

He started to drag her along with him.

The captain leaped to his feet with surprising grace for a man of his size. "His Highness, Prince Wulfric, has ordered me to accompany her everywhere."

"Come along then. You can watch."

She tried to tug away from his bruising grip. "I'm menstruating," she lied.

"Not according to the Guardian. Why do you think I waited until now?"

Clarke stepped in the way. "I have been ordered to protect her as well."

Duncan laughed harshly. "You misunderstood his purpose, Captain. You are not protecting *her*, you are protecting everyone else *from* her."

"You lie." Sapphire's tone was cold. For a moment, she thought he would hit her for her insolence. She stood ready to deflect the blow. He would not catch her unawares again.

"You forget your place, prisoner," he sneered. "You will address me as 'Your Highness,' and you will afford me the respect I'm entitled to."

"I am not a prisoner."

He laughed again, the sound even more grating than before. "Why do you think you're here in D'Ashier?"

She didn't deign to answer that.

"Let me tell you," he offered with malicious glee. "You're the daughter of Grave Erikson, the man who defeated us in the Confrontations. You are the favorite concubine of the Sarian king, our enemy. You're a great prize to us. We'll ransom you back for information and POWs. In the meantime, Wulfric's been enjoying the spoils of war and learning all about your father's lauded military strategies. Thank you, by the way, for being so willing to share his military expertise."

She recoiled as if he'd struck her.

The prince grinned smugly. "Wulfric keeps you locked away all day. Why do you think he does that? You're obviously capable of protecting yourself, so that can't be his purpose. Where do you think he's been the last few days? He's been arranging the ransom agreements. Soon, you'll be sent home and I intend to enjoy you before you leave."

He began to haul her toward the doorway again. This time she didn't resist, her mind skittering around what he'd said but unwilling to grasp it. Looking at the situation in that light made horrifying sense. Wulf's distance and distractions, the constant guards around her, the long hours he spent away from the palace, and the way he picked her brain for stratagems.

Could the proof of Duncan's words have been in front of her the entire time, with her too lovesick to see it?

Her hand went to her stomach as it roiled.

When Clarke tried to intercede, she threw him a warning look. He could not stand up to the prince. He didn't have the right or the authority. She would not see him punished because of her.

The captain followed with clenched jaw and fists.

Sabine intercepted them when they reached the doors. "Your Royal Highness." She prostrated on the floor. "Please, many of the other concubines are willing. Choose another, I beg you."

"Rise, Sabine," the prince ordered. "Prince Wulfric told me I could have the use of his concubines."

"If they are *willing*."

Duncan's smile was predatory. "We all know this wildcat likes to fight at first, but she's willing in the end."

Sapphire gasped. "I will never be willing for *you*."

Not conceding to argue his point further, Duncan pulled her out to the corridor, where two guards wearing his personal red and white colors waited. "Bring her to my rooms."

He started down the hallway, leaving her to the care of the guardsmen.

Sapphire moved quickly, having no other choice. She wasn't familiar with any other wing of the palace; therefore, if she hoped to escape, she would have to make her move here and now.

Fisting her hand, she whipped her forearm up and to the side, breaking the nose of the guard on her right. As he howled in pained surprise, she grabbed his arm and pivoted to the left, using his stumbling body to knock the other guard down.

Then she took off at a run, struggling to gain traction on the marble with her damp feet.

Remembering the day she'd arrived, Sapphire knew the transfer room was a few meters down the hallway from Wulf's rooms. It was a straight shot down the long corridor. If she could outrun her pursuers and gain some ground, she might be able to lock herself inside and transfer to safety.

Wulf's guards lined the hallway at regular intervals, protecting his wing of the palace, yet not one of them made a move to stop her. She flew by them, surprised at their abetting of her escape, but having no time to consider their motives.

A tackle from behind knocked the wind out of her. The heavy weight of a masculine body slammed her into the hard floor. Stunned, she struggled for air. As her assailant rolled her over, she was unable to breathe.

Duncan straddled her, his eyes alight with vicious lust.

"I'm going to enjoy this," he snarled, tearing at her filmy gown.

Sapphire swung hard and clipped him in the temple with her fist.

He roared, falling to the side. Twisting, she kneed him, aiming for his balls. He moved, causing her to hit his thigh instead.

"Bitch!" he hissed, bruising her upper arm in a viselike grip.

She ducked an incoming blow, but his greater weight pushed her to her back. He climbed over her. She clawed at his face, drawing blood with her nails. Pinning one of her hands beneath her hip, Duncan trapped the other over her head. Then he licked the side of her face from jaw to temple.

"Ready to scream?" he growled.

"Ready to die?" She lifted her knee again, this time grazing his scrotum and stealing his breath.

Duncan reared back, fist raised. She freed the hand beneath her hip and slammed the heel of her palm into his eye. His head snapped back and he screamed.

Abruptly he quieted, eyes widening before rolling back in his head. He slumped over her, a crushing weight. Clarke loomed above them, wielding his glaive-hilt.

Relief filled her. "Get him off me."

Grabbing him by the scruff, the captain threw the unconscious prince aside and held out his hand to her. He pulled her to her feet. She glanced around, noting how the hallway guardsmen kept their gazes carefully averted. Seeing nothing.

"I have to leave." She limped toward the transfer room.

"You don't know that Prince Duncan was telling the truth."

"I don't know that he wasn't. I've put my father and country at risk. For what?"

"For love."

She paused and gripped Clarke's massive hand. "Let me go.

Don't you see? I can't stay. I could never stay, even before this happened."

He hesitated, then nodded. "You'll need a change of clothes."

"There's no time. Duncan's guards will come with reinforcements soon."

Clarke looked back toward the *seraglio*. She followed his gaze. Wulf's guards blocked the hallway farther down, pretending to have some trouble with a door. Despite her anxiety, she had the presence of mind to appreciate the help these men were giving her. She'd made some friends that day of training in the courtyard.

"Come on," Clarke urged, breaking into a lope.

Despite the aches and pains she felt, she followed and kept pace. The doors to the transfer room opened as they approached and locked behind them with a curtly voiced command. When they stood inside, he ordered her to the transfer pad and leaned over the control panel.

"Damn," he muttered.

"What?"

"The controls are locked to allow transfers only within the borders of D'Ashier, and only from pad to pad."

"Why?" Her gaze stayed trained on the doors.

"Prince Wulfric was concerned that your father would track your transfer and locate you here."

Sapphire thought quickly. "Transfer me to Akton. I'll make my way over to Sari from there."

"Akton is like all border towns. It's not safe for you there, especially in your present state of undress." His shoulders straightened. "I'll go with you."

"*No*. You must stay here. Blame today's events on me. Tell them I wounded Prince Duncan and escaped on my own. Tell them you tried to stop me."

"Mistress—"

"You have to stay and tell Prince Wulfric I said he must release my *mästares*. I know he will." She glanced nervously at the doors. "Now enter the coordinates! We're running out of time."

Clarke looked prepared to argue.

"I can take care of myself," she assured him. "You know that."

When he reached for the controls, Sapphire managed a shaky smile. "Thank you, my friend. I hope one day we meet again."

Taking a deep breath, the captain entered a series of key-strokes on the console.

Sapphire blinked and found herself standing outdoors on the public transfer pad in Akton. The pad was packed with women, all in various states of undress like herself. Like a flock of colorful birds, females of every size and shape mingled in a dazzling array of diaphanous gowns. The natural breeze blew, carrying with it the scents of the desert and the savory offerings of the multitude of food vendors.

Startled by the proliferation of pedestrians, she searched her surroundings. A bright red banner stretched over the street fluttered in the wind and caught her eye:

CONCUBINE CONTRACT AUCTION EVERY TRINADAY

As apprehension welled, she mentally calculated the date. She winced. *Oh, hell.*

Chapter 13

"I warned you."

Wulf held Duncan pinned to his sitting room wall by the neck, his brother's feet dangling several inches above the floor.

"Wulfric, p-please," Duncan mumbled through his cut and swollen lips. "I'm sorry. I—I didn't realize—"

"Liar. I told you the cost would be grave if you touched her again." Wulf threw his brother into the corner in disgust, then turned to the captain of the palace guard. "Contact General Petersen. Tell him His Highness, Prince Duncan, will be joining the infantry. He is not to receive special treatment or consideration. He's to go through Basic Training with all the other new recruits. Once he's graduated, I want him to be given the most undesirable assignments for the next three years. I expect weekly reports on his progress directly from the general."

"God, Wulfric. No," Duncan moaned, curling into the fetal position.

The king stepped forward. "The thrashing you gave him is enough. He's your blood!"

"Don't remind me, Father. It's not something I'm proud of at the moment."

Wulf bent over Duncan, struggling to restrain his fury and helpless frustration. "You have no idea how lucky you are that you didn't succeed in your plans for Katie." He straightened and rolled his shoulders back in a vain effort to relieve the tension there. "I want His Highness dispatched immediately. He is not to use a healing chamber until he reaches his destination. Send him by transport, not by transfer."

"Damn it, Wulfric," Anders roared. "That's barbaric."

"And raping a woman isn't? Let the punishment fit the crime."

"He didn't succeed!"

"Not for lack of trying. Had Katie been a lesser woman, the outcome would've been very different." Wulf's hands fisted at the thought. "Now you know how it feels, Duncan, to be brutalized by an opponent considerably stronger than you. To use your strength on a woman is intolerable. You're spoiled and indolent, and I blame myself for that. I've been too focused on the state of the nation and paid too little attention to the vagaries of my own family. I'm rectifying that neglect now."

He motioned to the captain. "Take him to the landing bay, Captain, then return to me. We have much to discuss."

When they were alone, Wulf turned to face his father.

Anders stared at him. "I understand your need to defend what's yours and to teach your brother respect, but exile for three years is too harsh."

"Time will tell. That was the lightest punishment I could think of."

"Over Erikson's daughter." Anders began to pace. "That's what I don't understand. Why are you so quick to take *her* side?"

Wulf scowled. "She could have hurt me in a hundred different ways, but she's done nothing but care for me and protect me."

He looked away, his throat tight.

Katie was gone.

"Wulfric—"

Wulf cut Anders off with a slash of his hand. "No more,

Father. You're as responsible for this as Duncan. You poisoned him against her with your suspicions and hatred for Sari." He released his breath in a rush. "Just . . . go, please. We can discuss this later. Right now I have to go after her. She's alone, under-dressed, and injured. If something happens to her on D'Ashier soil, we'll have a war on our hands."

Anders hesitated, then he left without another word.

The captain returned a moment later. "Prince Duncan is on the transport. General Petersen thanks you for the trust you've placed in him."

Wulf nodded impatiently. "Have you traced her nanotach signal?"

He was grateful he'd had the foresight to implant the track-ing device in her right buttock on her first night in D'Ashier. She'd been exhausted by their encounter by the *seraglio* pool and had barely whimpered when he'd inserted it while she was sleeping. Aside from a brief mention of being sore for a day or two, she hadn't paid the discomfort any further thought.

"We have."

"Excellent. Let's go." Wulf's gaze narrowed when the cap-tain hesitated. "What?"

"It's not my place to gainsay you, Your Highness."

"If you have something to say, Captain, I give you leave to say it."

The dark chin lifted and massive shoulders pulled back, a defensive pose that set Wulf on edge. "I think you should remain in the palace and allow me to organize the retrieval and safe transport of Katie Erikson back to Sari."

"She's my responsibility."

"I can lead a squad to the uppermost border where we can release her servants near the Sarian outpost. A few kilometers' walk and they'd be home."

"No."

Clarke fell silent, his face impassive.

Wulf exhaled harshly. "This is a delicate political matter. It requires precise and skillful oversight."

"Forgive me, Your Highness," the captain said, "but you are not objective."

"My concern benefits her," Wulf growled.

"Only if it's selfless."

Wulf walked to the wall of windows overlooking the capital city below. He stood, hands behind his back, legs apart. He looked down at the country laid out before him. D'Ashier was a demanding mistress, pushing him, driving him to lift her up and make her great. Millions of people relied on him to provide for them and he struggled daily to fulfill their expectations. Given enough of his blood and sweat, D'Ashier could indeed rival all nations.

All he had ever aspired to be was a good monarch. He strove to be fair, to be strong, to ruthlessly protect his people's rights and their lands. He had learned to make rapid, life-altering decisions and he'd learned not to second-guess himself no matter what the outcome. A powerful ruler didn't have the luxury of remorse or self-recrimination. His word was law and the law could not waver.

Yet the biggest, most important decision of his life was one that he had put off making. Afraid to be vulnerable, afraid to be wrong, he had refused to see what was right before his eyes.

Wulf turned. "You think I should let her go?"

"She's a proud woman," the captain said, "intelligent and strong. She was wasting away during the days, waiting for you to come to her. She was bored and lonely. A woman with her wealth of talents needs to be useful. She might have sacrificed her home, her country, her family for you. I think she would have, if you'd offered to make her your equal, and prove your respect and affection for her." Clarke bowed respectfully. "I hope you don't take offense to my observations, Your Highness."

"You like her."

"Of course. There was nothing unlikable about her."

"You assisted her escape."

The captain said nothing, which was answer enough.

Wulf's gaze drifted to his bed in the next room. How would he ever be able to sleep without her curled beside him? How would he bridge the hours of the day knowing she wouldn't be there at night?

"I appreciate your candor, Captain, but I'm going after her," he said. "We leave for Akton immediately."

This was *not* happening.

Sapphire closed her eyes and prayed that when she opened them again the auction would become a figment of her imagination. She opened her eyes.

No such luck.

Damn.

If only she'd had the time to change into a *dammr*-suit. Then, it would have been quite clear that she was not an underclass concubine forced to auction her contract. Now, her explanation of the situation would delay her flight, taking up time she couldn't afford to lose. If Wulfric decided to come after her, he would move immediately and any lag on her part would lead to her recapture.

Deep in her heart she knew Duncan was wrong about Wulf, but that didn't mean he was wrong about what the royal family as a whole was considering doing with her. If the King of D'Ashier wanted to use her for leverage against her father, he would, and Wulf wouldn't be able to stop him. She couldn't risk it. She could never allow herself to become a liability to the people she loved, and as long as she stayed in D'Ashier, she was a liability to both her father and Wulf.

Goaded by that thought, Sapphire moved quickly, weaving among the crowd in her route to the street.

Unfortunately, her rapid flight drew attention. The obvious costliness of her gown kept that attention fixed on her. As she was about to separate from the throng of women, she was caught, her elbow held firmly by a man whose leer made her queasy.

"Unhand me," she ordered in a low, angry tone. "I am not here to be auctioned."

Her captor's dark gaze wandered leisurely down the length of her body, so readily visible through her diaphanous gown.

"Don't be shy, sweet," he coaxed. "It'll be over before you know it, and you'll be employed again. Beauty such as yours should snag a wealthy patron without any trouble."

Yanking free, Sapphire snapped, "I told you, I'm not here for the auction."

This time when the man reached for her, she laid him low with a quick backward jab of her elbow. His nose snapped beneath the force and he screamed, sinking to his knees with his profusely bleeding nose cradled between his hands.

"What's going on over here?" Another man, dressed in the same black and white uniform as the first, shoved his way through the melee.

"Damned woman 'it me in the nose!" The bleeding man's voice was muffled by his hands. "I think she broke it."

She glared at both men. "I told him I'm not here for the auction, but he wouldn't listen."

The man looked her over with the same insolent perusal as his coworker. "Quite a coincidence that you would be here, dressed in such a fashion, at the same time as the other women."

Her hands settled on her hips. "It wouldn't matter if it were a coincidence or not. My contract, if I had one—which I do not—would be mine to sell or keep."

"Not so," purred an oily voice from behind her. "You have caught the attention of one of my best clients."

"She's giving us trouble, Braeden," the uninjured man said.

"She'll get over it."

Snorting with disgust, Sapphire turned to face the owner of the unctuous voice. She was surprised to see that he was handsome, in an exotic sort of way. "Your best client will have to be disappointed and so will you. I am not for sale."

Braeden's smile made her skin crawl. "I'm afraid you're the one who will be disappointed. Karl Garner likes a little fire to warm his bed and your display of temper has whet his appetite. Whatever Karl wants, he gets."

"Karl can go to hell."

Braeden reached out and lifted the golden necklace that held her Guardian's chip. The pad of his thumb caressed the etched royal shield of D'Ashier before she ripped it out of his hand.

"It seems you're a thief," Braeden said, staring at her with cold, dark eyes. "I may be willing to resist turning you over to the authorities. *If* you cooperate with me."

"His Highness, Prince Wulfric himself gave this to me. I'm under his protection. For your own well-being, I suggest you allow me to leave quietly."

The crowd around them erupted in a wave of laughter. Humiliated and frustrated, Sapphire started to push her way through the throng. "You can check with the Captain of the Palace Guard if you don't believe me. In the meantime, since you have no authority to detain me, I'm leaving."

When the men tried to delay her again, she fought back. The women around her scattered with startled screams, providing a welcome distraction. Three more men dressed in black and white attempted to capture her, but all were soon lying in various states of injury on the transfer pad. Before the terrible situation could get worse, Sapphire took the stairs to the main thoroughfare and broke into a run.

It would have helped to know where she was going, but for the moment, anywhere away from the group of auctioneers was good enough. Rounding a corner, Sapphire spotted a group of public communicators. She selected the one farthest from the street and hid behind the privacy screen, peeking out cautiously to watch her pursuers run by. Then, she devoted her attention to activating the communicator.

She saw the slot for a credit chip, but that was of no use to her. She examined the top and sides of the machine to see if there was a way to hotwire the connections to make her call. It was when she felt along the bottom that she discovered the small round hole. As she leaned over for a closer inspection, her necklace hung away from her and brushed the machine.

It lit up.

Encouraged, Sapphire tried inserting the charm into the opening and became dizzy with relief when the three-dimensional hologram of the royal shield of D'Ashier spun in a slow circle above the communicator. Of all the available choices on the communicator pad, only SEND and RECEIVE were lit. She typed in the code to release the caller identification block, then entered her father's direction. With a silent prayer, she pressed the TALK button.

She was waiting for the line to connect when she was grabbed from behind. Screeching in fury and frustration, she was wrestled around to face the man named Braeden.

"Can't you take a—?" She gasped at the sting that pained her upper arm.

Agape, she looked down and watched a syringe withdrawing from her flesh.

She meant to scream, but the world faded into darkness.

Chapter 14

Wulf paced the landing strip at the military base on the outskirts of Akton. The strip was rarely used since it was much faster and more convenient to transfer. Still, the occasional movement of large machinery and weapons called for flight, and Akton's close proximity to the border with Sari made it a prime location to launch countermeasures when necessary.

It had been five hours, *five damn hours,* since Katie had left the palace. Five hours that seemed like five years. His fear for her welfare was aggravated by his need to tell her that Duncan had lied. Wulf couldn't let her go with the belief that he'd meant to use her. And if something happened to her before he found her . . .

He was going insane. His heart was thudding violently; his gut was knotted tight.

In just a few moments the sun would set and the city of Akton would turn into a maze of twinkling lights in the ebony darkness of the desert night. Where was she? Was she hurt or in danger? How could he have been so blind to the treachery of his own family?

He snarled.

The nanotach signal was faint, too faint for as close as they had to be to her. Since the nanotach was powered by her life-force, the weak signal meant one of two things: she was either unconscious and had been for some time, or she was close to death. Both of those scenarios made him wild. Feral.

"Your Highness!"

Wulf turned to face the young lieutenant who ran toward him.

The officer bowed at the waist before continuing excitedly. "I think we've found her!"

"Where?"

"There was a disturbance in the public transfer center this afternoon. A woman matching the Mistress's description stated that she was under your personal protection before being accosted by several men."

A growl left Wulf's throat. "Who were these men?"

"Employees of Braeden's Auction House."

Wulf stilled. It was Trinaday.

He immediately registered the import of the day. A woman as beautiful as Katie would be difficult for Braeden to pass up. Nearly naked, she would be irresistible. With an oath, he strode toward the hanger and the transfer pad inside. "Round up your men, Lieutenant."

Within moments he was standing in the foyer of Braeden's prosperous and well-appointed auction house. Familiar with the establishment from past patronage, he headed straight toward the back parlor.

He presented an intimidating sight, he knew, as he strode into the room, blood-red royal robes billowing behind him and a full complement of royal guards fanning outward to encircle the occupants. As the surprised men sank to the floor in obeisance, he waited impatiently. He said nothing, giving them no permission to rise, forcing them to remain at his feet.

"Your Highness," Braeden murmured slickly "I was unaware you planned to attend the auction today. I'm afraid the bidding is over, but I'm certain—"

"Where is she?" The dark threat threading Wulf's voice caused the proprietor to frown in confusion.

"I beg your pardon," Braeden stalled. "I don't know who—"

Wulf yanked him roughly to his feet. "You accosted a woman claiming my protection in the transfer center today. Where is she?"

The auctioneer paled. "Your Highness, I assure you, I had no idea she spoke the truth. Her attire was—"

"One more time," Wulf repeated with ominous softness. "Where is she?"

Braeden jerked his chin toward the staircase. "In the pleasure room at the top of the stairs."

As Wulf struggled to control a near-murderous rage, the arm that held Braeden shook. "Has anyone touched her?"

"I—I don't b-believe so." The auctioneer swallowed hard. "The winning bidder just went up."

Wulf tossed a glance over his shoulder and a guard quickly separated from the group and ran up the stairs. "Has she been harmed in any way?"

"I administered a small cocktail," Braeden admitted. "A combination of mild sedatives and an aphrodisiac that I use occasionally with skittish females." His voice rose. "She was wild, Your Highness! She injured five of my men!"

Wulf shoved him away. His voice was harsh when he spoke. "For your abuse of a person who claimed my protection, I am confiscating your business."

Braeden began to plead.

"Silence! For illegally abducting a woman and attempting to sell her favors against her will, you are to be taken forthwith to the nearest jail, where you will remain until you are tried for your crimes.

"You had best pray I find her untouched, Braeden. If I don't, I will castrate you myself."

"Then I'll have a go at you," the lieutenant added coldly. A murmur of agreement rippled through the ranks of his men.

Wulf reassessed the events of the long day, events he had been too distraught to notice earlier. He thought about how Sabine had attempted to intercede with Duncan, and how the other concubines had readily offered their services in lieu of Katie. He considered the way his own men had held off his brother's guards so that she could escape. He remembered his discussion with the captain who so obviously admired her. And the lieutenant and the men under his command who were expressing their desire to avenge her, if necessary.

In her short time with him, Katie had won the respect of his subjects. Even his father's distress, when taken in the proper context, revealed the monarch's fear of her growing power in the palace.

Katie was his perfect counterpart. A warrior like himself, a voluptuary, strong and supportive, a woman to admire and respect. A lover he could cherish. His heart ached at what he had almost lost—a prime consort for D'Ashier, the ideal companion for him.

He turned toward the staircase, filled with renewed purpose. He would bind her to him, so they would never be separated again.

Sapphire heard the door slide open even through the buzzing in her ears. Her thoughts were fogged, everything murky and disoriented.

Lifting her head, she strained to see through the filmy curtain that surrounded the bed. She spotted the broad, muscled back of a man as he disrobed, and she squeezed her eyes shut and dropped her head back onto the pillow with a moan.

She supposed she could turn her back to him—the muscle relaxant she'd been given made her languid, not immobile—but the aphrodisiac was driving her crazy. She forced herself to remain as still as possible, because the slightest movement caused a prickling sensation to burn across her skin, heating her flesh and laboring her breathing. She was completely naked, but she didn't reach for the silk sheet that she'd kicked off earlier. The feel of the fabric against her overly sensitized skin had been too much to bear and her modesty was not worth the torture of it.

"If I were you," she managed in a drug-slurred voice. "I would turn around and run for my life."

She heard a seductive chuckle that drifted across her body like smoke, inflaming every nerve ending. She gritted her teeth as the buzzing sound worsened.

"Crown Prince Wulfric will come for me soon." She hoped that was true. "He's a very possessive man. If you touch me, he might kill you."

"Do you belong to him?" The man's rich, deep voice echoed through her mind.

Sapphire meant to say one thing, but what came out was the truth. "Yes."

Through the maddening noise in her head, she thought she heard bare footsteps approach.

"From what I can see," he murmured, "a few moments in your arms would be worth the threat of death."

"Don't do this," she pleaded softly, her chest too tight to speak any louder. "I—I love him. I couldn't bear to be touched . . ."

She sensed his sudden stillness and the tension that radiated from his frame.

When he spoke again, his voice was deeply husky. "The prince? Is that who you love?"

She sighed, filled with deep longing. Rolling her body away from him, she moaned with the pain of unnaturally evoked desire. "He'll come . . . It's not too late . . . to go . . ."

The filmy drapes parted and the mattress dipped with the man's weight. He was so close, she could feel the heat of his skin, but he didn't touch her.

"Does he love you in return?"

Sapphire groaned against a wave of lust brought on by his close proximity and the evocative scent of his skin. "Go," she gasped.

"Does he love you?" he repeated.

"No . . . but he wants me . . . he'll fight for me."

"He's a fool, then. To have your love and not return it."

His hot, open mouth pressed against her shoulder, sending sensations radiating outward in a flaring sweep across her flesh. She pressed into the kiss against her will, her body anxious for relief from its drug-induced torment. As her heart pumped blood rapidly through her veins, the buzzing in her ears worsened. His tongue flicked across the side of her throat. "I want to love you," he whispered.

Sapphire laughed with soft mockery. "I'm certain you do or you wouldn't be in this bed. Eager to die."

The crisp hair on his chest brushed her back, making her breath seize in her lungs. "I want to make love to you." His tone was ardent, despite being muffled against her shoulder. "From the moment I first saw you, I had to have you. I'll take you slowly, deeply. I'll cherish you. Pleasure you until the sun comes up."

"W-what?" She arched into the aroused length of his body, feeling the heat and hardness of his erection against her buttocks.

"You're in pain. Let me help you."

Raised voices outside the door penetrated her dazed mind and sent her into a panic. "Please go," she urged. "I—I'm drugged. I don't want this."

His breath fanned across her cheek. "Just imagine that I am the man you love. Give yourself to me as if I were. I'll make you forget about the prince who doesn't deserve you. I'll wipe him from your memory so that all you can think of is me—a man whose only desire is to service you."

His tongue traced the shell of her ear and she purred with forbidden pleasure. "I need you." The voice was achingly familiar now that it was so close. "I need you like I need to breathe."

Her heart stopped.

How she had dreamed of having her passionate Wulfric back, the one who had hidden in the obsidian darkness of her bedroom in her home and taken her breath away with the totality of his possession.

With a hushed cry of surrender, Sapphire turned in his arms and pulled him against her.

"Wulf."

Wulf groaned, a low, deep sound of welcome and relief as Katie rolled into his embrace. How marvelous she felt, tucked close to him after the day's tormented search and worry for her.

She loved him. He couldn't help but squeeze her tightly and vow never to let her go.

Tonight he would share his affection with every press of his lips, every caress of his hand. He would promise her the world and spend the rest of his life striving to give it to her. His life, once an endless stretch of duty-filled days, and nights of meaningless sex, would become a life augmented by joy and love and sweet, breathtaking passion.

His mouth descended to hers and he pulled her tighter against him, until the ripe softness of her breasts was crushed against his chest and her lithe thigh was thrown over his. From somewhere deep inside, Wulf could feel the connection between them. From the beginning, he'd felt the link and had followed his passion for her into forbidden, frightening territory. He didn't regret it, regardless of the many difficulties ahead.

Katie struggled against him. Her flesh was so hot and sensitive from the aphrodisiac that she was trying to crawl out of her skin.

"Please." She rubbed her pussy against his thigh and left a

slick trail of moisture behind. It had been days since he'd had
her. To feel her melting was an irresistible lure, swelling his
cock painfully.

"Wulf, I need you inside me."

"Easy." Rolling, he tucked her beneath him and spread her
legs. "I'll give you what you need."

With a quick thrust, he was deep inside her and she was
coming, her back arching off the mattress, the slick walls of her
pussy rippling greedily up and down his length, her throaty
cry of relief filling the room. Filling his mind. Heating his blood
with the knowledge that he could do things to her body that
no other man could, take it places she hadn't known it could go.

"That's it," he crooned, gritting his teeth against the devastating pleasure. He withdrew and she gripped his hips with
steely fingers and yanked him back into her. She was scorching, dripping, and he groaned at the unbelievable sensation
of her sweet pussy eagerly suckling his cock.

At her desperate pleading, Wulf began to pump between her
thighs, riding her gently at first, then faster, more furiously as
she begged for more, always more.

The drugs drew out her orgasms. He'd never felt anything
like it in his life, her body milking his cock as he shafted her
hard and deep.

"Katie." He gasped as his balls tightened up, his cock throbbing violently. He needed this. To be joined with her, to be
deep inside her.

"Yes," she sobbed, her hips rising to meet his every thrust.
"That feels so good . . . so good . . ."

Throwing his head back with a fierce roar of pleasure, he
spurted thick and hot, his climax prolonged by hers, the convulsions of her delicious cunt coming one after another
around him. He clung to her, pressing grateful open-
mouthed kisses against her shoulder and tearstained cheeks,
finding a joy in lovemaking he never knew existed. Until he'd
found her.

★ ★ ★

Sapphire moaned as Wulf's cock withdrew from the trembling depths of her pussy. "Don't leave me."

"Never." He stretched out alongside her, the fingers of one hand pushing into the sweat-dampened roots of her tangled hair. His hand caressed her hip, sliding down in a callused glide.

She spread her legs wantonly, her hot face pressing into his neck where the spicy scent of his skin was so strong. She breathed him in with desperate gulps of air, her raging hunger only mildly appeased by the orgasms he'd wrung so skillfully from her tormented body.

"You're here," she whispered, her hand pressing against his chest. "So glad you're here."

"Shh . . . I'll take care of you."

Her spine arched as his fingers parted the bare lips of her pussy. He cared so much for her pleasure and needs. He made her feel as if she was the only person in his world, a woman he treasured and worshipped.

His thumb brushed over her clitoris and she gasped. Without the aphrodisiac, his touch was electric. With it, it was nearly painful, the rush of sensation overloading already tender nerves. His fingertips glided over the spasming opening of her pussy, teasing her.

"More," she begged. "I need you."

His head lowered to her breast, his tongue curling around an erect nipple.

"Yes." Sapphire lifted onto her shoulders, pushing the straining tip into the haven of his talented mouth. "Suck me."

With a soothing murmur, Wulf pushed two long, thick fingers into her. She whimpered, her hands fisting in the sheets. Every pulling draw on her nipple echoed in her pussy, her tissues clenching tight around the welcome intrusion.

His head lifted. As his fingers thrust inside her, he eyed her with a possessive glimmer. "You're drenched with my come. Filled with it."

Sapphire licked her parched lower lip, her throat working as he finger-fucked her slow and easy. "I love it when you finish in m-me. You get thick and hard, you push so d-deep."

Wulf growled, the rough sound rumbling through the room.

"You lose c-control." She gasped, her hips grinding into his hand. "You pound into me until I think I c-can't take any more. The sounds you make . . . as if it feels too good—"

"It does." His tongue thrust into her ear, making her cry out. "I wonder if I'll survive it. Then I wonder how quickly I can do it again, experience it again."

"I feel it when you come. So hot. Thick. Endless. I love it." Sapphire climaxed at the memory, coming around his fingers.

"You destroy me." He pushed three digits inside her, in and out, his tongue fucking her ear as he kept her taut and breathless in orgasm. "Tear me apart. I can't get enough."

"Wulf . . ." She released the linens and reached for him, needing to feel him over her, against her. Her palms pressed flat to his perspiration-slick back, her head lifting to connect her hot forehead to his shoulder.

"Inside me," she panted. "I need you inside me."

His forearm propped his weight while his fingers continued to stroke through her spasms.

"This is for you, Katie." His voice was dark and hoarse. "Not for me."

Tilting her head, she pressed her lips to his. Her nipples, so hard and sensitive, puckered tighter as they brushed across the hair on his chest. Her pussy rippled with the resonating delight, her entire body enamored with his. "Do it for me, then," she urged.

He loosened his grip on her hair and mounted her. She bit back a sound of protest as his fingers left her empty and greedy. She waited, breath held, as he moved against her, the thick crest of his cock gliding through their commingled fluids.

Poised and aching for the feel of him throbbing inside her, Sapphire was painfully aware of her vulnerability. The drugs made her crave sex. But her craving for Wulf came from inside her, independent of anything she could control. Nothing would be the same in the morning, while at the same time nothing would have changed. She couldn't keep him.

Wulf reached down and cupped the back of her thigh, dragging it over his own, opening her more fully. His hips rolled, pushing the barest inch inside her. When she put her other heel to the mattress and lifted for more, he made a chastising noise and caught that leg, too.

"Slow and easy," he purred, rising to his knees. Draping her thighs over his, he kept her angled upward, her pussy splayed wide and desperate to be filled. Stretched.

Her nails raked across the sheet. "Hard and deep."

His large hands moved to her breasts, the heated palms kneading the swollen flesh. "You'll get sore. We have hours ahead of us."

"I need you."

"Trust me." He thrust gently, working another wide inch into her. "I've got you."

She moaned, grateful for his care and attention, loving how he knew what she wanted and needed before she did but hating that he was right to be cautious. The desire was agonizing, goading her to writhe beneath him, to beg and plead, to cry and curse as he rocked his way into her with painstaking leisure.

"You're so damn hot," he bit out, sweat dripping from the long, dark strands of his hair. "I love fucking you. I love the look on your face when you come. Whenever I see you, I ache to see that look."

"I ache to show it to you." She locked her ankles at the small of his back and tugged, hissing in pleasure as he hilted.

Then the ride began. The sweet, slow glide. The push and pull. The exquisite feel of the furled underside of his cockhead as it stroked deliciously over hypersensitive nerves. She could swear she felt every pulsing vein, every gush of pre-come, every frantic beat of his heart.

Instinctive, needy cries spilled from her lips. Primitive sounds of surrender and hunger that stirred the dominant male in him. She saw it in his eyes, in the clenching of his jaw, in the way his chest heaved with effort despite his rigidly timed pace.

"Deeper," she begged. "Harder."

Wulf resisted the latter while indulging the former, moving her legs to his shoulders and coming over her. Her hips tilted higher, his dropped straight down, pumping his cock into her farthest depths. He bottomed out on every plunge, pulled out to the tip on every withdrawal. The feel of that long, thick penis pumping its full length into her brought her to orgasm swiftly and kept her churning in the climax like a sandstorm.

His arms wrapped beneath her shoulders and held her pinned as he worked, his breath gusting across her ear. Sapphire felt the growl before she heard it, sensed the tension that gripped him in the moments before orgasm. He kept to the tempo that had to be killing him, but his fervor grew. The slap of his tight sac against her buttocks grew sharper, spurring her pleasure.

Her fingertips clung to his straining back and she breathed, "Come in me. Fill me with you."

"Katie," he snarled.

He grew thicker, harder. She climaxed again at the stretching of her inner muscles and he exploded with a hoarse shout of her name, his large frame straining against her in the way she loved. The way that told her he was as helpless as she to the force of their need.

Wulf held himself still at the deepest point of her, grinding into her, emptying his lust in fierce, fiery bursts.

With his temple pressed to hers, he gasped, "I love you. God, I love you."

He came apart in her arms. She held him through the torrent that raged through them both.

Wulf held his torso aloft to look down at her. "Tell me what happened to you today."

She inhaled deeply. Her dark eyes were luminous and beautiful. "I don't want to talk. I just want to hold you."

He nuzzled the fragrant valley between her breasts. "We have a lot to talk about. Plans for our fut—"

"No. For the next few hours you are not a prince, you are simply my lover. There is no tomorrow or any other day after that. There is only tonight and this bed." Her pussy clutched at his cock, stroking it until he began to stir inside her.

"Duncan told me what he said to you. None of it is true."

"I know."

He took her mouth, his tongue sweeping inside and caressing hers, gratitude for her trust a deep ache in his chest. When she arched impatiently against him, Wulf rolled onto his back, tucking one arm behind his head. "Ride off those drugs."

"You are my fantasy." She smiled and everything knotted up inside him. "Did you know that?"

Straddling his hips eagerly, Katie took him to the root, whimpering with pleasure as she seated fully onto him. He held her gaze, his chest tightening at the sight of her outlined by the faint moonlight entering through the small window behind her.

"Never leave me again." His voice turned thick and unsteady. "I'll chase you to the end of the universe if I have to. I'll never let you go."

As she began to move over him, she bent at the waist and claimed his mouth with her own. She rode him slowly, tenderly. He savored the press of her body atop his—the feel of her breasts brushing against his chest, the velvet moistness of her body gliding up and down his cock, the gentle brushes of her hair across his shoulder.

Except for the soothing caress of his palm on her thigh, Wulf forced himself to remain still. His jaw clenched and he gripped the pillows as he felt her endless string of orgasms clench around him. Her lush body was tortured, tormented, wracked with artificially heightened sensations, and this was the only thing he could do to help her. To allow her to use his body to ease her pain. He wished he could do more.

She gasped, her body shuddering over and around him. The touch of her hands upon his skin was reverent. She made him feel special and important. She told him every day in countless ways how much he pleased her. The way she looked at him, kissed him, talked to him—all of it made him *feel*. He had never felt so much as when he was with her.

His eyes slid closed, and he held on to her with the thought that he would never let her go, never allow her to be farther away from him than he could touch.

Katie rode his body for hours, but finally sweat and activity burned the drugs from her body. Their final coupling was slow and tender. Just the two of them, alone in the world. Her body spread beneath his, her head tossing restlessly while he loved her leisurely and deliberately.

He took her with gentle desire, keeping her pinned and helpless beneath his lazy, rhythmic thrusts. He whispered endearments against her sweat-slick skin, praising her beauty, her passion.

How different it was to make love to her with his heart. He had never experienced sex like it before, a joining of more than mere bodies.

As the sun began its measured rise, he tasted a tinge of melancholy in the flavor of her kiss, but exhaustion prevented him from investigating further. His eyelids weighed heavily and he sank into sleep with Katie held tight in his arms.

It was midmorning when Wulf's carefully cultivated warrior's senses told him they were no longer alone in the room.

He moved instinctively to shield Katie with his body and was astonished at the speed with which a dark hand snaked through the drapes to slap a neurosignature badge against the skin of her upper arm. His body instantly dropped to the mattress.

Katie had been transferred right out from under him.

With a howl of rage, he rolled from the bed, slipping under the voluminous curtains and reaching for the glaive that rested atop his discarded trousers. He engaged the blade a scant moment before his aggressor's first offensive move nearly cut him in half.

Deflecting the blow and kicking out with his legs, he bought himself time enough to spring off the floor and land on his feet. He froze for an instant in surprised recognition then swiftly parried the next attack.

"General Erikson," he acknowledged tersely, relieved that Katie was in loving hands. Then he steeled himself to deal with her father's obvious wrath.

"Prince Wulfric."

Grave Erikson faced him with a glaive in each hand, the two glowing white blades spinning in opposite directions, creating an impenetrable shield for his body.

"Naked as the day you were born," the general growled, kicking aside an intrusive chair. "Fitting that you should end your life the way you began it."

With that ominous statement, he lunged, one blade thrusting, the other parrying.

Distantly, Wulf's mind registered the sounds of his guardsmen trying to enter the room. Altering his position, he faced the doorway and saw that Erikson had attached a disrupter to the controls. Wulf was relieved. If his men entered the room, the possibility that Katie's father could be injured would be greatly increased.

Sweat stung Wulf's eyes as he fought defensively; refusing to risk injury to the father of the woman he loved. It took all his skill to keep Erikson's blades from penetrating his defenses.

The fury that goaded the general's actions seemed endless. And deadly.

"Fight back, damn you!" Erikson yelled.

"I can't. Katie would never forgive me if I hurt you."

Suddenly, decisively, the general stepped back and disengaged his blades. Wulf cautiously did the same. Darkness descended upon the room as the laser light retracted and disappeared.

"You've improved much, Your Highness, since the last time we sparred," Erikson said, with just a hint of breathlessness. "And you were damn good then."

Wulf tilted his head in acknowledgment, his eyes wary, his stance tense with expectation. "Where are your men?"

"I came alone. Bringing men with me would have been a military incursion. I am here as a father."

"I need her back, General."

"You have no claim to her."

"I love her."

"Don't speak of love to me!" Erikson snapped. "Do you know how I located my daughter? Her abuse in the town square yesterday is today's gossip. If you can't protect her, you don't deserve her."

Wulf's face heated. "I would protect her with my very life."

"You *stole* her!" The general stepped forward, the fists holding his glaive-hilts white-knuckled with tension. "You took her from a place where she is revered and brought her to a place where she is reviled. Endangered from every side. A target for anyone who has a grudge against Sari."

Wulf straightened, shrouding his nakedness with regal dignity. "I've made many mistakes regarding your daughter, General, but I'm prepared to rectify them. Katie is precious to me."

"She is nothing to you. Forget she exists."

"Not a chance," Wulf vowed.

Erikson's gaze narrowed. "You'll have to get through me

to get to her. It would be far less painful to find a new D'Ashierian concubine."

Wulf stepped forward.

The belt on the general's waist beeped an alarm. "Time's up, Your Highness."

Executing a quick bow, Erikson transferred out.

Stunned by the sudden end to the conversation and the loss of Katie after she'd been so recently found, Wulf stood frozen.

Katie was gone without knowing he wished to make her his consort.

She'd left him yesterday and he had promised her nothing since then that would change her mind. Would his profession of love be enough to bind her to him? She'd refused to talk about tomorrow or the future, as if they had none. Her last bittersweet kiss still lingered on his lips. Despair ripped through him like the lash of a whip.

She wasn't coming back. He knew it, felt it in his bones.

Chapter 15

"I know he loves me, Daddy, but it's not enough."

Sapphire paced the length of her father's study, her chest plagued with a dull and throbbing ache.

"Do you love him?" her father asked gently from his seat on the damask-covered sofa.

She heaved out her breath and tossed him a self-deprecating smile. "Hopelessly."

Being apart from Wulf felt as if she was missing a part of herself. She missed his arrogant demands for her undivided attention and the way he could focus all of his on her. She missed his laughter and the sound of his voice, which could soothe or arouse depending on his mood. She missed the smell of his skin and the weight of his body over hers. She was addicted to him, sometimes wanting him so badly that she shook with it.

As she moved around restlessly, Grave's gaze stayed on her. "Do you want to stay here with your mom and me? Do you want to go back to your home?"

Home. Was it really only weeks ago that she'd been ecstatic over the gift of her freedom? It seemed as if a lifetime had passed. "It's not home, Daddy. It comes with conditions I'm not willing to meet."

"I understand. Perhaps a vacation, then?" His dark eyes were filled with concern. "An off-world trip? Sometimes, getting away is the best medicine."

She stilled, then broke into a wide smile. "That's a wonderful idea. I'm going to track down the merc responsible for the attack against Wulf."

"What?"

"I need to find out why Wulf was attacked, what the intent was. I need to know if he's still in danger."

"You're in no condition to go on a hunt like that," he protested. "You need your head on straight first, or you put yourself at risk."

"My head *is* on straight." Her gaze swept around the wood-paneled room, finding comfort in its familiarity. "I'll be thinking about Wulf no matter what I do. At least this way, I can focus that concentration on something positive."

Grave leaned forward. "This isn't a short jaunt you're talking about. It could take years for you to find Gordmere. I can't bear the thought of you being away that long."

Sapphire sank onto the sofa beside him. "This is for the best. I'm sure of it."

"Perhaps you should talk to your mother first."

She glanced down at her hands. "Mom is a romantic."

His smile was indulgent. "True."

"I have no regrets." Sapphire lifted her gaze to meet her father's. "You should see how driven he is, how much of himself he gives to D'Ashier. He is deliberate, focused, unwavering . . . except when it comes to me. It's worth the heartache to have been loved like that by such a man, however briefly."

Her father's hand came up and brushed the hair from her face. "I'm proud of you."

"Thank you, Daddy." She nuzzled into his palm. "Besides, Gordmere has to be stopped. I can do it. I'm more than capable."

"It's not like you to run from trouble."

They both looked toward the melodious voice coming

from the doorway. Sasha Erikson entered the room, bringing with her a palpable energy.

Sapphire wrinkled her nose. "You have no idea how determined Wulf can be, Mom, or how stubborn. The more impossible our circumstance, the more obstinate he becomes. Once I've removed myself, he'll have a chance to reconsider. Then, he'll realize this was the right decision for both of us."

"If you love each other, maybe—"

"It's impossible, Mom. His family . . . I deserve better."

"Of course," Grave soothed. "I would never allow you to be anything less than the most important person in your man's life."

She turned to her father. "Then you'll help me leave?"

"If that's what you really want, I'll see to it." Grave pulled her close and kissed the top of her head.

"Yes! I'll go pack." Sapphire leaped to her feet and bolted from the room.

Sasha moved toward her husband in the innately sensual glide that had made their union inevitable. He'd taken one look at her and knew he would have her. Not having her simply hadn't been an option.

She took the seat recently vacated by their daughter and rested her blonde head on his shoulder. "I feel for her, Grave. Why did she have to fall in love with the one man impossible for her to have?"

"It's not impossible, but it is exceedingly difficult and expensive. They'd both pay dearly."

"We'd pay, too."

"Yes. I'm not sure any of us is prepared or willing to afford it."

Tilting her head back, Sasha stared up at him.

He stroked the elegant curve of her spine. "It won't be long before the prince comes after her. He's in rut. He isn't thinking clearly."

"Maybe there is love with the lust? Why not keep her here until he comes, so they can find out?"

Grave exhaled harshly. "Because this isn't a fairy tale, Sasha.

To be with him, she'd have to give up everything. Renounce her homeland. Wulfric, too, may lose all he holds dear— including the throne. I refuse to make it easy for them."

"Poor Katie." Wrapping her hand around his nape, she pulled his mouth to hers. "I'll go help her pack, then."

Sapphire watched as the last of her trunks disappeared off the transfer pad. She'd already said her good-byes. Now there was nothing left to do but embark.

Leaving was harder than she'd thought it would be. She'd been off-world many times before, having traveled with the king for a variety of reasons. But this time was different. She was leaving her old life behind and she wondered how she would reinvent herself as time passed. She couldn't silence the part of her that wanted to return to Wulf and take whatever he was able to give her. But she knew she would never be happy with anything less than all of him, and he could never give her that when torn by loyalty to his family and his Crown.

Steeling herself with the renewed conviction that she was doing the right thing, Sapphire moved onto the transfer pad. She turned to signal the controller that she was ready to go to the ship, but blinked in surprise as Dalen stepped onto the pad beside her.

"What are you doing?" she asked.

"Going with you."

"I only needed you to help me with my luggage."

"But I *want* to leave with you, Mistress." He smiled. "I've always wanted to travel and you'll need help to get settled."

"I won't be settling anywhere. I'll be working, Dalen. It will be dangerous and tiring, there will be no time for comforts—"

"Sounds lovely."

"You just returned from D'Ashier."

"See? This trip will seem like a vacation after that."

Sapphire eyed the handsome blond man carefully. "Why?"

He understood. "You can protect yourself, but I'd rest easier if I were with you. My eldest brother was a captain under your father during the Confrontations. He swears the general saved his life. My family owes a huge debt to yours. Attending you is the least I can do."

"This isn't—"

"Necessary. I know."

"All right." She shrugged. "If you don't like it, just tell me and I'll arrange for you to return to Sari."

"Agreed." Dalen rocked back on his heels and grinned.

She signaled their readiness to the pad controller. Instantly they found themselves on the transfer bay of the interstellar transport *The Argus*. It would take two days to reach Tolan, where—according to intel—Tarin Gordmere was last seen.

Glancing at Dalen, she smiled at his boyish excitement. Perhaps it would be good to have someone she knew with her as she started a new life for herself.

A life without Wulfric.

"What do you mean you can't find her?"

Wulf's patience had run thin about an hour after Katie had transferred away. Now, a week later, his patience was gone.

The captain met his gaze without flinching. "We lost her nanotach signal yesterday and we've been unable to recover it."

"*Lost* it? What the hell does that mean?"

"Either she's removed the nanotach or she's out of range of our receptors."

Wulf drummed his fingers in rapid staccato on the desktop. "Out of range? How far would she have to travel to be out of range?"

The captain's lips pursed before he replied, "The nanotach signal would be detectable anywhere on the planet."

Wulf stood. "Are you telling me she's *off-world*?"

"It's a possibility, Your Highness."

"Damn it."

Here he'd been impatiently waiting for Katie to contact him. He had wanted to reach out to her, but worried that doing so would put her at risk with the king. He'd thought for sure she would remember their last night together and his declarations of love, and find a way to reach him.

He had no way of knowing whether she'd chosen to leave—or had been given no choice.

"Find General Erikson. *Now!*"

"Good evening, General."

Wulf watched as Katie's father casually lifted his gaze from his book. Lounging on a green sofa, the general didn't appear the least bit surprised to see Wulf, as if an enemy prince standing in his study was a commonplace occurrence. Of course, Wulf had made it clear that he wasn't letting Katie go without a fight. And he doubted the general was ever caught off guard by anything.

"Good evening, Your Highness," Erikson replied. "Nice to see you with clothes on. Would you care for an ale? Or perhaps something stronger?"

"No, thank you. I've come for Katie. Where is she?"

"You're too late." Erikson snapped the book closed. "I expected you a week ago."

"I couldn't risk contacting her and putting her in danger."

"Then why are you here?"

"I need to know if she's okay, General."

"She's gone."

"I know she's off-world. Where?"

"How do you know that?" The general's gaze narrowed.

Wulf ignored the question. "I have to speak with her."

Erikson shook his head. "She's moved on with her life, Your Highness. Go away. Find another concubine."

"General . . ." Wulf's fists clenched. Katie couldn't move on

with her life. Not until she heard him out. "Don't push me.
I'm not in the mood."

"Damn it all!" Grave threw the book down. "The way you
and the king carry on about Katie is downright pitiful. You'd
think—"

Wulf lunged across the low coffee table and tackled the
general to the floor. Erikson laughed, and the fight was on.

"Where the hell is she?" Wulf ducked an incoming punch
to the face.

"Wouldn't you love to know?" The general grunted as he
paid for that jibe with a blow to the ribs.

They scrapped like schoolyard boys, fighting for the sheer
animal joy of it as well as for the instinctive need to establish
the dominant male.

"I won't give up, General. Not now. Not ever."

"You better not," Erikson retorted, "or I'll kick your ass."

Wulf growled and lunged. The general caught him by the
shoulders and used his incoming momentum to toss Wulf
into a nearby chair, which broke under the impact.

"Enough!" The general withdrew. "We cause any more
damage in here and Sasha will have me sleeping on the couch."

Gasping, they both leaned heavily against the nearest intact
piece of furniture. Wulf glared, the general grinned.

"About time you showed some fire, Your Highness. You'll
need it in the days ahead."

Wulf snorted. "Where is she?"

Erikson pressed his palm against his ribs. "She's gone to the
planet Tolan, tracking the merc who arranged for the attack
against you—Tarin Gordmere."

Katie was protecting him. Again.

Wulf wiped the sweat from his brow. "Is it too late for us?"
he asked grimly. "Does she want me to let her go?"

"I wouldn't say that." Erikson's tone was dry.

"Thank you, General." Wulf straightened. "I'll find her, and
bring her back safely."

"The king won't concede her easily," Erikson warned. "He released her contract, but he hasn't released *her*."

"I understand."

The general stared at him intently. "We may yet find ourselves across a battlefield from each other."

Wulf nodded grimly. "I would turn my back to you, General."

"And I would turn my back to you, Your Highness."

They bowed in unison.

With a quick twist of his signet ring, Wulf left.

Chapter 16

"You're impossible, Wulfric," Anders snapped. "I command you to go to your concubines and work that Sarian woman out of your system."

Wulf concentrated on the depth of his breathing rather than the fury that bubbled so close to the surface. He knew his barely leashed temper made him miserable company, which was why he'd avoided his father as much as possible.

"If you don't like my mood, Father," he said with forced calm, "may I suggest you leave my chambers?"

The king paced. "I'm not the only one who finds you unbearable. The servants are afraid to come near you and the guards are drawing straws for duty assignments. This has gone on long enough."

Wulf rubbed a hand over his face. Katie had a week's head start and seemed to have disappeared without a trace. He didn't understand how she was surviving. She wasn't using credits. How was she paying for the things she needed? Food, lodging, transportation? Worry for her was eating away at him. Had she tracked Gordmere only to be hurt . . . or worse?

His jaw clenched. He knew she could take care of herself, but he didn't want her to have to.

When a soft beeping came from the door, he tersely gave permission for entry. The captain entered with a bow.

"Your Majesty. Your Highness." He straightened and his gaze met Wulf's. "The small group of guardsmen you requested are making the necessary preparations for the journey to Tolan."

Wulf nodded. "Excellent. I'll be ready shortly."

"You are not leaving with them," the king said with dangerous softness.

"I am."

"I request permission to accompany you, Your Highness," the captain asked.

"Granted."

With a bow, the captain left the room.

Wulf moved toward his bedroom, where servants were packing his belongings. He was halted by a powerful grip on his elbow. He looked at his father. Struggling to regain his equanimity after the surprise, he asked, "What are you doing?"

"The Manerian king and his daughter are arriving today."

"I know."

"You're to meet the princess in anticipation of a possible match."

"You'd better send for Duncan, then. I won't be here."

Anders's voice vibrated with anger. "I've stepped back, Wulfric, and allowed you free rein, but never forget that it is *I* who am king. You *will* obey me."

"Father, don't do this."

The king's mouth hardened. "A union with Maneria, Wulfric! Can you imagine the power and influence D'Ashier would have?"

"Yes, it would be an excellent match." Wulf placed his hand over his father's. "But the Manerian princess can wait. Katie is in danger because of me."

Anders growled. "I was certain you would always put D'Ashier first. I never imagined you could be so selfish."

"I'm sorry you feel that way." He pried his father's hand from his arm and moved away.

"Wulfric! You will not turn away from me until you are dismissed."

Wulf stopped in mid-stride. He turned carefully to confront his father, his face impassive.

"You will listen to me," the king ordered.

"I always listen to you. I have duly noted your thoughts on the matter of my departure."

"That's it?"

"That's it. Katie's on Tolan, risking herself to avenge me. I have to go to her."

"And if I command you to stay?"

Wulf gave a weary exhale. "You would have to imprison me, which wouldn't impress the Manerian king."

The king's hands clenched into fists at his sides. "And if I command you to marry the Manerian princess?"

"We can discuss Maneria when I return, Father."

"I forbid you to pursue Erikson's daughter!"

"I have to pack." He bowed, and turned away.

"Wulfric." There was an anguished note in his father's voice that stopped him again. "Why?"

He returned to his father with hands outstretched. "When I was in that cave . . . the slightest hint of a breeze across my skin was agonizing. When I awoke in the healing chamber and saw Katie there, I thought I'd died and she was my reward. I felt joy. Gratitude. From that very first moment, I knew she was mine. *Knew* it. And she looked at me the same way. Before she knew who I was. I was just a wounded man who had nothing to offer her."

"She knew damn well who you were."

"She didn't." Wulf made a slashing gesture with his hand. "I can say that with absolute certainty. I was there when she was told. I saw the horror and fear. The confusion. She didn't know."

"You talk as if she's the only woman to desire you," Anders scoffed. "All women want you."

"But I don't want all women. Since my capture, I can't bear

to be touched. I have no attendants. I dress and bathe myself. I maintain a safe physical distance from others."

"Except from the one person you need to stay far away from!"

"She makes me *feel*. I see her, taste her, smell her . . . Everything else is gray to me, but she's vibrant. I *need* her to touch me. I ache for the feel of her hands on me. Part of me died in that cave. Whatever is left exists because of her. I can't explain it any better than that. She's necessary to me."

Wulf dropped to his knees. "I beg you, Father, don't ask me to choose between D'Ashier and Katie."

"You've never begged me for anything," Anders said hoarsely. "I wish you'd ask me for something I could give you."

"Her father's support could facilitate the Sarian treaty we both want. Think of the future," Wulf said.

The silence that followed his words stretched endlessly. The waiting was torture.

"I am, Wulfric." Accepting Wulf's offered hands, the king pulled him to his feet. The forlorn sigh he released made Wulfric's heart ache. "Fetch her, if you must. But her presence in your bed makes the need for a powerful alliance even more urgent."

Wulf embraced him. "We'll deal with the logistics when the time comes."

Anders's face was lined with strain and disappointment, aging him drastically. "I'll do my best to pacify the Manerians. For your sake, son. Because I love you."

"You won't regret this," Wulf promised.

"I already do, but I can't think of any other way to hasten your boredom with her."

As Wulf turned his gaze toward the window and its view of his beloved D'Ashier beyond, his gut knotted. He remembered Katie standing naked in front of it, bathed in the reddish glow of the setting sun, her body soft and languid from his lovemaking.

He didn't know if he could live without either one of them.

His hand lifted to rub at his chest. "I have to go now. I'll return as soon as I can."

Sapphire moved swiftly through the urban darkness, her glaive-hilt gripped tightly in her hand. The mercenary moved with casual ease along the pedestrian strip, completely unaware that she shadowed him so closely. The traffic on the street was light—most likely owing to the earlier light drizzle—but there were enough people around to make her inconspicuous.

Breathing deeply, she relished the rare smell of a rainy night. Tolan was a lush planet, a stark contrast to her desert home-world. Covered in golden-leaved trees and seas of wild green grass, it was beautiful. A paradise. Sadly the perfection of the planet was marred by the massive cities, the favored metallic designs glaring in the light of Tolan's twin suns.

"Do you have a light?" Gordmere stopped a passing woman in order to ignite his cheroot.

Sapphire slipped beneath the shadowed overhang of a closed establishment.

After the two-day trip to Tolan, it had taken almost two weeks to track the mercenary down. Gordmere was wily enough to switch aliases constantly, which made it difficult to monitor him through the interstellar system. It might have taken longer to locate him, but she'd learned he had two powerful weaknesses—gambling and arrogance. He didn't fear anyone, and he couldn't seem to quit while he was behind. Some gaming hells were more forgiving than others. Once she'd established which hells would let players get deep in the hole, the rest had fallen into place.

In a way, Sapphire was grateful for the attention the hunt had required. The time spent tracking Gordmere had kept her busy enough to prevent pining over Wulfric, at least during the daylight hours. The nights were another matter.

As Gordmere continued on, Sapphire rejoined the foot traffic, her nostrils teased by the tendrils of fragrant smoke drifting over his shoulder.

He paused at a doorway and glanced from left to right. She walked right past him, careful to draw no attention to herself. Finding nothing suspicious, Gordmere disappeared inside.

"Dalen," she whispered.

The reply came through the tiny comm link in her ear. *"Yes, Mistress?"*

"He just walked in."

"I see him."

She sighed. It was difficult to leave so important a task to someone else, but it was a gentlemen's club and she wouldn't be allowed entry. "Make sure you sit close enough to overhear his conversation."

"I understand. Please don't worry. I'm very good at making friends."

"I'll be nearby, waiting for you."

Sapphire turned around and took the lift to the small room she'd rented overlooking the club. It was a hovel, but despite its condition, it still cost her two cases of Sari wine, far more than it was worth. But there was no help for it. She couldn't leave Dalen alone, untrained as he was. Something could happen, anything could go wrong, and she had to be near at hand just in case.

Entering the tiny lodging, she was suddenly overwhelmed by emotion and exhaustion. It happened every time she was alone with nothing to occupy her.

Nothing but thoughts of Wulf.

Staring out the grimy window at the club below, Sapphire wondered what he was doing. Did he ache for her, as she did for him? Did he feel as hollow inside? And she wondered again whether she'd made a mistake, if she should have returned to him, despite everything.

It was late when Dalen stumbled from the club with Gordmere, both men slightly tipsy from too much drink. They parted ways at the pedestrian strip and she exited the small lodging by way of the lift. She deliberately fell behind to be certain Dalen wasn't followed. When she was sure he was safe from prying eyes, she followed him up to their hotel room.

Like nearly everything in Tolan, their lodging was designed to look "modern" with sleek lines, metallic and stone accents, and neutral colors. She hated it, wondering why the Tolanites admired such lifeless surroundings when their planet as a whole was so warm and vibrant.

She found Dalen lounging on the beige chaise in the small living area, waiting for her. He reeked of perfume and sex, his dazed smile telling her that he'd had a good time with the club's concubines. Sapphire was happy for him. In choosing to travel with her, he had left everything he knew and loved, and she'd been horrid company; snappish one minute and crying the next.

As she sank onto the seat next to him, he grinned at her with boyish charm. "I think you'll be pleased with tonight's events, Mistress."

"Did he mention anything about Prince Wulfric?"

"No."

She groaned.

"But," Dalen continued, "he did offer me a job."

"What?"

"I repeated everything you told me to say. I told him how I'd been released from my employment because I was caught pilfering. I mentioned my resentment and lack of work. All of this information was unimpressive and boring to him, until I told him that I once worked in the D'Ashier palace. Then, he began to listen."

Sapphire leaned forward. *"And?"*

"He wanted to know more." Dalen yawned.

"You told him that you knew Crown Prince Wulfric personally?"

He nodded. "He was interested in everything I told him."

"How interested? Do you think you could talk to him again?"

"Even better." Dalen grinned. "He said he'd been hired to capture a figure of great prominence and that recent events had severely reduced his crew. He offered to take me on."

She blinked. "He offered to *hire* you? To capture a crown prince? He doesn't even know you!"

Dalen smiled smugly. "I told you I was very good at making friends."

"This is fantastic." She fell back into the cushions of the chaise.

There were a hundred scenarios she'd considered when it came to dealing with Tarin Gordmere, but working for him had not been one of them. It was, however, perfect. "Tell me everything."

"He says he must build up his crew before he can take action and he's been warned that his target is a warrior of great skill. He hesitates to make his move until he's certain he can succeed. This, apparently, will take a few more weeks."

She frowned. "Not if he's hiring strangers right off the streets."

Dalen laughed. "My work at the palace was quite important to Gordmere. He mentioned it several times. If I hadn't revealed that, he probably wouldn't have offered."

"I wonder if he intends to go after Wulf in the palace." Sapphire rubbed her temples, her mind struggling to puzzle out all the possible options and finding too many variables. She had to protect Wulf. If anything ever happened to him . . .

She shivered. Nothing was going to happen, because she would ensure that he was never in any danger.

"When do you see him again?" she asked.

"Tomorrow." Dalen's blue eyes lit with obvious anticipation. "You were correct about his gambling addiction, Mistress. He also has a weakness for women."

She smiled ruefully. "I can smell that on you."

"I expect that I'm going to spend the next few weeks getting to know him"—his smile was wicked—"and his rather decadent lifestyle."

She wrinkled her nose. She couldn't stand by doing nothing. She had to be involved in some way, no matter how minor. A thought came to mind, along with a slow grin that spread across her lips.

Dalen eyed her warily. "I've started to recognize that look, Mistress. It rarely bodes well."

"Nonsense," she scoffed. "You'll be pleased to know, Dalen, that you've just acquired a *mätress*."

"I'm going to have to do something about him," Sapphire muttered in Dalen's ear, her arm thrown around his neck.

Dalen's gaze followed hers, coming to rest on the bulky man who stood next to Gordmere by the club bar. Music thumped loudly as the singer on the stage belted out a popular dance tune. All around them, various patrons gyrated to the beat, creating an environment of wild, carefree decadence.

"Such as?" he asked.

"I haven't decided yet, but he doesn't like us, and if he continues his complaining, Gordmere might decide we're not worth the effort. Tor Smithson has been with him for years and we're just strangers."

Strengthening their appearance as an amorous couple, she threw her leg over Dalen's. "We have to stay involved long enough to discover who hired Gordmere."

"What do you want me to do?"

She watched Gordmere catch the eye of a pretty concubine, then move to charm her, leaving Smithson alone. Sliding off the seat, Sapphire pushed to her feet. "Keep Gordmere distracted."

Dalen grabbed her arm. "You're going to do it *now?*"

Meeting his concerned gaze, she offered a reassuring smile.

"It's been three weeks and he still hasn't told you anything about who hired him or details about the job. He doesn't trust you yet, and he won't as long as Smithson is filling his head full of doubt. We have to get him out of the way." She stood. "Besides, Smithson's one of the mercs who tortured Wulfric. He deserves what I can give him."

Dalen grabbed her wrist. "You're unarmed."

"So is he," she pointed out. "Don't worry. I'll be back in half an hour. If I'm not, *then* you can get worried."

"Your reassurances leave much to be desired," he muttered, but he rose from the small booth and made his way over to Gordmere.

Sapphire sidled up to the bar and flashed a smile at Smithson. She ordered a glass of Tolan brew, a potent liquor that Dalen enjoyed but she couldn't stomach.

"Why don't you go home?" Smithson's tone was harsh. "You've no business being here."

She perused him with an assessing side-glance, taking in the threat he presented while sizing him up. Her father had always advised her that being prepared was half the battle.

"I'd be bored at home," she complained with a pout.

Smithson's returning perusal was blatantly disgusted. "That's not my concern, my wallet is. Your boyfriend looks to you every time he's asked a question. A man who buckles under a piece of ass like that can't be trusted."

Sapphire looked over her shoulder. Dalen was talking animatedly with Tarin Gordmere, who faced away from her. The bartender set the brew she'd ordered on the counter and she moved quickly, while the time was still right. "Why don't you show me out?"

"You're leaving?" He studied her suspiciously. "Just like that?"

"Sure." She shrugged. "I don't want to cause any trouble. We need the money, you know?"

"Walk yourself out," he said coldly.

She sighed. "Fine. I'll stay. I can never hail a public transport by myself and—"

Smithson grabbed her elbow and hauled her toward the exit.

"What about Dalen's drink?" she whined, stumbling along behind him.

"I'll give it to him when I get back."

She hid her smile. "Okay."

The instant the doors slid closed behind them, Sapphire moved. Surprise was all she had, so she used it, rotating Smithson's arm with all of her weight, gritting her teeth when she heard the bone break. His howl of pain was deafening. She lifted her foot and kicked him in the ass, shoving him away from the door, where they might be overheard.

The entrance to the club was in an alley off the main thoroughfare, which made time a precious commodity. She was moments away from discovery, if that.

Smithson dropped and kicked in a sideways swipe, knocking her feet out from under her. Sapphire fell forward, landing on top of him. Before she could react, his good arm was around her neck, squeezing. Gasping and clawing, Sapphire fought to ease the pressure on her trachea. The mercenary was too strong. Spots drifted before her eyes, then blackness closed in. Seconds away from unconsciousness, she yanked his broken arm. As his agonized roar echoed through the dimly lit alley, she scrambled free.

Time. She was running out of it. Stumbling to her feet, she sucked air into burning lungs, her neck throbbing from his brutal grip.

Smithson snarled, rolling and somehow coming up onto his knees. "I'm going to kill you."

As he reached for his boot, she spotted the dagger-hilt he sought. His gaze locked with hers, filled with bloodlust and an inherent evil that chilled her to the bone. This man hunted humans for a living and tortured the helpless for the sick thrill it gave him. He'd almost succeeded in killing the man she loved.

"I'm relieved you said that." Sapphire steeled herself for the grim task ahead. "Killing a man in cold blood isn't my style."

He lunged for her, the wicked blade coming to glowing life in his hand. She kicked. Good fortune and a lot of skill ensured that her foot hit his wrist, sending the hilt spinning into the air above them.

She leaped and caught the weapon. With a diagonal slash, she severed his head. His torso hit the ground with a thud.

"But self-defense I can handle."

Chapter 17

"**K**atie Erikson is here, Your Highness."

Wulf looked away from the data screen as the captain strode into the room. "Did you see her with your own eyes?"

The captain nodded.

"How does she look?"

"Thinner, tired."

"Stubborn woman," Wulf groused, but he was nearly dizzy with relief. Six weeks of searching and Katie was finally close enough to touch. He stood to get ready, but a quick look around his quarters turned his anticipatory pleasure into a scowl of distaste.

Tolan was a relatively new member of the Interstellar Council. The planet's foray into high-automation was so new as to still be something flaunted with pride. Everything everywhere was stark and lacked color. He tried to picture his sensual Katie in such a dismal place and was unsuccessful. The fact that she was here in Tolan entirely on his account made his heart ache.

"Where is she now, Captain?"

"She and the *mästare* are at the concourse as specified by Gordmere."

Wulf began stripping from his robes. "I want to see her."

"Your Highness, I don't recommend that you come with me. What if you're seen? It could ruin everything. It's taken me weeks to reach this point."

"I'll keep a low profile and stay out of your way."

"Forgive me, but it's impossible for you to keep a low profile."

Wulf grinned. "It's not so difficult when you're around, Captain. You have a way of drawing attention."

A hint of a smile teased the corner of the captain's dark lips. "As you command, Your Highness. I'll remove her from the conversation. If I succeed, I suggest you and the Mistress depart the area and allow me to manage the rest."

"Taking her away won't bother me in the slightest, I assure you."

Within minutes, they were on their way to the concourse.

Sapphire draped herself over Dalen and ran her tongue along the shell of his ear.

"Umm," she purred. Arching her back, she pressed her breasts into his arm. One hand slipped across his bare chest and up through his golden hair. The fingers of her other hand walked across his muscled thigh and dropped between his legs. He groaned and turned his head, burying his face in her neck.

"Mistress," he panted. "Is all of this really necessary?"

"He must believe we're a couple. He's grown terribly suspicious since Smithson was killed."

"Y-yes, but . . ." His hand flew to her wrist and stilled its movements. "I'm only a man, and you are a well-trained concubine. There's only so much I can take."

Looking over her shoulder at the occupants of the small lounge in the Deep Space 10 Concourse, Sapphire noted the slender blond man who entered.

She moved over Dalen quickly, straddling his thighs and

wrapping her arms around his neck. "He's coming back." She nuzzled his throat. "You know what to do."

"I can't think when you're doing that!"

"Haggle with him a little on the price for your services," she whispered. "It's taken us weeks to get to this point, you don't want to seem too eager. And whatever you do, make sure you find out who hired him to capture—"

A deep voice rumbled behind her. "Get the woman out of here."

Sapphire stilled. She turned slowly, struggling to hide her surprise. She failed miserably, her mouth falling open at the sight of Clarke, who stood next to Gordmere as if they were old friends.

"We've no need of her services for this conversation." His dark gaze raked her insolently.

She blinked.

"Have you never seen a real man before?" Clarke asked scornfully, gripping her elbow and yanking her away from Dalen. He hauled her close, crushing her against his massive chest.

"When you tire of your pretty boy, come see me." He bent her over his arm and bit her earlobe gently. "Go to the exit," he growled, then he pulled her up and shoved her toward the door.

Sapphire stumbled away, glancing over her shoulder in amazement. *What the hell was going on?* Distracted, she ran directly into a rock-hard chest and was pulled out of the lounge into the crowded terminal beyond. "What—"

"*Katie.*"

She felt faint. Her gaze followed the golden hand that held her wrist and traveled up the muscular arm with lightning speed. She stopped for a split-second on the delicious lips that were presently pursed in anger, then her wide eyes met Wulf's furious ones. Tears welled at the stark relief and love that shined in the emerald depths. With a whimper of pleasure,

Sapphire leaped at him, locking her legs around his lean waist and taking his mouth.

He absorbed the impact easily and turned, pressing her into the wall of the corridor, his mouth open and ravenous under hers.

Her heart raced. She'd longed for him. So badly. Every night his memory would not be denied, demanding she dream of him.

"I've missed you," she gasped into his mouth.

Wulf thrust his hips into the open apex of her thighs, revealing the depth of his desire. "You and Dalen . . ."

A harsh, edgy noise vibrated in his chest.

"It's nothing." She arched into him, her blood raging.

He bit the vulnerable point where her neck met her shoulder. His touch was rough, barely controlled. "You were kissing him, rubbing against him . . . I'll tear him apart . . ."

"No." She moaned, pinned to the wall by his overwrought and powerfully aroused body. She was burning, on fire for him and his passion for her. "It was all for you."

"I don't care what your reason was. You're mine!"

"Yes . . ."

"You belong to me." His hand at her waist wrapped in her hair, pulling her head back to expose her throat. He nipped and licked along the tender skin, his other hand coming up to grip her breast, squeezing her nipple, tugging its ring until it puckered wantonly. "If my life depended on it, you will not ever touch another man."

"Jealous fool." Sapphire laughed, filled with joy to be in his arms. She hugged him with her thighs, but it wasn't necessary; his thrusting body kept her firmly in place. "I would do anything for you. I love you."

"You will be the end of me." Wulf pressed his forehead to hers. "You'll drive me insane . . ."

"Wulf." Her hands soothed the taut length of his back, understanding how he felt. She'd experienced the same when she'd sent the concubine to him. "There is only you."

"Never again," he muttered against her cheek. "Never touch another man again. I can't bear it."

Pulling back from the wall, he carried her swiftly away. "We have to get out of here."

"Dalen! I can't leave him behind."

"The captain will take care of him. Right now, you need to take care of me."

Sapphire leaned back in his embrace, his strong thighs flexing beneath hers as he strode easily through the crowds, his sheer commanding presence causing commuters to weave out of their path.

"What are you doing here?" she asked, breathless from his bold possessiveness.

A black brow arched. "Coming after you."

His face looked paler, his lips sterner, but he remained by far the handsomest man she'd ever seen. Only for him had she ever felt such a wealth of emotion. It was addicting, over-powering, intoxicating.

"Wulf. You take my breath away."

His chest expanded with a harshly indrawn breath. Tightening his arms around her, he quickened his pace. "You have no idea how much I've missed you. You're so damn beautiful. As many times as I've pictured you in my mind, it never did you justice."

Sapphire smiled. "I look like hell."

"You look like heaven." He pressed his lips to her temple and kept them there. His voice dropped. "I'll mend my ways. I'll change. I can make you happy."

Her arms encircled his neck. "I can't go through this again. You shouldn't have come."

"I couldn't stay away. I've never been able to. *I love you.*"

Tears slipped free, wetting both of their faces. "Wulf . . ."

"Hush. Wait until we're alone. I have something to ask you."

Pulling back, Sapphire looked into his face. His features

were so austere and intent, but his eyes were smoldering. She
flushed. "I know what you want."

His mouth curved in a sexy smile. "You don't know everything. But you can, if you just give me time to get out of here."

She spent the short hackney ride back to Wulf's lodgings
tucked against the warm strength of his chest. His hands caressed up and down her arms; his mouth pressed kisses along
her face and neck. They said nothing, both longing for the
moment when they could be alone. When the transport arrived at the hotel, they leaped out and hurried to his rooms.

Wulf led her directly into his suite. The outer foyer was
similar to the rest of the city—metallic with silver paint on
the walls and polished cement floors. Sapphire still found the
barrenness of the decor jarring. Sari and D'Ashier had long
ago re-embraced the beauty of the tactile. The need to celebrate what was human was what made warriors so revered
and concubines so prized.

"This way," he directed. She moved with him into the bedchamber beyond. Her breath caught at the sight that greeted
them.

Multicolored rugs decorated the floors; rich velvet counter-
panes littered the bed along with an array of jewel-toned
pillows. The glaring lights remained off, the room lit with a
profusion of flickering candles.

"It's beautiful," she breathed.

Wulf came up behind her, wrapping his powerful arms
around her waist. "Only because you're here." He turned her
to face him, then sealed his lips over hers.

She melted under his kiss. The heat that sparked between
them was hotter than before. The passion ignited every nerve
ending in her body, traveling from her lips to her toes. Dizzy
with longing, Sapphire pulled away to catch her breath and
was arrested by the sight of him.

He was flushed, his mouth moist and parted, his breathing
labored. But it was his gaze—fierce and determined—that

most aroused her. His effect on her was potent, aging like a fine vintage, becoming stronger the longer she knew him.

"I'm going to make love to you now." Wulf's tone was a sensuous whisper. His hand reached out to cup her breast, his thumb brushing over her nipple. "Then we're going to talk about our future together, and you're not leaving this room until I say what I have to say. Understand?"

Shaking, she kissed him passionately. It was astonishing, really, that this magnificent man loved her enough to pursue her.

"I adore you." She felt him shudder. Her words released something primal. Wulf's hands were rough as his fingers curled into her gown and rent the fragile garment in two.

Sapphire was as desperate as he, struggling to feel the warmth of his flesh beneath her hands, to know this was not another dream. She paused when she saw the gold chain carrying her Guardian's chip around his neck. She plucked it away from his skin with her fingertips.

He held her by the waist as she examined it. "We found it at Braeden's. I've kept it close ever since."

Her fingers caressed the warm metal. "I missed this tangible reminder of you."

He tugged off the remnants of her clothing and pressed her back into the bed. "You'll have no more need for reminders. For the rest of your life I'm going to spend every free moment buried as deep inside you as I can go."

She sank with a sigh into the rich velvet coverlets, the luxurious material no match for the silken texture of Wulf's skin. He covered her body with his own. She couldn't get enough. Her mouth pressed moist, open-mouthed kisses along the top of his shoulder. She licked and bit him. Her hands caressed, her nails scratched. Her legs wrapped around his hips and held him to her. She wanted to devour him.

"Hurry," she urged.

Wulf laughed. "I've been dreaming of this for weeks, let me savor it."

"Later."

With a lusty chuckle, he positioned the broad head of his cock at her entrance and began to push into her. "So tight, Katie."

He kissed her deeply, pressing inexorably into her. A low groan of pleasure rumbled up in his throat. "I've wanted you so badly, I thought I'd go mad without you."

"I love you," she purred as he lodged to the hilt within her. "I've dreamed of you, needed you so much."

His head dropped next to hers, his breathing harsh and ragged. He pulled out, then plunged deep. When she arched into him, rushing him, spur-ring him on, he began to fuck her like she needed, his hips churning, his cock shafting her with devastating skill. His mouth lowered, surrounding a straining nipple, suckling with such force she could feel the pull of it deep inside her aching pussy.

Helpless mewls of pleasure poured from her. It had been so long. Too long. The feel of him was exquisite, so thick and hard, pumping between her thighs with latent power.

"Yes . . . you feel so good . . ."

He mumbled something that sounded arrogant, then shifted his mouth to her other breast. Sapphire pushed her heels into the mattress and fucked him back, needing him to be where she was—lost in lust, desperate for orgasm, hope-lessly in love. She loved that he was so self-possessed, loved that she was necessary and important enough to him that she was his one and only vulnerability.

He took control, rising above her, hooking his arms under-neath her legs to better ream her. Her nipples were swollen, too tender, distended from the passionate assault of his mouth. He took her fiercely then, his hips pistoning, his massive cock shuttling through greedily clenching tissues.

Fast and hard, grinding and rolling his hips, Wulf deliber-ately drove her beyond sanity. The sight of him was stirring. His handsome face contorted in a grimace of pleasure.

Because he was connected to her in the most intimate way possible.

"I love you," he groaned.

His passion-slurred words pushed her over the edge, her spine bowing in climax. She whimpered as she convulsed around him, her entire body wracked with endless shivers.

"More," he snarled. The pounding of his cock into her heat was relentless. "Come again."

"No ..." she moaned, certain another orgasm would kill her.

Wulf reached between them, rubbing her clitoris with deftly skilled strokes. Her next orgasm came even more powerfully than before. As she writhed beneath him, she felt him swell. He shouted her name, clutching her to his shuddering body, lewd love words and praise tumbling from his lips as he spurted heavy and thick deep inside her.

Gasping, Wulf twisted over, pulled her to drape over him without separating from her. His strong arms held her tightly to him as their breathing slowed.

He kissed the top of her head. "I want to handfast with you, Katie."

She lifted her head and met his gaze, astonished. "Handfast?"

"We can make it work. We love each other, Katie. I never expected it or even wanted it, but it's happened. And I'm not sorry."

"Handfast?" she repeated.

"I've been doing some research. In the first years after D'Ashier established sovereignty, the monarch and his family were in great danger. To stabilize the throne, preserving lineage was a priority that took precedence over ceremony. If a member of the royal family wished to marry, they couldn't always wait to do it properly. Not in times of war and treachery."

She nodded. "I understand."

Wulf caught her hand and held it over his heart. "The tradition of the handfast was established—an informal, yet binding agreement as strong as a marriage. It doesn't require the blessing of the king the way a formal joining would. It only requires that both parties be willing."

"Wulf." She bit her lower lip. "You would circumvent your father in something so important?"

His grip on her hand tightened. "He would still have the last word. If he never gives his blessing, the binding would become a morganatic marriage. You'd be my consort, not my queen, and our children could never attain the throne."

"Our children . . ." Longing pierced her chest with such force she shivered with it. Her eyes and throat burned. She would lose all that she had now, but gain something so precious she hardly dared to dream of it. Marriage. A family. *With Wulf.*

His green eyes were brilliant and laser-focused. She'd rarely seen him look so determined. "You deserve more, Katie. I wish I could promise you more. But this is all I can offer now—my heart, my bed, the respect and prominence of royal consort, and the promise that I will do everything in my power to sway my father and gain his blessing. I believe it's possible. And if he never concedes, you would still belong to me. I would belong to you. Nothing could break the vows we make to one another."

Sapphire linked her fingers on his chest and rested her chin upon them. "I don't want to be responsible for causing a rift between you and your family."

Tucking a pillow beneath his head, Wulf locked his gaze with hers. "I need you in my life to be happy. It's as simple and as complicated as that. I can deal with anything, as long as you're mine. As long as you love me back."

Tears fell. "My father . . . If there was another war . . ."

"I've made overtures to the King of Sari," he said swiftly. "And he has agreed to meet with me to discuss the possibility of cease-fire agreements and new treaties. I won't say there will never be another war, but I swear to do my best to prevent one."

"It's impossible."

"It isn't." Wulf's strength of will was so powerful it charged the air around them. "I won't lie and say things will be easy. I can't promise you a happy ending, where everything is wonderful and our families coexist peacefully. I can only promise to love you, to make time for you, and cherish you. I'll never give you cause to regret the sacrifices you'll make to be with me. We'll survive the trials together. We'll find a way. And when we can't, we'll still have each other."

Her heart ached. "I love you."

"That's all we need. Say yes."

Sapphire nodded, her throat too tight to speak. He wanted to bind himself to her, at great personal and political cost. She couldn't refuse. She wanted him just as badly.

He flopped backward in an exaggerated collapse. "Good."

She managed a smile. "You look so relieved."

Wulf's returning smile was sinful, yet ardent.

She sat up, taking his thickening cock to her deepest point. "What would you have done if I'd refused you?"

Wulf flexed inside her. "Moved to Plan B."

"Which was?" Though she suspected she knew.

"Kidnapping you again and keeping you trapped in my bed until I convinced you to marry me."

She released a mock sigh. "I should have held out for Plan B."

One black brow rose. Wulf gripped her hips, lifting her. "Well . . ." He pumped upward in a breathtaking thrust. "Just because Plan A worked doesn't mean we have to forgo Plan B."

Her head fell back on a low moan. "I'm all yours."

"Yes," he purred, taking her. Loving her. "You are."

Wulf was starving. Seated at the small metal table in the sitting area, he plunged into his meal with gusto. He looked at Katie and his heart ached. Her lovely lips were curved in an indulgent smile, her dark gaze filled with love as she watched him. He thought about their future and how he would see this same vision every day for the rest of his life. He hadn't thought such joy was possible.

There was a soft beeping at the door. He called out permission to enter. The captain and Dalen walked in. They bowed, then straightened, looking grim.

"What is it?" he asked. "What did you learn?"

The captain stepped forward. "Your Highness. We have identified the target."

Katie stood. Her voice was tight when she spoke. "The prince is in danger, isn't he?"

Wulf rose and went to her, drawing her into his arms.

The captain shook his head. "Gordmere was hired to capture *you*."

Chapter 18

"**I**'m the target?"

Wulf looked down into Katie's pale face and his gut knotted. He held her tighter, his gaze moving between Dalen and the captain.

"It's extremely fortunate that you left the terminal before the courier from Sari arrived," the captain continued. "Gordmere was given a disk with video footage of his target, whom he knows only as 'Katie Erikson.' When he views the data, he'll realize Dalen's *mätress* and Katie Erikson are one and the same."

"I don't understand." She frowned. "They were after Prince Wulfric before . . ."

"That was a different assignment, which was interrupted when Gordmere was captured by Sarian troops. Smithson exchanged His Highness for Gordmere, forfeiting that bounty."

"Who hired him?"

"I don't know. That information is something Gordmere guards very carefully. I believe he's the only one of the group who ever knows where the money is coming from."

"So someone out there still wants Prince Wulfric?" Katie asked.

Dalen nodded. "Gordmere intends to use the credits he earns with your capture to finish that previous job."

"How many buyers are there?" Wulf asked. "Is it one person after both Katie and I?"

"Why would anyone want me?" she queried. "I'm not important."

"You're important to men of importance," Dalen pointed out. "However, my understanding is that these are two separate assignments."

Wulf looked at the captain, who nodded. "I agree, Your Highness."

Katie's hand clutched his forearm where it crossed beneath her breasts. "So what do we do?"

"Dalen's out of commission now that his motives are known," the captain said, "but I'll remain with Gordmere and learn what I can. I don't think he'll give up the job, even though his group has been infiltrated. Once he watches the disk and sees how well his quarry can fight, he'll realize she's the one who killed Tor Smithson. From what I've gathered of his personality in these last weeks, Gordmere will hunt her merely to avenge his friend."

Wulf stared at Katie. The forthrightness in her returning gaze answered his unspoken question. He reeled at the knowledge that she'd killed a man for him. The man who'd tortured him until he prayed for death.

Pride swiftly overcame his shock. He would kill for her, die for her, do anything necessary to keep her safe. She'd proven again and again that she felt the same way. He gripped her convulsively, his insides squeezed in the grip of fear. He hated the feeling of having so much to lose. "Does Gordmere know *why* this person wants her?"

"No." The captain exhaled harshly. "Frankly, he doesn't care. His orders are to bring her to a drop-off point that has yet to be specified and that's all he's concerned with—where, and how many credits are involved."

Wulf pressed his lips to the crown of Katie's head, holding her extra tight in response to the surprising way she clung to him. He was out of his depth here, away from his home and the safety it represented. "If we have to battle a malicious force, I would prefer to do it on ground I'm familiar with."

"I agree. It's not safe here on Tolan."

"Go back to Gordmere. Katie and I will depart in the morning."

"As you say, Your Highness." The captain bowed. "I'll contact you whenever I find the opportunity."

Wulf turned to Dalen. "It's too risky for you to return to your previous lodging. You'll stay here tonight. The servants will see to your comfort. I owe you a great deal for your support."

Dalen bowed. He looked at Katie and offered a reassuring smile. "You're in capable hands, Mistress. Not that you need them. Your own hands are sufficiently capable."

Katie managed a faint smile. None of them understood what was happening.

Wulf wouldn't rest until he knew.

Crown Prince Wulfric Andersson of D'Ashier was hand-fasted to Katie Erikson, a common citizen of Sari, with little fanfare in the Interstellar Council Embassy on the foreign planet of Tolan.

He wore no crown, only a simple travel robe. The consort-to-be wore a deep red gown with long bell sleeves and slender waist. A golden girdle hung low on her hips with a length of chain that fell to her knees. Dangling from the end was the jeweled crest of the royal house of D'Ashier. They'd bought the gown and girdle off the rack at a local shop. The jewel-encrusted crest had been brought by the prince from his homeworld.

The only other person in attendance was the embassy cleric, a thin man with a bored expression which altered when he reviewed the license.

"Your Highness." He bowed. "I am honored to preside over your marriage. Come with me. I have a much more suitable venue for such a momentous occasion."

They could have been wed in a transport cargo bay for all

the prince cared. It was the bride herself who mattered to him. But he followed with a hand at her elbow, eagerness lightening his steps.

The massive embassy ballroom stole Sapphire's breath away. The ceiling rose at least four stories above them. The chandeliers that lit the room were the size of small antigrav-crafts. Silver and gold satin ribbons crisscrossed the skylight above them, dappling the sunlight, which glittered on the marble floor.

The brief ceremony passed in a daze. She remembered little of the proceedings, only the soothing timber of Wulf's voice as he vowed his troth and the sharp prick of the needle in her fingertip as they placed their palms on the blood collector to seal their marriage in the interstellar records.

Awareness began to set in when Wulf lifted her hand and slipped the gold and talgorite promise ring on her finger. On her right hand she wore a signet ring like Wulfric's, only much smaller—her means to transfer back to the D'Ashier palace, just as Wulf had done when he'd first stolen her away.

Then he was kissing her with passion, his arms wrapped around her, warm and protective. Everything came into crystal clarity. Wulfric was hers. Forever.

"I love you," he whispered against her lips.

Tears streamed down her cheeks. "I love you, too, my darling Wulf."

D'Ashier, the Royal Palace

"Nervous?"

Sapphire nodded in answer to Wulf's gentle query, although nervous didn't come close to describing the turmoil she felt.

He pulled her closer to his side, offering her the support of his powerful frame. "Just be yourself."

"The last—and only—time I met your father, it didn't go well," she reminded him.

"You were an enemy's concubine then. Now, you are a Princess Consort of D'Ashier."

"I'm pretty sure that isn't going to make me more likeable," she muttered, her slight confidence faltering.

He grinned and kissed the tip of her nose. "Every time you start to have doubts, I'm going to remind you that it's too late to change your mind."

"It's never too late for a woman to change her mind."

"It's too late for you," he growled.

Her lips twitched. "I love you, my arrogant prince."

"Much better. Now smile and show my father how thrilled you are to become my wife."

She turned her gaze to the double-doors that led to the king's wing of the palace.

It was time to face Wulfric's family.

Fingers linked with Wulf's, Sapphire entered the informal receiving room, a part of the palace she'd not been allowed to see before.

Sunlight flooded the intimately sized chamber and illuminated the dark-haired man who stood within a golden halo. The royal palace in Sari was beautiful and many centuries old. The D'Ashier palace was much newer, using more advanced technology in the design, which allowed the use of massive windows without compromising security or cooling efficiency. The walls were made of a beautiful white stone, heavily decorated with multicolored jewels of all shapes and sizes.

Sapphire fought the urge to spin around and gape in wonder at the magnificence of the home—a residence that was now her home as well. She promised herself to explore every millimeter of it at her first opportunity.

Turning her attention to the sovereign who awaited them,

she tensed against her will, feeling a profound pressure to make this meeting pleasant for Wulf's sake.

The King of D'Ashier was impressive. A handsome man, every bit as virile and healthy as his sons, both of whom looked so much like him. Tall, dark, and barrel-chested, he was formidable, a monarch who easily commanded respect with the force of his presence alone. The lines of strain around his mouth and eyes didn't diminish him, but they did betray how he felt about the news Wulf had broken to him earlier.

Sapphire was about to prostrate before him when her movement was checked by Wulf's hand at her elbow. She shot him a quizzical glance.

He shook his head.

"Don't start me off on the wrong foot," she pro-tested.

"Father." Wulf raised his voice. "I have advised Katie to curtsey, as befits her new position."

The monarch's full mouth, so like Wulf's, thinned. "You'll do whatever you like, as usual."

She hid a wince and curtsied. "Your Majesty."

The king studied her carefully, from her head to her toes. "I think my son is wrong about you. But Wulfric is stubborn and does as he pleases. I have to trust that he will manage you when that becomes necessary."

"I love him. He is the most important thing in my life. I will do everything in my power to keep him safe and happy, and to make him proud."

Sapphire wasn't surprised that Wulf's father said nothing and continued to look at her with enmity, but it still hurt. Her grip on Wulf's hand tightened.

"Excuse us, Father," Wulf said, his voice harsh. "Katie and I need to make arrangements for our *shahr el 'assal*. We will be leaving after breakfast tomorrow."

"Wulfric." The monarch's voice carried a note of steel. "You are the Crown Prince. The people want a union they can celebrate, one that would strengthen them. Not one certain to take them to war."

"The binding is done, Father," Wulf reiterated. "Certified in the interstellar records for all to see. You may arrange a reception with dignitaries and other important persons, if you like. Hell, arrange a second wedding if you want the people to celebrate. Choose whatever day you like, but the marriage stands."

Sapphire was stiff. She felt the corresponding response in Wulf, he was so attuned to her.

The king's face reddened. "This is intolerable."

"We appreciate your felicitations," Wulf said dryly, leading her away. "Good night."

"That was horrid," she whispered as they exited the room.

He squeezed her hand. "Lucky for you, I'm worth it."

She leaned into him. "I hope you think I'm worth it."

"You're worth far more to me. I'd fight any war for you."

As they walked the length of hallway toward their rooms, she asked about Prince Duncan, knowing that was yet another battle he would face to be with her. "Why wasn't your brother with the king?"

After a brief explanation of the drafting, he said, "By all accounts he has adapted to military life. He'll be commissioned First Lieutenant soon."

"Your punishment hasn't adversely affected his feelings for you?"

"At first, it did," Wulf admitted. "Basic Training is difficult and he was singled out by my order for the harshest assignments. Now, he says he appreciates my decision."

"Will he resent me?" Sapphire had her own resentments to overcome and doubted her ability to do so, even for Wulf's sake. She'd found no redeeming qualities in the young prince.

"No more than you do him, I imagine." His fingertips caressed the center of her palm. "He understood when I sent him away how important you are. Everyone will afford you the respect you deserve or they will answer to me. I assure you, no one is eager to try my patience. Duncan especially."

Later that night, Sapphire slid from their bed and padded

over to the massive windows overlooking the capital below. She stood there, shadowed in darkness, and wondered if she was up to the task she'd accepted by agreeing to become a royal consort.

She'd dreamed of the happiness inherent in claiming Wulfric as hers and hers alone, but she'd naïvely considered him only as a man, not as a monarch. She saw him as her lover, but the rest of the world revered him as a fierce crown prince, a warrior whose skills were legendary. She was a match for the man. Was she equal to the king he would become?

"I love you," Wulf murmured, his warm arms wrapping around her from behind.

Wondering—not for the first time—how a man of his size could move so silently, she leaned into him and asked, "And love conquers all?"

"You're damn right it does. You can't change your mind now. You made it clear that I couldn't have you as anything other than my wife. I made the commitment, now it's your turn."

"You don't have to sound so disgruntled about it," she protested.

"Disgruntled? Katie, I knew that night in Akton that I was going to propose to you. If your father hadn't interceded, we could have been spared a lot of suffering. After six weeks of torture, I have a right to be *disgruntled* with you."

He tugged her away from the window. "Come back to bed. I can't sleep when you're not next to me and we have a busy day tomorrow."

"Ah, yes. You're going on a honeymoon tomorrow," she teased, following him.

"I'm taking you to my favorite place in the universe. I'm going to lay blankets on the sand and make love to you under the stars. I'm going to fuck your luscious body until you can't move, can't think of anything but me and how much I love you. And how much you love me back."

She smiled. "Do I have to wait until tomorrow?"

Wulf swept her off her feet and carried her back to bed.

Chapter 19

They raced across the desert with reckless abandon.

As the *skipsbåt* skimmed the desert dunes at high velocity, Katie clung tightly to Wulf's waist and laughed with joy. The cooling wind whipped through their hair and the setting sun glimmered off the shifting sand. Their hearts light, they hurtled through the air to the spot where he'd promised to take her.

This oasis had always been Wulf's favorite place, his retreat where he rested when winding down. After tonight, it would be "their" place, their shared escape from the problems of the world, a refuge for their love when the demands of their lives became too great.

Guardsmen were all around them, flying alongside in various antigrav-crafts. Ahead, the oasis was encircled with soldiers, the scene already set to his specified design. But all would keep their distance, allowing Katie and him the illusion that they were utterly alone.

Just the two of them in a world of their own.

As he heard her delighted laughter, Wulf sped up, anxious to hold her and revel in the fact that she was finally his.

The sand undulated gently in the firm breeze. He loved their planet and his beautiful country, almost as much as he loved the woman destined to share both with him. They crested the next rise and he heard her exclaim in wonder. He smiled. Their destination stretched out before them, an oasis kilometers wide with a rare spring-fed pond in the center and lush greenery all around, a verdant haven in the midst of the sweltering desert. A white tent fluttered in the zephyr, shielding their food and bedding inside.

Wulf slowed to a halt and released the handlebars to cup her hands, now resting on his thighs. "What do you think?"

"It's gorgeous," she breathed. "Oh Wulf, I think it's my favorite spot in the universe, too."

He twisted around to look at her. Her cheeks were flushed from the ride, her dark eyes shining with happiness and love, her lips moist and parted in a beautiful smile. Wulf slid off the bike and caught her to him, spinning her around in his delight at being alone with her. She threw her head back, laughing, and he laughed, too, knowing he was grinning like a besotted youth and feeling as carefree as one. For tonight, at least, there would be no danger, no tension, no work. Tonight, there was only Katie.

He knew she was hurt that there had been no reception, no joyful family dinner. She'd had to tell her parents about her marriage after the fact, an announcement that had been met with tears and distress. But he was determined to make her forget all the unpleasantness, to make her so happy that such things were mere inconveniences in a life otherwise filled with his love for her.

Wulf set her down and they ran to the pond, tearing off their clothes and diving into the sun-warmed water in unison. Katie laughed like a mischievous water nymph while she splashed him. He dove under the surface to catch her about the waist. The talgorite that adorned her piercings glittered in the water, and unable to help himself, he took her smiling mouth, drinking her in when she opened for him.

Katie embraced him and he groaned, madly in lust with her. Her legs came up, wrapping around his waist, and he thrust his hips into her softness. Her mouth parted from his and she licked along his jaw, murmuring hot, erotic words.

He knew from her tone and her touch that she wanted to be in control and he was helpless to deny her.

"Carry me to the shore," she whispered in her throaty voice. He did as she asked, moving with swift strides.

Wulf laid her gently atop the profusion of blankets, then lowered his body over hers. She caught him close and rolled, taking him with her until she was on top.

She straddled his hips, smiling. "My prince," she cooed, her fingers caressing his chest and drifting across his nipples. "How I love your body and the pleasure it brings me."

"Katie." He groaned. She tortured him daily and he loved it, wanting her attention to remain focused on him forever. The enjoyment she received from his body was as valuable to him as the pleasure he found in hers.

She lowered herself until her nipples pressed against his chest. She moved, wriggling until the head of his cock was lodged at the slick entrance to her body.

"See how ready I am for you?" she whispered against his mouth. "How wet you make me just looking at you?"

Her lips left his as she slid lower, sheathing his aching dick within her lush pussy.

His eyes slid closed on a ragged groan as pleasure burned through him with potent force. He shuddered, his love for her and their recent vows making the moment all the more devastating.

"Watch me." She rose, using her weight to anchor her, her denuded labia clinging to the base of his cock. "Watch me ride you."

"Katie." As he watched her with heavy-lidded eyes, his fingers flexed restlessly. "You're killing me."

She lifted her hips, her gaze locking on the place where they joined. He rose up onto his elbows, and his eyes followed hers, seeing his cock glistening with her juices as it slipped from her body. Katie moaned his name before sheathing him again. "You feel so good."

"Witch." The sensation of heat, so hot, deep inside her was

driving him mad. He, a man who had once fucked for hours without strain, was on the verge of exploding after only a few strokes. Because he loved her, and had no defenses against her.

And she knew it. He could see it in her eyes.

Wulf gritted his teeth, his fists clutching the blankets. She rode him with brilliant skill and excruciating leisure, her head downcast, watching as she impaled herself on his throbbing cock again and again.

"I love the way you feel inside me." The awed note in her voice made him agonizingly hard and thick. "I love the way you fill me."

"I was built for you." Sweat dampened his hair. She began to move on him with feverish, violent passion, their thighs slapping together as she took him without restraint. "Made for you."

"You're mine," she gasped, her nails raking his chest. "Mine."

"Yes." His muscles grew taut as pleasure seared him, swift and sweet. He'd been hers the moment he first saw her from the healing chamber.

Raw, carnal words poured from her mouth, goading his lust until he was mindless with the need to spill inside her. His balls were drawn tight and aching, his fingers cramping from their grip on the blankets. "Katie . . ."

"Me first."

Her hands moved from his chest to dip between her thighs. She began to rub her clitoris in time with the frenzied thrusting of her hips, the talgorite in her promise ring catching the light of the torches around them. The ripples started inside her, the first signs of her pleasure, and Wulf took control with a snarl, rolling them over and pumping savagely into her, swelling further, stretching her until she screamed his name into the desert night.

When Katie settled limp and pliant beneath him, Wulf slowed, relishing the tiny pulses that rippled through her sated pussy. Stroking slow and deep, he gentled her, even as he built his own desire to a raging need.

Her fingertips brushed across his knee. "Wulf ... ?"

"I'm not done," he bit out, rolling his hips as he pushed into her. She was tighter after her orgasm. Hotter. Plusher.

She stretched, arching her ripe body like a gift. The sight of her made his chest ache. "I'm all yours."

"Never forget that."

In the simulated torchlight, her dark eyes glittered up at him. "You captured me," she purred. "Stole me. Naked."

"I'd do it again." He continued the measured plunge and retreat, working her with his stiff cock, rubbing the spots inside her that would arouse her again.

"You locked me away and took my body." Her lower lip stuck out in a pout. "You are a wicked prince who forced pleasure on me."

Wulf's smile was feral. Drunk on endorphins, his consort wanted to play. In his present mood, burning with lust and on the knife's edge of control, he was more than willing to play the role of pillaging conqueror. "You flaunted yourself before me."

"You tempted me to do it."

"I'll tempt you again, captive," he growled. "Before I'm through with you, you'll beg to sate my lust."

"Never," she cried, her arms crossing her breasts to cover them. "I'll never beg. I'll never give in to you. You'll have to *take* what you want."

The sight of her shielding herself demurely while daring him with her eyes fired his blood. She was strong and skilled, able to fight him to the death if she chose. He loved that about her. Loved how it added a layer to the game they played. Loved that she used sex to bring them closer together in more ways than just the physical. Raging with lust and possessiveness, he thrust harder into her than he intended. She gasped.

"Please," she begged, digging her heels into the earth and

pushing back from him. She slipped free of his dick and his lungs heaved.

"Katie." Wulf fought the primal urge to fall on his mate and fuck her until the churning need inside him quieted. "Did I hurt you?"

Her dark gaze was riveted on his ruddy cock, gleaming from her climax and straining upward. He was so hard, the ropy veins stood out in harsh relief, throbbing. It was brutal even to his eyes and he'd just rammed it into her without finesse.

She rolled over and began to crawl away from him, her beautifully pink pussy a nearly irresistible lure. Looking over her shoulder, she winked.

A reassurance . . . and a blatant challenge to come and get her.

With a growl, he lunged for her. Katie slipped away in a rush of satin limbs. He caught her ankle and she squealed, a sound that would have been more effective if she hadn't been laughing, too.

"You need to be taught a lesson in subservience," he said gruffly, tugging her back. "I am the master. Your sole purpose is to keep me sated."

"But you're never sated!"

Wulf climbed over her, his chest to her back. He nipped her earlobe. "Try harder."

Cheek pressed to hers, he caught her hips and hefted them, angling her to take him again. He notched his cockhead at the tiny entrance of her silken cunt and yanked her onto him, stealing her balance and hitting the end of her.

Her moan drifted on the night zephyr.

He straightened. Pulling back, he thrust again, groaning in pleasure. In this position she was tilted in a way that let him go deep. Deep to where she narrowed into a plush, suctioning fist. His cock was so enamored with that part of her, it filled her with small spurts of semen he couldn't hold back.

"Please," Katie's voice came slurred with pleasure. "No more."

"But you're mine," he growled. "By your own admission. Why shouldn't I do whatever I want to you?"

"Because . . . you'll make me come."

A rough, edgy sound escaped him. "Damn right."

There was nothing like the feeling of her climaxing on his dick, the tiny muscles shivering around him, squeezing him so tight he thought his head would explode with the pleasure of it.

Holding her hips aloft, he pulled free in an agonizingly slow glide. Wulf paused at the cusp, the broad of his cock spreading open the clutching mouth of her sweet pussy. The expectation was both torture and the keenest of pleasures. The feel of her trembling, the breathless pleas.

Katie pushed back with her hands, trying to reclaim him. Although she was strong, he held her at bay, his lust tempered by admiration for the power of her body. There was nothing about her that he didn't love to distraction.

Biting back a groan, he thrust into her.

"Umm . . ." Her cheek was on the blanket, her eyes closed, her hands fisted beside her shoulders.

Too far away.

His hands slid up her flanks and pushed beneath her breasts. She wriggled her ass against his loins and complained, "Don't stop."

"But you wanted me to stop," he drawled, catching her close and straightening until he was upright and kneeling. "You begged me to stop."

She whimpered when he settled her in his lap, her legs tucked behind her on either side of his knees. His hand moved up to wrap around her throat. The other slid between her legs, his fingers splaying around where they were joined. He mantled her, covering her from behind while the lushness of her front and the carnality of his claiming were bared to the night sky. Wulf pictured how they must look—her ripe courtesan's body dominated by his larger warrior's frame. His skin so much darker and hair roughened. Her legs spread to show how her snug little hole stretched tremulously around the thick, heavy cock shoved deep inside her.

Katie reached behind her and cupped the back of his head, her fingers threading through his hair. Leaning back, her mouth sought his and he gave her the kiss she wanted, his tongue gliding into her mouth while his fingertips teased her tender clitoris.

"Wulf," she breathed into his mouth, undulating against him in an effort to find the friction she needed. "Have mercy."

He nudged into her, the crest of his cock stroking the spot inside her that caused her to tremble. As he worked her body from head to toe, she began to writhe. His focus was on making her insensate with desire, creating a scorching need in her that only he could quench.

"No mercy, Katie." His voice was hoarse from the effort he exerted to stave off his rising orgasm. "I want all of you. Everything."

"You have it. You always have."

"Are you sure?" He rolled his hips, stirring into the thick juices that bathed his cock. "Show me."

She whimpered, grinding onto him but having no leverage. He knew what he was doing to her, what it meant to her to have no control at all. For Katie, pleasure had always been work. Something that took concentration and focus. After that first night in her bed, he'd determined to strip her control every time he had her. To take her beyond reason until only sensation and he existed. Sex was a means to that end; a journey, not the destination. Their connection to each other was the eye of the storm they'd face. It had to be stronger than blood, more valuable than water, and rooted deeper than skin.

"Do you know how you feel to me?" he murmured darkly,

his lips to her ear. "How slick and tight? How hot? You burn me, Katie. Destroy me. When I saw you from the healing chamber—rubbing against the glass, your eyes eating me alive—I pictured you like this. Hungry. Helpless. Mine. All mine."

"Y-yours . . ."

"I wanted to live for you. So I could give you what you were asking for. So I could feel you pressed against me without the glass between us."

Panting, she offered kiss-swollen lips to him. "Nothing between us . . ."

"I needed to feel your hands on me. Healing me—"

"Karisem." My love.

"Katie . . ."

With his tongue in her mouth, his cock in her cunt, and his fingers deftly rubbing between her legs, she climaxed with a broken cry. Quaking violently. Sobbing. Milking him with rippling pulses. He growled in pure male satisfaction, his arms tightening around her.

Lightning tore down his spine and fisted his balls. Semen churned and boiled until it shot along his aching erection and erupted in a ferocious flood. He turned his head and set his teeth to her shoulder, groaning against her skin as the orgasm tore through him, ripped from a place inside him that she had created. A place that she replenished until it overflowed and drowned him.

Wulf took her down, blanketing her, pumping fast and shallow. Her knees slipped out from under her and he followed, rutting in her with a primitive need to mark her, mate with her, join with her. His fingers linked with hers. He stretched her arms over her head so that he covered her from fingertip to toe. The sand gave way beneath her, cushioning her as he fucked her like an animal, wild in his need. Katie was right there with him, coming and coming, moaning his name with every plunge into her.

"Katie."

As the fisted grip of his climax eased, Wulf felt the bite of her ring band digging into his finger. *She belonged to him.*

"Mine," she gasped, as if she'd read his mind. "You're mine, too."

He nuzzled his sweat-slicked forehead against her temple. "Yours," he vowed. "Always."

Beyond the golden circle of torchlight, the black of the desert night swallowed the world, creating a tiny paradise for the two sated lovers on the shore.

Wulf's fingertips drew patterns on the bare flesh of Sapphire's thigh. "What are you thinking?"

"That it's a good thing you pursued me, because the sex is unbelievable."

She giggled when he growled and tugged her beneath him. "You bonded with me for the *sex*?"

Blinking innocently, she asked, "That's not a good reason?"

Wulf nipped her bottom lip with a love bite. "If only it was that simple. Then I'd have some hope that it would burn itself out. Become more bearable."

"Promise me that it'll never burn out."

"I've made several promises to you and I intend to keep every one of them, including that one. I love you too damn much. Even if it were halved, it would still be excessive."

She brushed back a stray lock of raven hair from his forehead. "You promised to care for me."

He arched a brow. "Don't I?"

"You haven't fed me since lunch." Her mouth made a moue. "Then you drained me with your ravenous lovemaking."

The second dark brow rose to join the first. "*My* ravenous lovemaking? If I remember correctly, I was the one who was ravished first tonight."

She tapped her chin, feigning deep thought. "I don't remember that."

He pinned her down and tickled her. He wouldn't cease even when tears streamed from her eyes and she pleaded with him to stop.

"Remember now?"

"Wulf!" she gasped. "Let me go . . . I'll do anything . . ."

He paused. "Anything?"

She nodded, knowing she'd love whatever he came up with.

"I can't resist that," he said, freeing her with a wicked smile.

She scrambled to her feet. "Horrid husband, abusing me to get your way."

He reclined on the blankets and tucked his hands beneath his head. Deepening his voice, he said, "Wife, fetch some food."

Her hands went to her hips and he laughed. "Please," he added with a wink.

For that arrogant comment, Sapphire swayed her bare hips seductively as she moved away, tossing him a mock glare over her shoulder before she entered the white tent.

Inside, she gathered sealed bio-packs of provisions and a large flagon of wine. She'd taken a few steps out of the tent before she realized they were no longer alone.

Wulf caught up one of the blankets and crossed over to her, covering her nude body. She noted that he made no effort to hide his own state of undress. He stepped aside, revealing their visitor—a soldier she recognized from the palace.

The young officer bowed to her. "Forgive my intrusion, Your Highness."

"Has something happened, Lieutenant?"

Wulf set his arm around her shoulders. "Remember I told you I was making overtures to Sari in an effort to stabilize relations between our countries?"

She nodded. "Of course I remember."

"The lieutenant has come with news from the palace. An emissary from Sari arrived unannounced this evening with a message from the king. It appears Gunther is willing to meet with me. But it must be tomorrow and it must be at the coordinates he specified."

"Is that normally how such matters are arranged?"

"No. Summits take months to prepare for. The king has declined to meet with me these last six weeks. Now, he's had a change of heart and wants to see me immediately."

Sapphire turned under his arm to face him fully. "I don't like it. It doesn't feel right. I don't want you to go."

His thumb circled soothingly against her neck. "I promised you to do my best to resolve this rift. The king is hot tempered and rash. He's already shown his willingness to go to war over matters that could easily have been mediated. If I don't go, I could exacerbate an already combustible situation."

"Then, I'm going with you."

"No." His gaze narrowed. "I won't have you anywhere near him."

"Wulfric. You and I are bound. What can he do?"

"I don't want to find out."

"I'm coming with you, or you're not going."

A reluctant smile tugged at his lips. "Is that so?"

"That is."

Wulf looked at the lieutenant. "You heard the Princess Consort. Go to the palace. I'll rely on you to gather our formal attire and accoutrements. Return in the morning with everything we need to progress from here to the location specified for the summit. Sabine will assist you. And send a battalion to the coordinates to ready the site for our arrival."

The lieutenant bowed. "I'll see to it, Your Highness."

"Excellent. Good night, Lieutenant."

"We're staying?" she asked as the officer departed.

Wulf's gaze was both tender and filled with seductive promise. "The king's not ruining my binding night."

"Good, because I'm famished."

"For me?"

She hefted the bio-packs and flagon. "First food. Then Wulf."

"They warned me about marriage," he grumbled.

Sapphire huffed back to the blankets, allowing the one draped over her shoulders to fall to the ground. She heard him whistle appreciatively and she tossed a smile over her shoulder. "You haven't seen anything yet."

Chapter 20

Raising the field-sight lenses to her eyes, Sapphire scanned the profusion of blue domes only a few kilometers away and the large force of troops just beyond them. She pivoted slowly, moving the lenses in a wide semicircle, studying the terrain while mentally mapping vulnerabilities and strengths. She knew her father was responsible for determining the location; the tactical advantages were overwhelmingly in the Sarian camp's favor.

She lowered the lenses and released a deep breath, her stomach churning. Here she stood, firmly on the side of D'Ashier, while her beloved father made the necessary arrangements to engage her husband in war—should that become inevitable. Wulfric was also preparing, his camouflaged domes a sign of his warrior's mind-set. When she'd left him—just moments ago—his handsome face had been grim and the mouth that had pleasured her mere hours before had been tight with tension.

"This is hard for you, isn't it?" a deep voice murmured behind her.

She stiffened at the familiar but unwelcome intrusion. Turning to face her brother-in-law, she retorted, "Of course it is." She couldn't bear to be around Duncan, so she moved to pass him.

"Wait!" he said hastily. "Please."

Pausing, she stared at him. They both wore *dammr*-suits to protect them from the fierce sun. The tiny gold stitches around their lapels subtly proclaimed their status as members of the royal family. She studied him carefully, noting that his boyish frame had filled out with muscle since she'd seen him last. He remained smaller in stature than Wulfric, but that would change. Already, she could glimpse the man he would become. He'd be handsome, like Wulf. A pity that his looks would exist only on the outside.

"What do you want, Duncan?"

"To apologize."

Sapphire turned away again.

"Damn it!" he snapped. "Listen to me for a moment."

Her lips thinned. "Who do you think you're talking to?"

"No one, because you won't stay still long enough." He ran his hand through his hair and for an instant he looked like Wulf. That brief flash was enough to remind her how important it was that she at least *attempt* to tolerate him.

"I'm begging you." He met her gaze directly. "Give me a chance to say my piece."

"I'm listening."

"Thank you."

Duncan turned away from her then, looking out over the landscape as she had just done, although from this distance he couldn't see the Sarian camp without the aid of lenses.

"I'm sorry for the way I treated you, Katie, and for the things I said. They were lies, every one of them." He released his breath in a rush. "I was jealous."

"Why?"

"You're an only child. You have no idea what it's like to try to live up to an older sibling. That alone would be hard enough, or so I've heard." He shot her a glance over his shoulder, his mouth curling derisively. "With Wulfric, it's impossible. He has always been the best at everything. Not just better than me, but better than most men. He won't do anything if he can't do it precisely."

Sapphire watched Duncan as he spoke, noting the slightly defeated slump to his shoulders and the hint of despair that colored his words. To compete against Wulf was folly. When Wulfric put his mind to something, nothing less than perfection would do. And this young boy had attempted to compete with that. Something Wulf, most likely, still didn't know.

Duncan returned his gaze to the endless dunes. "From the time my brother was a young man—younger even than me—it was obvious to everyone that he was born to rule. Our father is too hardheaded and rash to be an effective monarch. He gladly passed responsibility over to Wulfric. From that day on, D'Ashier was everything to my brother. He had no time for anything else."

"No time for you," she amended.

The young prince barked out a derisive laugh that did nothing to hide his pain. "Wulfric is only a decade my senior, but he's always seemed like more of a father to me. I wanted him to teach me how to be more confident, more talented with a glaive, more appealing to women . . . Damn it, more like *him*. But he never had the energy when his day was over." He crossed his arms over his chest. "Until you came along."

He kicked the sand. "Suddenly he talked of nothing but you. Your aptitude for stratagems, your intelligence, your fighting skills. He was so damn proud of you, like he'd never been of me. When his day was over, he seemed more energized than when he'd started and eager to get to *you*, not me."

Duncan looked at her over his shoulder. "I hated you for being the one he cared about. Then, he chose you over me and sent me away, and I hated him, too."

"Wulf loves you. Surely, you know that." The picture he'd painted of a young boy with a hero who had been too absorbed to spare even an hour or two with him was moving, but her antipathy would not be so easily soothed.

"I do know that, Katie. I knew it then, too, but I just . . ."

He faltered and swallowed hard, before continuing with fervor. "I don't know. I just wished he'd eat dinner with me at times, search me out like he did you and talk with *me* for hours. I took my frustration with him out on you and I'm truly sorry for that. My behavior was unforgivable, but I must ask you for forgiveness anyway. I love my brother. I want him to be happy, and you make him happy."

"You abused me, Duncan. You deliberately set out to wound me in every way possible. You tried to destroy me. That isn't something I can forgive offhandedly."

"I know." His dark green eyes were open and earnest beneath his furrowed brow. "But if you'll allow me, I'd like to attempt to repair the damage I've done. For Wulf's sake, as well as ours."

"Why now?" she asked bluntly. "What's changed?"

"We're family. We'll be living and working together for the rest of our lives."

Sapphire rubbed the space between her brows, fighting the tension headache that was quickly forming. It was still difficult to grasp the thought that she and this petulant boy were related now, but the fact remained that they were and Wulf loved him.

There was a huge gulf of anger and animosity between them. The distance between her and the royal family weighed heavily on Wulf, and she knew that if she could mend the rift, it would bring him peace.

"We'll start over," she conceded. "Forgiveness is earned with me, Duncan, not just handed over in exchange for a few words of regret."

"I'll earn it," he promised.

Sapphire nodded. "Then, I'll give you a chance."

"You're not going with me, Katie. That's final."

Wulf watched his wife's chin lift in the stubborn cant he

adored. He smiled. Katie would never be tamed. It was one of many reasons why he loved her so much.

"You think this is amusing?" She turned away, her hands clenching into fists. "You won't find it funny when you sleep alone."

His grin faded. Now, that was a threat he'd be doing away with immediately. "Don't push me, Katie. I have sound reasons for insisting you stay behind."

"Perhaps I have sound reasons for sleeping in my own dome."

Wulf tugged her into his embrace. He stared into her beautiful upturned face with its clever brown eyes and lushly carnal mouth. A mouth that did things to his body that enslaved him. He meant to berate her and teach her a lesson. He meant to firmly establish that he would lead and she *would* follow.

Instead, he kissed her senseless.

He kissed her until she went limp in his arms, kissed her until her curvy body melted into his, kissed her until her fists unclenched and her fingers entwined in his hair, holding him close. He kissed her until his body ached with it, until he couldn't think or remember what they'd been arguing about. When he'd accomplished all that, he pulled away and nuzzled his nose against hers. "I need you here in case something goes wrong. You'll know what to do to protect the camp and the troops. It would be one less thing to worry about, knowing they were in your capable hands."

"General Petersen is here for that," she grumbled, her eyes opening slowly. "But I'll stay. That was underhanded of you, Wulf. You know I can't think straight or stay mad at you when you kiss me like that."

"I feel much better myself."

Katie attempted to push away, but he held her tight.

A frown marred the space between her brows. "I don't see why I can't accompany you."

"Because I don't trust him." He licked her lower lip.

"Then don't go."

"I have to." He brushed her hair back from her face. "If he's serious and I reject his offer, we may never see a treaty signed in our lifetime. This feud has already continued for generations. I want to spare our children as much of it as possible."

The palm of her hand came to rest over his heart. In her expression, he could see her love and worry for him. Despite his nagging uncertainty regarding the meeting ahead, he felt a deep peace that all was well between Katie and himself at last.

"You think the king still wants me?" she asked.

"Yes. I can't take the risk that his decisions could be affected by his feelings for you."

"Will you return by this evening?"

He brushed his mouth across hers, relishing the feel of her wrapped in his arms. "Of course. I have no intention of ever spending a night away from you. Negotiations won't be finished today, but I'll return to you, regardless."

Her lips clung to his, conveying a wealth of feeling. "Promise me."

Wulf lifted her feet from the ground and deepened the kiss. "I promise."

Wulf had been gone for hours and the sun was slowly beginning to set. Sapphire paced the dome, her dinner untouched.

"You need to eat," Duncan said from his seat at the small dining table.

She shot him a quelling glance.

"You're worrying yourself sick." He attempted to act nonchalant. He failed. "Wulfric knows exactly what he's doing."

"It's not Wulf I'm worried about." She stilled her fevered pacing. "I can't shake the feeling that something's off, and I always trust my instincts."

"I feel it, too. Something isn't right. They didn't care for each other before. Once the Sarian king learns that you're bound to Wulfric, that dislike will worsen."

"I hate this. I—" She paused, cocking her head. "Do you hear that?"

"Hear what?"

"That buzzing!" She exited the cooled dome to the heated desert outside. The noise grew louder.

Spinning, Sapphire scanned three hundred and sixty degrees, attempting to discern where the sound originated from. The volume rose and her sense of foreboding increased along with it. Shielding her eyes from the setting sun with her hand, she saw it—a black cloud rolling in with ominous speed. She sprang into action.

Rushing back into the dome, she passed a startled Duncan and pounded her fist on the alarm. The wailing of the siren rent the quiet desert dusk.

"What's happening?" he shouted, freeing his glaive-hilt from its holster.

"We're under attack!"

She grabbed the dangling facial shield of her *dammr*-suit and covered her nose and mouth before bursting out of the dome to help rouse the troops. As General Petersen rushed to meet her, she engaged her blade.

His voice crackled through her mask headset. *"Skipsbåts. A hundred or more by the sound of them."*

"His Highness—?"

Petersen set a large hand on her shoulder. *"I heard them coming a moment before you sounded the alarm. I've already dispatched two companies of men to extract Prince Wulfric."*

She nodded, but the fear that gripped her didn't ease. Wulf was at the neutral meeting dome halfway between the two encampments, but if the King of Sari was willing to arrange this bold attack, what else would he be willing to do?

Sapphire didn't have time to contemplate the danger further, because the skips were upon them, thick like locusts in the air, their guns blazing blaster fire.

By necessity she tuned out the screams of wounded men and the acrid smell of smoke, concentrating instead on saving her own life and the lives of the men who battled alongside her. Some of her adversaries wore the Sarian uniform, but most did not, and she understood that mercenaries had been hired to supplement this assault.

It was difficult fighting in the sand, despite her lengthy training in similar situations. She needed a skip if she hoped to be most effective, but all were in use. When an enemy rider approached at a moderated attack speed, she took the opportunity presented.

Sapphire ducked and rolled when he attempted to cut her down, then swung her blade as he passed over her, cutting the line that connected the throttle to the engine. The sudden loss of speed sent the driver flying over the handlebars. He was quickly captured by D'Ashier troops, freeing her to commandeer his skip.

Mounting the bike, Sapphire reached into the engine compartment and transferred the throttle signal from the right pedal to the left, which was an emergency brake. Testing the success of her hotwire with a tentative push of the pedal, she smiled grimly when the skip leaped forward. Pulling back on the handles, she forced the bike to climb into the sky at full speed.

She circled and approached the battle from the north, hunched low to make herself less of a target. She was preparing to swing at an oncoming rider when the rear of her bike was rammed by another skip, sending both her and her bike spinning violently. Losing her grip, she fell to the sand. As she rolled down the steep slope of a berm, her glaive fell from her hand and her mask dislodged.

She cursed as she came to a stop at the bottom. Her body ached from the force of the crash, but the pain was mitigated by adrenaline. She leaped to her feet and searched for her weapon.

"It's lovely to see you again, Sapphire."

She tensed at the sound of the familiar voice. As the blond man approached her, she instinctively reached for the glaive-hilt that was absent from its holster.

"Surprised to see me?" His smile didn't reach his eyes. "You and I have unfinished business. You had to know I'd come for you."

She wanted to find her weapon, but knew it would be a deadly mistake to take her eyes off him. She pulled off her mask to reply. "Not here. Not like this."

"No one expects to die when they do."

Her returning smile was grimly determined. "Well, Gordmere, that won't be a problem for you."

"Oh?" The mercenary palmed his glaive-hilt.

"You can expect to die now." Sapphire lunged at him.

Wulf drummed his fingers atop the ridiculously long table and glared at the king seated some distance away at the opposite end. The whole meeting was slightly ridiculous, right down to the separate twin entrances, as if they couldn't enter the summit tent the same way. Presently, the monarch was stalling. Wulf had more productive things to do.

He stood. "Perhaps you should study my proposal in private," he suggested.

The king arched a blond brow. "In a hurry, Wulfric?"

"As a matter of fact, I am."

"I thought this treaty was of great importance to you."

"They are *all* important to me," Wulf reiterated, "but it's unnecessary for me to sit here while you read."

"Maybe I'll have a question to ask," Gunther pointed out with suspicious innocence.

"Write it down. I'll answer it in the morning." Wulf turned toward the exit, gesturing to his guardsmen to follow.

"Your manners still need improvement," the king bit out.

Wulf laughed. "Let's wrap this up so we can get on with—"

The door burst open and a large contingent of D'Ashier

guards poured in. The commanding officer, a captain, made a quick bow before speaking.

"The camp is under attack, Your Highness." He shot a venomous glance at the Sarian king. "Some of the men wear Sarian uniforms."

Wulf rushed to the exit and caught a faint glimpse of black smoke rising from the direction of his camp.

Katie.

"Where is the Princess Consort?" he demanded.

"She fights with the soldiers."

No. His heart stopped. If something happened to Katie . . .

He faced the king, who paled beneath his artificial tan.

"You son of a bitch!" Wulf leaped onto the table. "This was never about treaties."

He ran toward the king. Gunther pushed to his feet and stumbled backward . . . straight into Grave Erikson, who rushed in through the secondary door.

"Come no closer, Your Highness," the general growled, "or I will be forced to stop you."

Wulf paused mid-stride, seeing the stark tension that tightened the older man's features.

"Go to Katie," Erikson ordered, his bloodless grip on the king speaking volumes. "Find her. Keep her safe."

Wulf nodded. Without hesitation, he turned and ran the length of the table to the exit.

"Wait!" Gunther shouted after him. "If you give her back to me, I'll sign every treaty."

Wulf's stride didn't break and within moments he was seated on a skip, flying across the rapidly darkening desert toward his wife.

Chapter 21

Sapphire feinted to the left when Gordmere parried her lunge with a defensive swipe of his glaive. The sun was dipping behind the dunes at her back. With the biggest source of illumination coming from the light of the mercenary's blade, she could see nothing besides Gordmere, which made searching for her glaive-hilt nearly impossible.

She had only one advantage and that was her ability to see him while she could hide in the gathering darkness.

"Why prolong the inevitable?" he jeered.

She knew better than to reply and reveal her position. If he wanted her dead, he'd have to work for it.

Circling him, she secured her mask.

The mercenary swung in a circle, using the blade light to locate her. His grin was pure viciousness when their gazes met. He began to press his advantage with a series of wild swings. Twisting and leaping, Sapphire managed to stay in one piece, then she hit the upward curve of the berm behind her and tripped.

Rolling in an effort to stay a moving target rather than a stationary one, she fought the embrace of the shifting sands. As Gordmere used the elegant weapon as a blunt force instrument, hacking into the desert floor, she staved off panic by ignoring the heat of the laser, which could only be felt in close proximity. He was getting too close. She kicked out blindly and felt triumphant when she connected.

"Bitch!"

"Asshole."

Kicking out with both feet, the heels of her boots connected squarely with his shins. She heard the thud of his body hitting the ground, then the darkness was complete as he lost his glaive, the blade disengaging as it broke contact with his palm.

For the moment, at least, they were almost even.

They both lunged in the general direction of the glaive-hilt. Gordmere landed almost on top of her. He shoved her face into the sand. She thrashed beneath him, gasping into her mask.

He was so heavy, too strong, and he killed for a living. She felt his weight shift, his knee digging into her spine with paralyzing intent. She hissed into her mask, her fingers clawing at the sand, searching for his lost weapon.

She felt it.

With the last of the strength she had, she shifted him enough to catch the hilt in her fingers. The blade engaged, turning the surrounding sand to glass and startling Gordmere into leaping back, freeing her.

Sapphire rolled, wielding the glaive in an arc above her. Gordmere bellowed as she nicked him. He kicked out and the hilt was dislodged from her hands, sailing over the berm far beyond her reach. She scrambled away. He leaped and caught her ankle in his hand, tugging her back down.

Kicking with her free leg, she fought for freedom. The heel of her boot made repeated and brutal contact with the top of his head and shoulders. Still, he came at her, climbing over her.

She writhed to get away, her strength fading in the face of his greater might. If he made it on top of her, she'd never survive it. Her head made contact with something hard, a rock or other protrusion. Gordmere pinned her in place. Reaching up, she dug for the object with nimble fingers, hoping she could use whatever it was as a weapon. If she could bash him in the temple with it, she might knock him out. Or kill him.

When she managed to thrust her fingers beneath it, she was surprised at what she found.

Her glaive-hilt. Or perhaps it was his, and hers had flown over the berm.

Either way, it would save her life. She ripped the mask aside.

"I wanted to interrogate you first," she gritted out, her hand gripping the hilt.

Gordmere straddled her hips and loomed over her, laughing.

"Sadly"—she engaged the blade—"you'll just have to die."

In the white glow of the laser, she saw the fear register in his eyes. Then his head was gone, severed by her swinging glaive.

His torso swayed for a moment above her. The smell of burnt flesh from the cauterized wound made her stomach roil. She pushed at the body with her hands and it fell backward, tumbling down the side of the berm.

Sapphire lay there for a moment, gasping and crying, the grip of fear reluctant to release her.

"Mistress!"

In the obsidian desert night, Clarke was invisible, but she would know his deep voice anywhere.

She struggled to a seated position. "Captain! I'm over here."

"Are you unharmed?" As he climbed over the rise, the sound of his voice strengthened. "I saw the light of a glaive."

"I'm fine. Gordmere's dead."

"Give me your hand."

She reached blindly and found him. The captain pulled her to her feet and pushed her toward the faint glow of flames visible just beyond the rise. "We must get you back to camp. Prince Wulfric is going mad looking for you."

Hearing that, she ran. She scrambled up the side of the dune, following the orange glow of destructive fires just beyond. She reached the top and looked out over the D'Ashier encampment. And saw a nightmare.

Every dome was ablaze and damaged skips lay crashed and burning, releasing thick smoke to pollute the air. Bodies littered the valley floor and horrific screams tore through the night.

War. She'd never seen it firsthand like this. She would never forget it.

Searching through the fighting forms below, Sapphire caught sight of two glaive blades cutting a large swath through the camp. The deadly beams moved with obvious impatience, and the arms that wielded them, while swinging precisely and with a minimum of exertion, betrayed the bearer's panic.

Wulf.

She stumbled down the steep side of the dune, her heart racing. She fought off the same confusion and worry she knew he was feeling. Snatching a glaive-hilt from the hand of a dead man, she engaged the blade without a hitch in her stride. She threw herself into the fray with a singular madness, furious at the betrayal that had needlessly cost lives.

Sapphire fought her way through to Wulf, shouting his name all the while, but the din was deafening and she couldn't even hear herself above it. She was close, just a few feet away, when he turned and caught sight of her.

His face was pale beneath his tan, lines of worry and tension rimming his eyes and mouth. He strode toward her, his ceremonial robes billowing behind him as he fought his way through to her. His gaze never left her face, despite the smoke that stung their eyes and made them water. She battled her way toward him as well, the path clearing as more of the mercenaries fled and the D'Ashier force overtook the Sarian soldiers who remained.

As they closed in on each other, she saw the fury in his gaze and the bloodlust. His was a frightening countenance of torment and she ran to him, leaping over a falling enemy soldier when he crumbled to the ground in her path.

"Wulf!"

He disengaged his blades the instant before she threw

herself at him. He crushed her to his chest. With the ringing in her ears and her face pressed tightly to his skin, it took her a moment to realize they were in the palace transfer room.

Wulf shook her until her teeth rattled. "What the hell were you still doing out there?"

She blinked, her mind faltering from the shock of the day's events. He crushed her against him again, and her hands wrapped tightly around him.

"Damn you." His hands moved feverishly over her body, checking for injuries. "Why didn't you come back here? When I couldn't find you, I thought . . ." He choked. "I almost lost my mind."

"Gordmere blocked the ring." Her voice was hoarse from yelling.

"I was going mad searching for you!"

"I was over the rise. Gordmere's dead." She stared up into his face, noting that he was still so pale. "I can't believe he arranged all of this. He's—"

"It was Gunther."

"*What?* He wouldn't dare start a war—"

"He did. And he has. He knew you were with me." Wulf exhaled harshly. "As long as you're safe, I can manage the rest."

Her hand slid up to cup his face. As her touch left a trail of blood behind, she gave an alarmed cry. She pulled back, searching for wounds.

Ripping open the clasp to his robes, she found the deep gash in his right side. "Dear God, no!"

"It's nothing." He attempted to pull her closer. The fact that she easily resisted his strength belied his words and made her stomach knot.

"You need a healing chamber, my love."

He nodded wearily.

"You should have left when you were injured," she scolded, but her voice was shaky and she knew she sounded more frightened than chastising. She was terrified.

"I couldn't leave without you."

Her hands shook as she applied pressure to the wound. "And I can't live without you."

The deep red color of his robes had hidden the amount of blood lost, but now she could see that he was bleeding copiously. His *dammr*-suit was soaked on the right side down to the knee and the stain was spreading rapidly. She gestured to the guardsmen surrounding the room's perimeter. They rushed forward to assist their prince.

"Take him to the medical wing," she ordered. "Hurry."

The guards moved him toward the door.

"Come with me, Katie," Wulf slurred.

"Nothing could keep me away."

Covered in an icy sweat, she followed him to the healing rooms. Once he was safely inside the tube and she verified for herself that his vitals were stabilizing, she relaxed, her forehead resting against the glass door. Dizzy with relief, her heart finally slowed from its frantic rhythm.

Fingertips tapped against the glass and she lifted her teary gaze to his. Their gazes locked—his fierce and possessive, hers filled with love. Wulf rested his open palm against the glass and she lifted her hand to press opposite his.

The moment was similar to the first time they'd met. The moment they'd first fallen in love. Sapphire could see in the tenderness etched on his features that he was remembering, too.

She pressed her lips to the glass in a soft kiss.

I love you, she mouthed, placing her hand over her heart. The emotion that crossed his face at her words made her chest ache. She loved him so much she could scarcely breathe.

This was the last time she would allow something like this to happen, the last time she would ever come close to losing him. She'd had enough.

And she knew just where to go to put an end to it all.

Sapphire backed away, and Wulf, who knew her so well, understood what she intended. He shook his head furiously, his black hair blowing around his face in the swirling air pressure. She looked at his wounded side and watched his injury healing. She didn't have much time before he came after her. Knowing the clock was ticking, she blew him a kiss and rushed from the room.

As she made her way to the transfer room, the flat heels of her boots tapped in rapid staccato on the marble floor. She passed the bowing guards and headed straight to the keypad to type in her desired coordinates and her personal identification code. Stepping onto the pad, she waited the brief fifteen-second delay she'd programmed, then found herself in her father's office in the Sarian palace.

The palace Guardian system still accepted her transfers.

The last time she'd transferred in, she had been returning from a visit with her mother. She'd been coming home. Now the reason for her presence wasn't so benign.

In fact, it was murderous.

Grave watched with barely restrained fury as his king paced the length of the massive throne room. Good men had died tonight, for this one man's folly.

"I cannot believe you sent Wulfric after Sapphire!" Gunther raged.

"I can't believe you started a war over her! Have you any idea what you've done? The lives that will be lost?"

The king pivoted, his features contorted with rage. "You *knew*. You knew they were together, yet you said nothing to me."

"How was I to know that you would do something so damned idiotic?" Grave snapped, his blood thrumming with frustration.

Another war . . . it made him nauseous.

"You forget yourself, General. Remember that you are speaking to your king."

"I never forget it, but I'll speak my mind regardless. I'm only valuable to Sari if I dedicate myself completely to her safety. No lies. No reservations."

The monarch ran a hand through his blond curls and sighed wearily. "Why didn't you tell me, Grave? All this time she was gone, you knew she was with him, didn't you?"

"Not at first, but yes, later I knew. You'd released her from her contract. Your right to know anything about my daughter was severed by your own choice."

The king growled. "She's angry with me and hurt that I released her without saying good-bye. We argued the last time I saw her. If I have a chance to speak with her, we could work this out."

Grave choked on an incredulous laugh. "You don't seem to comprehend the gravity of the situation, Your Majesty. It's *over* between you. Forever. She's in love and—"

"She can't love *him*," Gunther roared. "It's not possible. She's been with me for years. She has only known him for weeks."

"Months."

They both turned at the sound of Katie's voice.

"But it took me only a moment to fall in love with him," she said.

As she entered the room behind the Queen of Sari, Sapphire offered a reassuring smile to her father. Her glaive-hilt was held loosely but securely in her hand. The front of her *dammr*-suit was stained with blood, as were her hands. She saw the concern in her father's eyes and shook her head, silently telling him not to worry.

"Katie." His tone was wary. "What the hell are you doing?"

She lifted her chin. "I'm ending this, Daddy. Now." Her narrowed gaze moved to the king.

The monarch took a cautious step back.

"The Crown Prince of D'Ashier was gravely injured tonight," she said in a low, dangerous tone. "It won't happen again. Leastwise, not by your hand, Your Majesty."

She shoved the queen forward with the flat of her palm. "Tell him what you did."

The queen stumbled, then regained her footing. Shooting

an incredulous glance over her shoulder, she pushed her silvery blonde hair out of her face. "I do not answer to the dictates of a *mätress*!"

"You may call me 'Your Highness.'" Sapphire's lips curved without humor. "On further thought, since you were the one who introduced me to my husband, I give you leave to call me 'Princess Consort Katie.'"

The king choked. His gaze shifted rapidly from the queen to the general, then back to her. "What are you talking about?"

Her father nodded grimly. "Yes, Your Majesty, she's telling the truth. About both the bonding, and the queen's involvement."

The king rounded on his queen, his face mottled with fury. "What have you done?"

The general hastily stepped between the two.

The queen's shoulders went back, and regal hauteur covered her from head to toe. "Did you think I would do nothing and play the martyr forever?"

"What the hell are you talking about?" He lunged toward her.

Grave intercepted the attack, then continued to restrain the king as he fought to reach his wife.

The queen's icy demeanor intensified, lowering the temperature in the room by several degrees.

"You're a fool, Gunther." She lifted an imperious hand when he opened his mouth to retort. "Listen to me, *for once*. I had my choice of suitors—rulers from larger, more powerful countries. You may find me lacking, but I assure you, other men find me beautiful. I could have been cherished. Instead I married you, because I wanted you." Her brilliant blue gaze raked him from head to toe. "You remain the handsomest man I've ever seen. The thought of sharing your life and your bed filled me with such excitement, I could hardly wait for our wedding night."

The king stilled, staring at his wife as if she were a stranger. She laughed, a cold and bitter sound. "You look so surprised."

"I assumed you hated me." His gaze shifted away. "When I bedded you, you were stiff and frigid. Afterward, you cried. Why in hell would either of us wish to repeat the experience?"

"I was a virgin!" The queen's fingers clenched rhythmically as if she longed to do violence. "And you lay on the bed and expected me to pleasure you like a concubine! I am a *queen* and *your wife*. You should have made concessions for my innocence. In my country, virginity is a prize revered. You detested it."

Gunther flushed. He shot a beseeching glance to Sapphire. She crossed her arms and said nothing, did nothing.

"Don't look at her!" The queen's beautiful face contorted with hate and jealousy. She rounded on Sapphire, hissing pure venom. "I thought the prince would *kill* you. I was certain of it. How could he resist? You, the lover of his enemy and daughter to Erikson. Instead, he married you. The idiot."

"I take offense to that," drawled a deep voice from the doorway.

Sapphire pivoted to face Wulf. "You shouldn't have come. It's too dangerous."

Wulf's emerald gaze remained locked on her. His long legs ate up the distance between them. "We're going to have to have a long talk about obeying orders."

"How did you get in here?" the king barked.

Wulf snorted. "As if anything could keep me out while my wife is here."

"Guardian!" Gunther bellowed.

"I'll kill you just as soon as look at you," Wulf warned with deadly softness, "and leave here without a scratch on me. It's your choice, but if I were you, I wouldn't call the guards."

The queen's smile was spiteful. She glanced back at her husband. "I admit the outcome is not as I intended, but regardless, she's permanently out of your reach."

"You would have seen her killed, Brenna?" the king asked, clearly astonished by the thought.

"You have no notion of the things I've done to win your regard."

As Wulf drew to a halt beside Sapphire, he wrapped his arm around her waist. She felt the combat readiness he hid beneath the casual façade.

"Care to explain to us how and why I ended up in my wife's possession?" he asked.

The queen gave a brittle smile. "You're stepping into the conversation belatedly, Prince Wulfric."

"A brief refresher is all I require. I catch up quick."

The queen moved to the dais and sat regally upon her throne. "After I realized my husband had no intention of sharing my bed, I understood that drastic measures were necessary. When the patrols reported a disturbance just across the border in D'Ashier, I dispatched several of my guards to investigate."

"Without advising me," the general muttered.

"I knew you had no knowledge of it," she said, "and I hoped that my handling of the matter on my own would please Gunther. Tarin Gordmere was captured and—"

"You said nothing of this to me!" The king resumed his fevered pacing. His hands clenched into fists.

Brenna shrugged. "I intended to tell you. I thought you'd be pleased that I'd caught the bounty hunter, especially since his men offered me Prince Wulfric in exchange for his release. You had agreed to retire the *karimai* from her contract. I was thrilled, thinking this would be a new beginning for us, then I saw how distressed you were over her loss and realized you loved her."

The queen settled back in her throne with both arms laid elegantly atop the armrests. "Until that point, I'd believed that luring you back to my bed was all that was required to win your heart, but your love for the *mätress* would never allow that to happen." Her smile turned feral. "The solution came to me in the form of Prince Wulfric. He would rid me of the *mätress* and take all of the blame for her demise. I, of course, would console you in your grief."

"You heartless, conniving bitch!" the king spat.

"Oh, I don't know," Wulf said. "It's deviously clever, considering the information she had to work with. I can't find it in me to be too angry, since the end result is my marriage."

The king paused, his robes swirling to a halt around his legs. "You truly love him?" He directed his question to Sapphire.

"Yes," she replied. "Very much."

He winced. "Why?"

"Who can say how these things happen, Your Majesty? It was simply meant to be this way."

"I thought you were angry with me for releasing you. I thought we could get past this and be together again. I love you; it never occurred to me that you didn't feel the same."

"There was a time when I wanted to love you," she admitted. "But you saw only what you wanted to see in me and disregarded the rest." She leaned heavily into Wulf, exhausted. "I wish our contract had ended amicably. Now thousands of people will suffer."

"It's nothing we can't—"

"Nothing?" Anger gave her strength. "Good men died tonight and I nearly lost my husband."

"I didn't plan the attack." The king turned away and sat in his throne next to the queen. "I trusted the details to Gordmere."

Brenna gasped. "Tarin Gordmere?"

"Yes. I hired the bounty hunter to find Sapphire."

"He found me," Sapphire said grimly. "He nearly killed me."

The horror on the monarch's face was clearly genuine. "That was never my intent! Gordmere was only to bring you to me, unharmed. I urged him to make haste because I knew Prince Wulfric had you. I'd hoped you would find it romantic that I would go to such trouble to rescue you. I knew nothing of the attack on the D'Ashier encampment until it happened."

"You lie!" she accused him. "You insisted on the summit."

"I thought Gordmere meant to find you without incident," he protested. "I was attempting to distract Prince Wulfric. That was all. I would never hurt you. You must know that."

"If you don't want to hurt my wife, leave her alone," Wulf growled. "Forget she exists."

Gunther's fingertips beat a rapid, agitated staccato on the armrest. "You say it so simply, as if I weren't tearing my heart out and giving it to you. Imagine having her in your bed for five years, then returning her to me. What would *you* do? How would you feel?"

Wulf's chest rose and fell in rapid rhythm. He glanced down at Sapphire, then his gaze swept around the room. It returned to the king. "We're leaving."

He gripped Katie's elbow. "Did you get the answers you were looking for?" he asked her.

"I'm not leaving until everything is settled." She looked at the king. "What will happen to my father?"

"Don't worry about me," the general answered.

"He's in no danger," the king replied, but the tone in which he delivered the pronouncement set her on edge.

Grave crossed his arms over his chest. "I won't lead a war over this."

"There won't be a war." Gunther ran a hand through his disheveled hair. "There are ways to cover this up." He looked to Wulf.

Wulf inhaled sharply. "We'd have to withhold the information of what happened in the desert from our peoples. The fallen soldiers' families would have to be misled. They'd insist on vengeance."

"But the survivors will know," Grave argued. "They won't understand why they're being asked to hide the knowledge. Rumors will spread. We can't contain it fully."

Gunther waved his hand carelessly. "We have no other choice."

"I hate lying to my men," Grave raged. "They deserve better!"

Wulf turned his gaze to Grave. Neither of them said anything, but Sapphire sensed a silent communication flowing between them. Later, she'd question Wulf about it.

After a long moment, her father nodded. He came to her, wrapping her in a tight embrace.

"Come with us," she whispered.

"I can't." He pressed his lips to her forehead. "They'll never let you leave if I don't stay. I'm their new leverage."

"What will you do?"

"Whatever I have to."

She rose to her tiptoes and kissed his cheek. "You and Mother aren't safe here."

"We'll be fine. I can't say more." He crushed her to him. "But trust that nothing will come between us, Katie. Ever."

She felt him stiffen against her and his breath hissed out between clenched teeth. Alarmed, Sapphire pulled back.

Wulf's hand rested on her father's shoulder. "My apologies, General," he murmured, tilting his hand to Sapphire to reveal a tiny injector cradled in his palm. "My ring was damaged in the battle and has a sharp edge."

A nanotach. Her lower lip quivered as she looked at her husband, loving him more in that moment than she'd ever thought possible.

"I'll take care of her," Wulf promised.

"You damn well better." Grave's dark eyes were filled with warning.

Sapphire linked hands with Wulfric and tugged him backward toward the door, her glaive-hilt held at the ready in front of her. "It's been lovely, but we have to go now."

The queen smiled with pure malice. "Until we meet again."

Chapter 22

Wulf stood in the darkness in his room, staring out the window at the sparkling lights of the city below. At the moment, everything seemed peaceful, but he knew the illusion was fleeting. Tomorrow was another day. More work to be done, alliances to be made.

Satin-skinned arms encircled his waist the moment before lush breasts pressed to his back. He wrapped his arms over Katie's with a pleasured sigh, his cock hardening just from the touch and scent of her.

Her warm breath gusted across his skin. "We still have to find the person responsible for hiring Gordmere to capture you. I won't be able to rest until I know who it is and what they want with you."

"We can't ever lower our guard around you either. The King of Sari is like a petulant child, and I've stolen his favorite toy. He's the type who would prefer that the object he covets be broken, rather than allow anyone else to have it."

Turning in her embrace, Wulf gazed down into Katie's luminous dark eyes. His back blocked the light from the window and cast her beloved features into shadow, but the lack of illumination didn't matter. Her face was forever etched in his mind.

"As long as he lusts for you," he continued, "the queen's hatred will fester."

"I worry about my father." Her voice was small.

Wulf rested his cheek atop the crown of her head and drew her tighter against him. "As do I. His nano-tach signal is being monitored, but in the morning, you and I will have to plan a better way to protect him. Knowing your father's location is only half the battle, and he'll fight us the rest of the way. He loves you, but he's wary of me. He'd remove the nanotach if he knew it was there."

Katie sighed. "No happily-ever-after, you said."

"No. Probably not."

Pressing her cheek against his heart, she said, "I don't have any regrets."

"Neither do I."

"None?"

He smiled into her hair. "I wish I'd proposed to you sooner."

"What will you do to make up for your delay?"

His cock swelled eagerly between them. With a wicked grin, Wulf lifted her and descended into the pillowed seating area. "I'll spend the rest of my life pleasuring you."

"Umm . . . Sounds promising," Katie purred, welcoming his weight with open arms.

As he settled between her spread thighs, Wulf's heart ached with love for her. "You haven't seen anything yet."

If you love Sylvia Day's writing, don't miss her historical romances, available now in print and digital forms. Read on for a sampling of two favories, *Seven Years to Sin* and, from the story collection *Scandalous Liaisons*, "Stolen Pleasures."

"Mr. Caulfield," the object of his obsession purred. "Did no one teach you to knock?"

One long, slender, very *bare* leg stretched out over the rim of a copper slipper tub. Jessica was flushed from the heat of the bathwater and too much claret . . . if her slurred words, lack of modesty, and the bottle on the stool beside her were any indication. Her hair was piled haphazardly atop her head, giving her a disheveled, recently tumbled look embodying every carnal imagining he'd ever had about her. He was more than satisfied with the lush figure on display for him. She had lovely peaches-and-cream skin, breasts fuller than he'd pictured, and legs longer than he'd dreamed.

Bloody hell, his decision to indulge her by storing extra barrels of water for bathing had been a stroke of genius.

As his inability to speak drew out, Jessica arched one brow and asked, "Would you care for a glass?"

Alistair walked over to the stool with as much aplomb as he could muster with a raging cockstand. He collected the bottle, then drank straight from it. There was little remaining. And as excellent a vintage as it was, it failed to dull the sharp edge of his hunger, which was aggravated by his new vantage—he could see every inch of the front side of her.

Her head tilted back, and she looked up at him with

slumberous eyes. "You are notably comfortable witnessing a
lady's toilette."

"You are notably comfortable being witnessed."

"Do you do this sort of thing often?"

Discussing past lovers was never wise. He certainly was not
going to begin now. "Do you?"

"This is a first for me."

"I'm honored." He moved to one of the chairs at the table
and wondered how best to proceed. The territory was unfamiliar to him. Yesterday, he'd pushed too far too soon. He
could not afford to make a similar mistake today, and yet he
was presented with a naked, inebriated, uninhibited woman
he had been lusting after for years. Even a saint would be
sorely pressed for restraint, and God knew he was far from
saintly.

As Alistair sat, he noted the case of claret by the foot of the
bed. The quantity spoke of a woman who occasionally sought
oblivion. It troubled him to think she'd been so attached to
Tarley. How could he compete with a specter? Especially one
who had so perfectly suited her in ways Alistair never could.

"Are you preparing to join us for supper?" he asked in as
casual a tone as he could manage.

"I shan't be joining you." Jessica leaned her head back
against the rim and closed her eyes. "And *you* should not be
joining me in my cabin, Mr. Caulfield."

"Alistair," he corrected. "So ask me to leave. Although you
should have someone here to assist you. Since your maid has
been dismissed for the evening, I would be happy to make
the substitution."

"You learned of my solitude and pounced straightaway.
You are so reckless and impetuous and—"

"—apologetic about the upset you experienced yesterday."

She sighed. He waited for her to explain. Instead she said,
"My reputation is very important to me."

Although it wasn't said, he understood the implication that

it was not a concern they shared. "Your good name is important to me, as well."

One gray eye opened. "Why?"

"Because it matters to you."

That lone, assessing eye might have been disconcerting if he hadn't been determined to be completely honest with her. With a nod, the eye closed again.

"I enjoy the feel of your gaze on me," she said with surprising candor. "That enjoyment is quite distressing."

He hid a smile behind the rim of the bottle. She was an honest drunk. "I enjoy looking at you. I always have. I doubt I could change that. You are not alone in this attraction between us."

"It has no place in either of our lives."

Stretching out his legs in front of him, Alistair said, "But we are not in our lives now. Nor will we be for the next few months, at least."

"You and I are very different individuals. Perhaps you think my paralysis that night in the Pennington woods hints at some deeper, more intriguing aspect of my character, but I assure you, nothing of the sort exists. I was confused and mortified; there is nothing of note beyond that."

"Yet here you are. Traveling alone a great distance. Not by necessity, but by choice. I find that very intriguing. Tarley bequeathed you a source of great income. Why was he so determined to see you not merely taken care of, but exceptionally wealthy? In doing so, he provided you with the means to go in any direction you choose, while also forcing you to conduct business on a large scale. He shielded you with one hand, while pushing you into a new world with the other. I find that intriguing also."

Jessica drank the last of the wine in her glass and set it on the stool where the bottle had previously been. Sitting up, she wrapped her arms around her bent knees and looked at the door. "I cannot be your mistress."

"I would never ask you to be." He draped one arm over

the tabletop, his focus narrowed to the wet curl adhering to the pale curve of her back. He was hard as a poker, throbbing and on display due to the tailored fit of his breeches. "I want no arrangement with you. I do not want to be serviced. What I desire is your willingness, your needs, and your demands."

She turned those big gray eyes on him.

"*I* want to service *you*, Jessica. I want to finish what we began seven years ago."

British West Indies, February 1813

H e'd stolen a bride.
Sebastian Blake gripped his knife with white-knuckled force and kept his face impassive. If the beauty in front of him were to be believed, he'd stolen *his own* bride.

He watched as her chin lifted with defiance and her dark eyes met his without fear. She was tall and slender, with blonde curls tumbling down from a once-stylish arrangement. Her lovely watered-silk dress was torn at the shoulder, revealing a tempting display of creamy breast. A sooty handprint marred her flesh, and unable to help himself, Sebastian reached out and rubbed the offending mark away with gentle strokes of his thumb. She stiffened, and lifted her bound hands to knock his away. He met her gaze and held it.

"Tell me your name again," he murmured, his hand tingling just from that simple contact with her satin skin.

She licked her bottom lip, and his blood heated further. "My name is Olivia Merrick, Countess of Merrick. My husband is Sebastian Blake, Earl of Merrick and future Marquess of Dunsmore."

He lifted her hands and stared at her ring finger, noting his crest etched in the simple gold band she wore.

He scrubbed a hand over his face and turned away, striding to the nearest open window for a deep breath of salt-tinged air. Staring out at the water, he espied the debris from her ship bobbing in the waves. "Where is your husband, Lady Merrick?" he asked, keeping his back to her.

Hope tinged her voice. "He awaits me in London."

"I see." But he didn't, not at all. "How long have you been married, my lady?"

"I fail to see—"

"How long?" he barked.

"Nearly two weeks."

His chest expanded on a deep breath. "I remind you that we are in the West Indies, Lady Merrick. It is impossible that you were married only a fortnight ago. Your husband would not be able to await you in England if that were true."

She was silent behind him, and finally he turned to face her again. It was a mistake to have done so. Her beauty hit him with the force of a fist in his gut.

"Would you care to explain?" he prodded, relieved he sounded so unaffected.

For the first time, her bravado left her, her cheeks flushing with embarrassment. "We were married by proxy," she confessed. "But I assure you, he will pay whatever ransom you desire despite the unusual circumstances of our marriage."

Sebastian moved toward her. His calloused fingers caressed the elegant curve of her cheekbone and entwined in her hair. Her breath caught, and her lips parted in response to his gentle touch. "I'm certain he would pay a king's ransom for beauty such as yours."

Through the smoky smell that clung to her, he could detect the arousing scent of soft woman, warm and luxurious. He reached for the blade strapped to his thigh and withdrew it.

She flinched away.

"Easy," he soothed. Sebastian held out his hand and waited patiently for her to step forward again. When she did, he sliced through the rope that tied her hands together, and sheathed his knife. He rubbed the marks on her delicate wrists.

"You are a pirate," she murmured.

"Yes."

"You have taken my father's ship and all of its cargo."

"I have."

Her head tilted backward on the slender neck, and she gazed up at him with melting chocolate eyes. "Why, then, are you being so kind to me, if you intend to rape me?"

He caught her fingers and placed them on his signet ring. "Most would say a man cannot rape his own wife."

She glanced down and gasped at the heavy crest that mirrored the one on her own band. Her eyes flew up to his. "Where did you get this? You can't possibly . . ."

He smiled. "According to you, I am."